Working for his ex and his boy

Dino is caught off guard when his ex shows up out of the blue asking for help. His current lover, Seth, is pushing him to find dirt on his sister's boyfriend. Juggling between two cases – and his boyfriend and ex – isn't easy, but what choice does he have?Working with his ex takes Dino on a trip down memory lane, raising a few doubts and stirring up Seth's jealousy. Now he must save his ex's restaurant and his relationship with Seth before it's too late.

Books by Elle Parker

Dino Martini Mysteries
Like Coffee and Doughnuts
Like Pizza and Beer

Published by Kensington Publishing Corporation

Like Pizza and Beer

A Dino Martini Mysteries Novel

Elle Parker

LYRICAL PRESS
Kensington Publishing Corp.
www.kensingtonbooks.com

First Electronic Edition: October 2010
eISBN-13: 978-1-61650-195-2
eISBN-10: 1-61650-195-2

First Print Edition: October 2010
ISBN-13: 978-1-61650-899-9
ISBN-10: 1-61650-899-X

Printed in the United States of America

This book is dedicated to the many people who helped make it possible. Family, friends, readers, editors and publisher. Your support is valued and appreciated.

Chapter 1

It wasn't the first time I'd found myself standing alone outside Ed's Garage wondering what to do next. I was supposed to meet Seth here for dinner, but he was nowhere to be found. Seth Donnelly is my best friend and my mechanic. He also happens to be my boyfriend. If that's what we're calling it now. I still don't know for sure. I'd already tried to call him once, but it went to voicemail. None of this would be especially unusual, except he was the one who'd suggested the date.

I got out of the car and went to peer through the office windows. I already knew the doors were locked up tight from the first time I'd been here. On the off chance I had the details wrong, I'd gone back to my place to see if Seth was there. He wasn't.

My cellphone rang, and I pulled it from my pants pocket, answering without looking. "Dino Martini."

"Hiya, sexy," came Seth's voice.

"Where in the hell are you?" I snapped. "I'm at the garage, and you're not. The last time I got a call from you when you were supposed to be here, but weren't, it didn't go down well for us."

That time, the call had led to the two of us chasing illegal drugs all over Miami while gun-toting thugs chased us. Just to make it interesting, one of Miami's big baddies expected us to do it all in record time or suffer the consequences. He'd given Seth a taste of what those might be so everyone was clear, and the whole thing still made me a little edgy.

"Relax. This is going to go down just fine for both of us. In fact, if you play your cards right, I might go down for you."

"That would be easier for you to do if we were in the same place."

"Which is why you need to come to me, because where I am is better than where you are."

"So, where are you?" This was starting to sound like a vaudeville act.

"Not telling," Seth said with a smug voice.

I sighed. "Then how am I supposed to come to you?"

"You're the detective, you have to figure it out."

"Seth, what the hell are you talking about?" I walked out into the parking lot and looked around to see if I could spot him hiding or watching me from an upstairs window.

"If you want me, you have to find me. It's like a scavenger hunt, and I'm your prize." He sounded exceedingly pleased with himself.

"You're not serious."

"Oh, yes I am. I'll even give you a hint. I'm *not* at Mama Gets anymore." He hung up on me before I could fish for more information.

That was fine. Mama Gets is a great sandwich shop within walking distance of Seth's place. It's also about halfway to the beach, and since I heard the surf pounding in the background during our phone call, I had a pretty good idea where he was. It made sense. With Seth's patience level, he wasn't going to make it too hard to get to him.

I pulled Matilda into a proper parking space and locked my briefcase in the trunk. Matilda is my burgundy 1966 Mustang convertible, named after the old ladies she resembles when her white rag-top is up.

The weather was gorgeous, so the walk to the beach was pleasant, and only took me fifteen minutes. When I got to the end of the sidewalk at the public access, I kicked off my shoes and socks and rolled up the cuffs of my slacks before heading off over the sand to find Seth. The sun hung low over the Gulf, and it was hard to spot him in the fading light, even with his telltale red hair. I finally found him camped out on one of the wide rental beach chairs scattered along the coast. He had the shell up, but given the hour, I gathered that was more for privacy than shade.

"You pay for this?" I asked, dropping my shoes in the sand and sitting on a corner of the chair.

"Sort of," Seth said, grinning at me. "I do work for the guy who owns these, and he told me to feel free to use them anytime. You got here pretty quick. I'm impressed."

"Well, you didn't make it real difficult to narrow down your general location. But, how were you expecting me to find you out here in the dark?"

He held up a lighter and snapped on the flame, waving it around in front of me. I rolled my eyes. He said, "Not only would you have found me just fine, but since you don't consider it a real date without symbolic fire involved, I'm covered on that score too."

"Lots of people put candles on the dinner table. My ma lit candles for dinner every night of my life. You don't get to make me out to be some kind of romantic sap until I light candles in the bathroom and shove you into a bubble bath."

Seth shook his head and opened the large bag sitting on my side of the chair. He produced two wrapped sandwiches, two bottles of beer and a bag of chips. "You like Mama's seafood salad, right?"

"Yep. Thanks." I moved the bag so I could sit next to him and look out across the water. Orange and pink streaks filled the sky, and two pelicans flew past.

"Listen, I need to ask you a favor." Seth licked a gob of mayonnaise off his wrist.

"Oh? What kind of favor?"

"A professional one. I intend to pay you in blow jobs."

"Are you serious? You mean like hire me for a case?"

"Yeah."

I could tell by his demeanor we weren't talking about strong-arming someone who'd welshed on a bet, or doing collections. I did those kinds of things for him all the time.

"So, spill it," I said. I took a sip of beer and shifted to face him.

"All right. You know that jackass my sister's been living with for the better half of forever?"

Seth's sister, Molly, was about four years older than him chronologically, and at least forty in terms of maturity. There was no mistaking the family resemblance. She had the same blue eyes and the same red hair, which she wore chin length and usually as out of control as Seth's. She worked as a lab tech for a hospital in Tampa, and Seth often referred to her as the white sheep of the family.

"You mean Frank? What's he done this time?"

Molly and Frank had been shacking up for about three years, in spite of Molly's wish to be a regular middle-aged wife.

"Same old shit, only I think he's doing it worse than ever." He took a swig of beer. "Molly's been complaining because money is tight, and the other night she let it slip that he's been more secretive than usual. She usually tries to hide that stuff."

"What are you thinkin'?"

"I don't really know. I mean, he's a sleazy guy and he's always onto some kind of get-rich-quick scheme or making shady deals. I don't want him getting Molly in trouble."

"So, what do you want me to do?" I asked.

He shrugged and drank more beer. "Poke around, get some dirt on him. Do what you *do*, Dino."

"The goal being?"

"To nail the bastard, what do you think?" He eyed me sharply. Then he sighed. "Maybe if we can dig up enough shit on this guy, Molly will finally see him for what he really is. She keeps hanging on, thinking he'll settle down, but she deserves better. She sure as fuck is smarter than that. I don't know what the hell her problem is."

"You're a good brother. I'll see what I can find." I wadded up the wrapper from my sandwich. "Does she know you're asking me to do this?"

Seth shuddered and widened his eyes. "No way, man. She'd kill me if she knew."

"I didn't think she was the killing type."

"Big sisters are always the killing type, you know that."

I thought of home and nodded. "True enough."

The breeze was warm and humid, and we talked about our day, comparing notes and discussing plans. It was dark when we finished. The only light came from the glow of the condos behind us, and the flicker of moon on the surf.

Seth took the empty beer bottle from my hand and dropped it in the bag with the rest of the garbage. He pushed me to my back and settled next to me, slipping a hand under my shirt. His fingers were cool, but his lips were warm against my neck, and his breath was heavy. I turned to kiss him and he pulled me closer, pressing his groin against my hip with a soft groan. Within minutes, he was all over me.

I caught him by the shoulders and held him back. "You're not gonna try to have sex with me out here, are you?"

"No," he said, shaking his head. "I'm going to make out with you until you can't see straight, and then I'm gonna try to have sex with you in your apartment."

"Yeah, all right, I can live with that." I let go of him, and he stretched out on top of me with his usual brand of easy sensuality. He's everything I'm not—wild, easy and free, completely uninhibited. It's been a big adjustment for both of us.

I slid my arms around him and held tight, opening my mouth as he kissed me. He flicked the tip of his tongue along my lower lip and moaned quietly when I ran my hands over his ass. I loved the weight of his body and the smell of him. A unique blend of spicy deodorant, warm male, and auto shop. Who knew there would be a time in my life when the scent of motor oil could get me hard.

The pounding of the surf blocked out every noise but his hot breath in my ear, and it gave me a sense of timeless isolation. I reached up to thread my fingers in his hair, angling his head to run my tongue over the skin of his neck. He moaned and pressed into me, arching his back so he could grind his hips on mine. The hard line of his erection dug into my hip and he moaned again, louder and more desperate.

"God, Dino, you are hot," he panted. He thrust in a lazy rhythm, rubbing against me through his jeans. The heat of his cock soaked through our clothing. It made me shiver, and I thought about getting him home.

I pulled him tighter to me and butted my hips, meeting him thrust for thrust. He swore and his breath grew ragged. He had his hands hooked under my shoulders, and his fingers clutched at my shirt. He tried to kiss me but was panting too hard and had to break away for air after only a few seconds. I smirked and licked the edge of his ear, biting softly.

"Oh, shit, I lied," he gasped.

"About what?"

"About trying to have sex with you here." He began to thrust in earnest, rubbing off against me like a horny teenager.

"There is no way in hell I'm getting naked with you on a public beach. I don't care how dark it is."

"You don't have to. I can do it just like this." He ground his dick into me and moaned loudly for effect.

"With all your clothes on." I narrowed my eyes at him.

"Just takes a little imagination to make up for the direct contact."

"Seriously."

"Dino, shut up and work with me here."

"Mmmm..." I held him by the waist and rocked my hips against his. "And what are you imagining while you rub off on me at the beach in the dark?"

"All kinds of stuff. You fucking me in my bed, jerking you off in a crowded club in Miami, my cock in your mouth..."

My skin flushed hot, and I moaned. Hearing that kind of stuff in Seth's voice was still something of a novel experience, and it never failed to turn me on. "You have a very active imagination," I said.

"You have no idea."

I could see his face in the dim light and his eyes were shut tight, intense concentration etched on his forehead and in the lines around his mouth. He only remembered to inhale about every third breath, and his body was taut with effort. He was gorgeous.

Elle Parker

"Come on," I said, "I wanna see you. I want to watch you lose it right here, like a high school virgin."

"Oh my God," he groaned, pumping harder and burying his face against my shoulder.

"That's it, Seth, come for me." I slipped my hand under his shirt and ran it up his bare back, still matching pace with him. I didn't think there was any way I'd get off like that, but helping him do it was hotter than hell.

He gritted his teeth, and a hint of frustration crept into his moans. I tugged on his hair and whispered in his ear, "The next time I fuck you, I want to do it in the backseat of my car."

He cried out and clutched me with a death grip, bucking his hips wildly while he muttered a string of curse words. The relief was plain in his voice, and the tension eased from his body when he finally slowed. He was nearly laughing as he fought to catch his breath.

"Oh, man," he said, after a couple of minutes. He rolled off to the side and gave me a huge grin. "I don't think I've done that since I was fifteen."

"I don't think I've ever done that."

"Dino, I'm amazed you're willing to do it doggie style. How old were you when you finally got laid? Thirty?"

"You know what? Screw you. I'll have you know I did *just fine* with my sex life before you came along."

The argument was one we had often and it had turned into a kind of pillow talk, but there was a time when I nearly let that difference split us up. Fortunately, the chemistry we had was more than I could resist, and Seth isn't nearly the tomcat he likes to make himself out to be.

"Yeah, I'll bet that was a hell of a weekend too," he said with a grin. He grabbed some napkins from dinner and sat up on his knees, reaching down the front of his jeans to clean up what he could. When he was done, he tossed them in the bag and straddled my hips, looking down at me with smug glee. "I think you should put your money where your mouth is."

"What do you mean?" I was still hard as hell, and the warmth of him sitting squarely on my dick made it difficult for me to think.

He slid back a couple inches and popped open the button of my slacks.

"Hey!" I made a grab for his hand, but he yanked it out of my reach. "I thought we had an agreement here."

"I didn't agree to a damn thing. And if you're claiming not to be uptight, then you won't mind a little public display of perversion."

"No way. I am not getting naked out here, someone will see."

"Dino." He leveled a gaze at me. "I just wanna give you a hand job, and no offense, but your dick isn't that big. No one is going to see anything." As he spoke, he wormed his hands into my pants and pushed my shorts out of the way. Being the horny pushover I am, I let him. "Besides," he said, caressing my cock, "you don't really want to walk home like this, do you?"

I licked my lips and swallowed hard, shaking my head. "No, not really."

The air was cool on my skin and his fingers were warm. He wrapped them loosely around me and stroked lightly, teasing me. I was already halfway there. In spite of my protests, watching him get off like that had me wildly turned on, and I wanted to come so bad I could taste it.

"Come on, don't be a jerk," I said, thrusting up into his hand.

He raised an eyebrow, but closed his hand tight and picked up the pace. I hummed with pleasure and sat up enough to kiss him, bracing myself on my hands. All I could think about was his hot mouth on my neck and the grip of his hand, working me steadily. The crashing of the waves drowned out everything else.

Seth grinned and licked my ear. "Look at you, all wild and exposed on the beach."

"Don't remind me," I panted. It didn't actually matter anymore, though. Being lightheaded and on the verge of orgasm goes a long way toward lowering my inhibitions.

I rocked my hips and pushed up into Seth's hand, moaning with pleasure. It felt so good I was shaking. The salt breeze and the surf heightened every sensation to a fever pitch, and I bit my lip as Seth sped up. The outdoor thing definitely tripped a few triggers for me, but unlike most people, I did not enjoy the ever present threat of getting caught.

"More," I said. "Come on, please." I reached to plant a kiss on the side of his neck.

He squeezed tighter and I was there, coming hard and trying to keep my voice down as I groaned with relief. I damn near knocked him off the chair. When the last of it was over, I slid down to my back and lay there panting, staring up at the stars. It was a beautiful night.

Seth cleaned us up and buttoned my pants for me, then dropped onto my stomach, peering close enough to see my face in the dark. "I told you no one would see."

"You don't actually know that," I pointed out.

He shook his head and kissed me long and slow.

* * * *

The walk back to the garage was nice, and I had to admit I was glad not to be doing it horny and hard. Once I was no longer half naked on the beach, I would also say I'd probably remember that dinner fondly in my old age.

"I still get to come home with you, right?" Seth asked.

I cast a sideways glance at him. "There's no way I'm sleeping in your bed."

To say Seth's apartment was generally a mess was seriously underestimating the situation, and while I was trying to influence his habits, safe sleeping there usually required a Hazmat suit. My place, on the other hand, is clean, and usually smells like pot roast or cinnamon buns due to the old ladies who live in the other two apartments in my building.

We climbed into Matilda and headed for my apartment. It's only a short way, but I'd rather move the car at night than have to make that walk in the morning.

I live in the upstairs front apartment over an old hardware store, which shares the street with a plumbing outfit, a mini-golf course, and the CVS. The hardware store's been closed for years, and I had recently gotten the go ahead to renovate it into an office for myself. Finding the time to do it was another story.

When I pulled up to the building, there was an unfamiliar black Mazda parked in my usual spot. I didn't recognize the car, but I sure as hell knew the woman who climbed out of it. Ten years ago, she'd been the love of my life.

Chapter 2

Seth and I climbed out of the car, and he looked quizzically from her to me and back. She was a tall, attractive woman, mid-fortyish with straight brown hair that fell past her shoulders. She pulled her scarf tighter across her shoulders and came around the front end of her car with a nervous smile. My heart was in my throat and memories, both good and bad, came flooding back.

"Hello, Dino," she said, searching my face for a reaction.

"Gigi." Out of the corner of my eye, I saw Seth stop short. "It's been a long time."

"Yes, I know. How are you?"

"I can't complain. Things are pretty good lately. You?" Seth cleared his throat meaningfully and I caught myself. "Oh, ah, Gigi, this is Seth Donnelly. He's a good friend of mine. Seth, Gigi Sapora, also an old friend."

She smiled ruefully and nodded at Seth. "Hello." She turned to me and said, "I'm not so good. I came here because I need your help. As a detective. You're not easy to find, I had to call Ernie to find out where you're living now."

Ernie's a used car dealer I do repo work for, and we were all friends back in the day.

"Yeah, I just moved about a month ago. I still have the same phone number though."

"Well." She looked awkward. "I thought it might be better if I just came in person."

"Okay, sure. Let's head inside and you can tell me what's going on."

She looked relieved and said, "Thank you, Dino. I didn't know who else to ask."

I nodded and led the way to the front door, passing Seth who had an inscrutable look on his face. I had an uneasy feeling this would go badly for me one way or another. The three of us went in and climbed the stairs in awkward silence.

Behind us, I heard two of my neighbors, Della and Ruth, come in the front door chatting, and I realized they must have been sitting out on the patio the whole time. I ushered Seth and Gigi down the hall, because I was no shape to make another round of introductions and small talk.

I unlocked my door and held it open for them. Inside, the mood was even more awkward if that was possible. I turned on the stereo to cut the silence. The oldies station came on, and Gigi smiled. "You still like that old music."

"Can't beat the classics," I said, pulling a chair away from the table for her.

Seth yanked open the fridge and brought two bottles of Corona to the table. He looked at Gigi. "You want a beer or a drink? I make a great Sex on the Beach."

His tone was a little blunt, and she looked startled. "No, thank you."

"I have amaretto," I told her. I gave Seth a hard look.

She smiled. "I'd love some, thanks."

Seth scowled and dropped into the chair across from her, while I went to pour her drink. I hoped like hell he was planning to behave himself. Seth and I didn't become good friends until about a year after Gigi and I split up, but he knew who she was, and had heard some of the stories. I could only imagine what was running through his head at the moment.

I set Gigi's glass on the table and sat down with them. "So, tell me what's goin' on. You don't look so good."

"I'm not, Dino." She took a sip of her drink and shook her head. "The problem is, I don't really *know* what's going on. I might just be paranoid, but something's not right."

Seth sighed, and I have him a sharp look. "Come on, Gigi, what's up? If it's nothing then we find out it's nothing, but if it's not and you ignore it..."

"Right," she said. "Well, I think someone's sabotaging the restaurant."

"How so?" Seth asked.

"It's a lot of little things. We've been having a few problems lately, and at first I just thought it was a run of bad luck, but we've never had this much trouble before. It started with a couple of very bad reviews, which were unfair and not at all accurate. Then we found out there were rumors going around about us. They were saying our chef was unsanitary, or that he was crazy and might do something horrible to the food." She paused to collect her thoughts and ran a hand through her hair. "This all sounds so silly, Dino."

The restaurant was an Italian bistro she owned and ran, located down the coast in Pass-a-Grille. It sits right on the edge of the Intracoastal Waterway, and you can park your car in front or dock your boat in back. It was called Salvatore's in honor of her grandfather who built the place. I'd eaten my fair share of fine meals there, but not in many years.

"Is there more?"

"Oh, yes." She nodded and took another sip of her drink. "We've been reported three times for health code violations we didn't have, someone challenged our liquor license, and one night several dishes were ruined because cayenne pepper was put in place of paprika. It's like someone's been playing pranks. It's a lot of little things that can be explained away."

"But you don't think these are just pranks?" I asked. Under her annoyance, I thought I detected something deeper. Something more like fear.

She shook her head. "No. It's starting to affect business, and I'm afraid our reputation will be ruined. And, Dino..." She paused, and she looked almost embarrassed. "I think I'm being followed sometimes."

That got my hackles up. "By who? Is someone threatening you?"

"No, no threats. I don't even know for sure. It's just a feeling I have, like someone's watching me. I think I keep seeing the same dark green car a lot. I don't know, like I said, maybe I'm just being paranoid because things are going so badly right now."

"Do you have a lot of enemies?" Seth asked. I narrowed my eyes at him, and he blinked. "What? It's a fair question. One *you* would generally ask."

"None that I know of," Gigi said.

"How about the employees?" I asked. "Anyone been acting suspicious? When's the last time you hired people?"

"We hired three new servers over the summer, but one has already quit and the other two are marvelous, I can't imagine they have anything to do with it. Everyone else has been around for nearly a year or more, long before any of this trouble started."

"Fire anyone recently?"

She shook her head.

"What about the server who quit?" I asked. "What's the story there?"

"It's not Kevin," she said with a smile. "He was awarded a scholarship he wasn't expecting and quit to go to school in Miami."

"How about pissed off customers?" Seth asked.

Gigi sighed. "Yes, we've had a few of those, but they all seem to be as a result of the problems. I've tried to think if there was anyone who might have had a reason to do this *before* all the trouble started, but I haven't come up with anything yet."

"You keep workin' on it," I told her.

"Do you think you can help, Dino?" She took a sip of her amaretto.

"Yeah, I do. I don't think you're paranoid, either. Someone is definitely screwing with you. I want you to be careful, all right?"

She nodded. "What do we do now?"

I slid a card out of my wallet and handed it to her. "Here's my number, if you need it. I'm gonna stop by tomorrow, and then I'll start digging around."

"Thank you, Dino. I really appreciate this."

"Hey, I'm always willing to help out a friend."

She smiled and stood up. "It's late, and I should be going. I'll see you tomorrow then?"

I got up too, and said, "Yep. I'll walk you down to your car."

I led her to the door, while Seth took care of the bottles and Gigi's glass.

Outside on the street, she stood by her car and turned to me. "It's good to know I still can count on you, Dino. It means a lot to me."

I shrugged and grinned at her. "I'm just that kind of guy."

Then she stepped forward and slipped her arms around my neck, giving me a warm hug. I squeezed her back. She wore different perfume than she used to, and I wondered what else had changed about her. Ten years was a long time.

She kissed me on the cheek and smiled with relief. "I feel better already," she said. "At least I know I'm not just imagining things."

"You're not," I assured her. "I'll figure it out, I promise. Are you going straight home?"

She nodded. "Marco is closing the restaurant tonight, so it should be fine. I hope."

"Okay, then, drive safe." I held the door for her while she climbed into her car and watched as she drove off. When she turned the corner, I waited a few more minutes and went back inside.

Upstairs, Seth was standing by the front windows. He turned as I shut the door. "So that was the infamous Gigi."

"Ah, yes it was. And you could have been a little nicer, for the record."

"Hey, I was fine. I was not about to fawn all over your ex the way you were."

I rolled my eyes. "By no stretch of the imagination was I fawning over her. I was polite, like I always am to ladies."

Seth pushed away from the windowsill and looked down his nose at me. "I saw you playing kissy face out there."

He had slipped into what he calls his "extremely gay" persona, which I was glad to see, because he's incapable of being very serious when he does. I was willing to cut him some slack, because I supposed being face-to-face with your boyfriend's ex when she's playing the damsel in distress could be a little unnerving.

"Oh, for Pete's sake," I said. "Come here, I'll show you what playing kissy face looks like."

I reached out to grab the collar of his t-shirt and pulled him into as hot a kiss as I could muster. He moaned and melted against me, so I figured I had it right.

When we broke, I asked, "You didn't happen to notice if it looked like anyone followed her, did you?"

"I did notice," he said, "and I didn't see anyone. If there was, they were too crafty for me, because I was watching for that."

"So was I. That's good, I'll tell her tomorrow."

"You think she's in danger?"

I shook my head. "I have no idea. None of the stuff sounds physically threatening, but I do think someone's messing with her, and it could escalate."

"Well, man, you know I'll do anything I can to help, right?"

"I appreciate that," I said.

"Damn straight. Now let's go to bed and play kissy face."

Chapter 3

When I finally chased Seth out of my apartment the next morning, it was ten past eight. He was late for work, but it was too early for me to get started. I fixed coffee, showered and dressed, and ate a quick breakfast. That used up an hour, and I still had a few more to kill before Salvatore's would be open and I would be able to get to work on Gigi's case.

In the meantime, I could get a start on Seth's. I poured another cup of coffee, sat down at my desk and switched on the laptop. My commute was still the length of my living room because progress on the office downstairs was slow, and I had to fit his job in between paying work.

I ran a few basic background checks on Frank. I have some software and a couple of internet services I subscribe to, because they all have slightly different areas of effectiveness, and I can usually save a lot of time running several searches at once.

Not surprisingly, his credit was trashed. He had way too many credit cards, all maxed out, and the bulk of those had missing payments. One of them had already filed an order to garnish his wages. Not like that would do them a hell of a lot of good. The guy bounced from job to job. He was currently listed as a part-time employee of a remodeling company, but I knew for a fact he did a lot of his work for cash under the table. Just to round things out, he also owed back taxes.

Frank didn't have too much of a police record. Mostly it was traffic violations, including a decent number of speeding tickets. Maturity must have seasoned him, though, because those were several years ago.

To get a really accurate picture of just how bad things were, I also ran a credit report on Molly. Her rating was starting to show signs of decline as well, and I figured Seth had good cause to be concerned. It was my experience, however, that cause or no cause, women didn't typically give up a man until they were good and ready to. I didn't bother with police records on her, because I knew damn well they would be squeaky clean.

I took out my notebook and wrote down the address where Frank worked, his truck's license plate and description, since Seth had only ever referred to it as "that cheap-ass piece of shit," and a few other pertinent details I thought might come in handy.

This was one of the more delicate cases I'd handled. Mostly because I knew Seth and Molly, and they were like family to me, but also because Molly stood a good chance of getting hurt. For whatever reason, she loved this guy, and making her see him for what he really was wouldn't be fun for her. Personally, I thought he'd been using her since day one, but it wasn't my place to say. We would have to tread lightly.

Gigi's case beckoned, and either way, it was time to hit the streets. I was still a little early, but I thought it wouldn't hurt to do some of the preliminary leg work, so I grabbed my phone and keys and went downstairs to the car.

The ladies were out on their patio, so I went around the corner of the building to say hello.

"Good mornin', sugar," Della purred with a broader smile than usual. Which is saying something, because Della Vinson Owen is a Southern belle who learned her craft well and has never once said anything to me that didn't have at least a hint of innuendo in it. "Don't you look all chipper and satisfied this morning."

Ruth gave her a stern look and turned to me. "Dino, good morning. Wonderful day, isn't it?"

"Ah, yes it is," I said, watching the silent, but not entirely subtle battle of wills between the two. Ruth Fletcher is Della's roommate, and they live upstairs next to me. She is ordinarily as down-to-earth and practical as you can get.

The other two women at the table were Adele Triggs and Fern Quigley, her sister-in-law, who shared the ground floor apartment. Adele owned the building and ultimately ruled the roost over all of us. She took a deep drag of her cigarette and blew out smoke. When I turned to her, she said, "Della wants to know who that woman was last night, and Ruth thinks she should mind her own God damned business."

Adele is nothing if not blunt, but for all her gravelly ways, she's a decent lady.

Ruth said, "Well, I wouldn't phrase it like that, but yes, I have been trying to convince Della that we can't be prying into Dino's affairs. Especially considering the line of work he's in."

"Oh, *is* it an affair, sugar?" Della clasped her hands together with girlish glee. "She's very lovely, and the two of you made quite a picture."

"Della!" Ruth shook her head.

I chuckled and slipped my hands in my pockets. "She's a client, Della, nothing more."

"Oh, but *she* said you two were old friends," Della countered, eyes twinkling. She's not stupid, and she knew exactly what kind of friends we were. That was all I needed.

"You spoke to her?" I asked.

"I did my best to keep Della from grilling her," Ruth told me. "We were having a nightcap out here last night when she came up to the door. She asked if we knew whether or not you were at home, that's all."

"I offered her a glass of wine," Della said, "but the poor dear looked nervous and said she'd rather wait in her car."

Adele coughed and said in her sandpaper voice, "You don't think she was just trying to get away from you?"

Della thrust her nose in the air. "I was only tryin' to be *polite*."

"Polite, my ass. The FBI is polite compared to you."

"Well, I *never*."

I laughed and held up my hands. "Ladies, it's all right, really. Gigi's a tough woman, she can hold her own. Della, don't quiz my clients, or I won't have any left."

"I'm sorry, sugar," she pouted. "Normally, I wouldn't dream of it, but you know I can't help myself when there's romance in the air."

"There is no romance in the air, only detective work." I looked at my watch. "And speaking of detective work, I better get started on it. You ladies have a lovely day."

They all wished me a good morning, and I turned to walk out to the car.

* * * *

I drove up to Clearwater, heading for the county courthouse. To start with, I planned to build a background file on Salvatore's. I knew most of the history of the place from having dated Gigi, but I wanted to make sure there weren't any surprises, and it didn't hurt to cover old ground. You never know what you're going to turn up.

I pulled into the lot of the Pinellas County Courthouse and found a little slice of shade to park Matilda in. I generally try to hit places like this before the lunch hour when the clerks are in a more helpful frame of mind. In this case it paid off, because the girl behind the counter was as perky as I could have hoped for. I was third in line, and by the time I got to the window, I had a pretty good read on how to approach her.

"Hi there," I said, flashing my most charming smile. I set my briefcase on the floor and leaned against the counter casually.

"Good morning. How can I help you?"

"Well, I need to get a report on a piece of property I'm interested in."

"All right. Address, please?" I gave her the address for Salvatore's, and she started tapping away at her keyboard. "Okay," she said, scanning the screen, "if you have specific questions, I can answer those, or for ten dollars you can get a printout. I should tell you that you can also look up most of this stuff online for free if you want to."

I knew that already, and I didn't want to, because I don't care what anyone says, you don't get complete or accurate information that way. The internet is great for all kinds of stuff, but some things are still better done the old-fashioned way.

"Is there a lot there?"

"There's standard property information, which I'm sure you want, but there's also all the business statistics. There's licensing details, plus a list of all complaints and inspections."

"Really," I said. "What can you tell me about the complaints? Are there a lot of them?"

"There aren't a ton of them, but quite a few are recent ones."

"Does it say who made the complaints?"

She shook her head. "Sorry, that's confidential. But I can tell you *what* the complaints were. That's a matter of public record."

"Yeah, okay, can you just add it to my printout?"

"I sure can," she said with a smile, punching a few more keys. "Now, are you the same person who requested these reports a month ago, or do you need the full set?"

That caught my attention. "Ah, no, I am not that person. Does it say who requested the report?"

Again, the head shake. "Sorry, no. There's just a timestamp telling me when the last report was run."

"I don't suppose you could find out what other records were run with it?"

"I don't know," she said, furrowing her brow. "No one's ever asked for that." She started typing again, clicking through various screens. "Well, the best I can find is a list of all the records requested on that date, for all the stations here. It's pretty long."

"Are we talkin' ten pages or a hundred?"

"Looks like eight," she said.

"Can I get you to print that too?"

She chewed the edge of her lip. "We're not really supposed to do stuff like that. We're only supposed to supply public records."

"Aw, come on, please?" I said, flirting. "I've had my eye on this place for a while, and I don't want to get scooped by my competition. If I can figure out what other properties he's been looking at, I'll have an advantage, see?"

She considered that for a moment. "Look, just don't tell anyone, all right? I don't know if this is allowed or not."

"My lips are sealed, I swear it." I gave her a genuine smile this time. "You're doing me a great favor."

She grinned and looked pleased with herself as she scooped the sheets out of the printer tray and straightened them up. She slipped everything into an official looking envelope and printed off a receipt for me to sign. I thanked her and gave her the ten dollars.

Outside in the car, I pulled the reports out and flipped through them. The official stuff was mostly all information I already knew, and the complaints matched Gigi's story. I turned my attention to the other list she'd given me. The list was a whole lot of names, addresses and report types, in no discernable order. I looked through it a few times, and I found Salvatore's listed there, but otherwise it didn't look like anything meaningful. That was all right. I hadn't been expecting a whole lot, but the list gave us a starting point to check things against as new bits of information came along. Something always clicked eventually.

Chapter 4

It was nearly lunchtime, so I turned south and headed in the direction of Pass-a-Grille. I could check out Salvatore's, touch base in with Gigi, and get a damn fine lunch all at the same time.

Gulf Boulevard runs along the beach the whole way, and it's a fun drive. You can't see the water, hidden behind of the line of condos and hotels, but there are always groups of tourists crossing back and forth, and the general atmosphere is festive. I like it because it's a reminder that I live someplace special.

When I pulled into the parking lot, there were only a couple of cars. It was still early yet, and the lunch rush wasn't due for another hour at least. I sat there for a few minutes and looked at the restaurant, letting my mind wander down memory lane. God, I spent a lot of nights in that place. Not in a long time, though. Finally, I pulled myself together, climbed out of the car and headed for the door.

The outside was pretty much the same as it looked when they built it, but inside there was new furniture and the decor had been updated to match. Salvatore's had a reputation for being classy but comfortable, and Gigi kept with that theme. The walls were painted a rich gold, and the carpet had been replaced with gleaming dark wood.

The bar was my favorite part. It was along the side, halfway back, between the two dining rooms, and aside from new stools, it looked like it always did. At the end of it was a set of sliding glass doors leading out to the patio in back, and another section of bar if you preferred to have your drinks alfresco.

I took a seat inside and flagged down the bartender. When he came over, I ordered a beer and said, "Can you tell Ms. Sapora that Dino's here to see her?"

He poured my beer and passed along the message to a waiter who disappeared into the back area of the restaurant.

A few minutes later, Gigi came out looking poised and professional as usual. Aside from the hairstyles and the furniture, it was like I'd gone back ten years. Part of me missed it. I stood up to give her a hug as she approached. "Hey, how're you doin' today?" I asked.

"I'm better," she said, nodding. "It feels good to be doing something about it. Where do you want to start?"

"Let's sit down and talk. Maybe out on the deck so we have a little privacy. Besides, I could use some lunch."

She smiled. "Should I bring a menu?"

"Do you still do a good pasta pomodoro?"

"Always have."

"Then, no, I don't need a menu."

She caught a waiter and gave him the order and told him she'd be in a meeting for a while, then led me out to the deck. We sat down in the shade, where a large ceiling fan slowly churned out a light breeze overhead. It was warm, but not oppressively humid, and there was a fair amount of activity on the waterway which runs between all the islands and peninsulas that make up the area. Across the channel were strings of houses on Vina del Mar, and beyond that, Tierra Verde.

"Okay, first of all," I said, "I went up to the courthouse this morning to do a little background work, and I found out I'm not the only one. About a month ago, someone else was digging into the public records of Salvatore's. Do you know anything about that?"

Gigi looked surprised. "No. There's nothing we're involved with that would give anyone reason to do that."

"Might be nothing," I said. "They're public for a reason. But it's the timing that's got my interest. That fits pretty well with the start of your problems, doesn't it?"

"The false reports were about six weeks ago, so yes, I'd say it does."

"Great. That's good news," I said, taking a sip of my beer.

"Good? How so?"

"Because it points to Salvatore's being the target here, not you."

"What about the car that's following me?"

"You're the owner. If someone's going after the restaurant, it stands to reason they're gonna be interested in you too. I'm not sayin' you shouldn't be careful, or that you're not in danger, but I don't think we're talking about a stalker or anything like that."

"I'm still in danger, but this is good news?" She looked irritated.

"That's not what I said, and you know it. My point is if someone was going after you specifically, we'd probably be dealing with some nut job and that would be a real problem. On the other hand, there are a lot of non-psychotic reasons to try to take down a business, and we can deal with those."

She made all the right noises of agreement, but I could tell she wasn't buying it yet. Salvatore's was her home, and she didn't see the distinction I did.

The waiter came out with our pasta and a basket of bread, and we spent a couple of minutes eating in silence. Finally, Gigi spoke. "I take it you weren't able to find out who was looking at the records, or who might have filed the complaints?"

"Sorry, no. They don't give that stuff out to the average Joe. I got some other information on things requested that day, but I don't know if it'll help."

She sighed. "It's more than I had yesterday."

"Trust me, it always seems like you're floundering around in the beginning."

"I remember. I hope for my sake you're still as dedicated as you were back then."

It was my turn to sigh, because this had been a point of contention between us. My job was a big part of our break up, and the reason why I hadn't been too eager for a serious relationship afterward. "Ah. Yeah, I am actually."

She nodded, but didn't say anything.

The pasta was delicious and I told her so while I mopped up garlic and tomato juice with a chunk of bread. That seemed to break the awkwardness. The waiter came to clear the plates away, and I took a notepad out of my briefcase.

"I want to go over each of the strange events with you more closely," I said. "Give me as much detail as possible, and see if you can't remember anything else odd, even if it didn't seem odd at the time. We'll try to build a timeline and see if there are any patterns."

We spent about an hour working out a list, and by the time we were done, Gigi was practically spitting tacks. If it weren't such a serious situation, it might have been kind of cute.

"Okay," I said, turning over a fresh sheet of paper, "tell me about the staff. Let's start at the top and work our way down."

"Well, there's me, of course, and there's Marco, my manager."

"How long has he been around?"

"Marco's been with me for six years, there's no way he's got anything to do with this. He's as upset as I am."

"Relax," I said, "I'm not accusing anyone, I'm just tryin' to get a feel for who's around."

She nodded and went on. "Angelo is our chef now. He's worked here four years. He's a good man too. He's very devoted to his work. We're lucky to have him."

She went on to tell me about the line cooks, prep cook, waiters, hostess, busboys and bartenders. Of all those people, only Felix Dempsey had been there when I was hanging out at the restaurant a lot. He was one of the bartenders, and a hell of a great guy.

"Hey, how is Felix these days? He's gotta' be getting up there, isn't he?"

Gigi smiled. "He's still going strong. He only works part time now, on the weekends when it's busier, and once in a while he'll cover a shift to give someone the day off. I'm sure he'd like to see you again."

I was pretty sure he'd get the chance.

"All right," I said, "tell me about your schedule. I need to know what your regular routine is and where you go during the day."

"I'm usually here or at home these days." She sipped her water. "Especially since the trouble started. I work at home in the mornings and come down here around opening. I close a few nights a week, and Marco does the rest."

She filled me on the specific times, and details like her dry cleaner and where she grocery shopped.

All that was left was the hard part. I started another page and said, "Now's the bit you're not gonna like. Tell me about your ex-boyfriends and anyone you're seeing now."

"Oh, you'd like that, wouldn't you?"

"I gotta' ask, Gigi. Who's a better candidate for screwing with you than an ex-lover?"

She chewed her lip and said, "Well, there is one guy."

"Yeah?"

"He's tall, skinny, speaks with a New York accent..."

I slumped in my chair. "Would you be serious, please? This is a legitimate request. It's not like I'm diggin' for dirt to amuse myself."

"I'm sorry," she said, laughing into her hand. "This is just such a bizarre situation."

"Look, you don't have to give me a lot of details, just tell me if you think there's anyone who might be capable of this. Have you had any real bad break ups, or anything like that?"

She shrugged and toyed with her napkin. "There have been a couple of guys that were serious but didn't work out. I don't think they have anything to do with it. There have been a few losers too, I guess. I'll think about it and keep my eyes open. If something occurs to me, I'll let you know."

"Fair enough," I said, not wanting to pry any further.

"What about you?"

"What about me?"

"What have you done with the last ten years? Are you seeing anyone?"

Her eyes met mine, and my blood ran ice cold. I know it was a perfectly valid question, but I wasn't prepared for it. "Well, yeah, I'm... seeing someone."

"Is it serious?" She leaned forward, waiting for an answer. As far as I could tell, she was enjoying the hell out of herself.

"You know what, you're right, this is too bizarre to talk about." I glanced at my watch. "It's getting late, and I think I've taken up enough of your time today."

"Dino, come on," she chided. "I was only giving you a hard time. Don't be like that."

"You weren't too happy about coughing up details, either."

"I know, I know." She cocked her head at me. "At least tell me this, are you happy?"

"Yes. I would say that I'm happy. Are you?"

She thought about that a minute. "Yes. Aside from my current troubles, I'm pretty happy. I haven't been single very much of my life. It has its advantages."

"That's what I've always told people."

There wasn't a lot of ground left to cover, and it actually was getting kind of late. Business was picking up, and I figured I'd better let Gigi get back to work. More than once during our interview, I'd noticed various staff members peering around the corner to see if she was available yet.

We said our goodbyes, and I told her I'd get in touch after I'd done some more digging. I headed back up the coast, but stopped at a dumpy bar about three-quarters of the way home. I needed to have a good stiff drink and wrap my head around seeing Gigi again. Sitting there with her was way too much like old times, and it brought back a whole lot of memories, good and bad. I didn't want to face Seth while I was still dealing with that.

* * * *

I still wasn't especially clearheaded when I turned onto my street and parked Matilda in front of the hardware store. I was tired and needed more time, plus I wanted to sit down and try to get a handle on the case. As I walked up the path, I pulled out my cellphone and dialed Seth.

"Hey, dude." He threw a sultry tone into his voice, and it felt a bit like being yanked forward in time. It was disconcerting to say the least. "How was your day?"

"Ah, it was all right," I said.

"So what do you want to do tonight? I could get some burgers, and we could put in a little time on your office."

"I don't think I'm up for construction work right now. It's been kind of a long day."

I snagged my mail as I went through the door and climbed the stairs, still feeing odd and disconnected.

"That's okay," Seth said, "we could just find a movie on TV or whatever. I'm easy."

"Look," I said, as gently as I could, "I just got home and I've kind of had it. I think I might take a shower and flop on the couch for a while. I need to figure out my next step with the restaurant, and I'm not sure I'd be very good company tonight. Can I take a rain check on those burgers?"

"Oh. Well, yeah, you could." He sounded disappointed, and I felt like a heel. "There's something you should probably know, though..."

I frowned. "What's that?"

I had just reached the top of the stairs and as I turned down the hall, my front door opened, and Seth stepped out, looking sheepish. He closed his phone against his thigh and said, "I'm already here."

"Hi," I said. He was wearing a t-shirt that said *iSwallow,* and he looked good. My sense of time shifted again.

"You want me to go?" he asked.

I chuckled. You don't get to your forties without knowing there's only one right answer to a question like that. Besides, I really didn't. "No, of course not. You're just gonna have to put up with me, that's all."

We went inside and he shut the door. He sidled up behind me and purred, "That's okay, I have ways of putting you back in a good mood."

"Yes, you do," I said, turning to drape an arm around his shoulders. I gave him a kiss on the forehead. "Want a beer?"

"Yes."

"Good, get me one while you're in there."

He snorted and headed to the fridge. "So what have you been up to? Did you find anything on Frank yet?"

"Nothing much. I ran some checks on him, but I don't think it's anything you didn't already know," I said. "Actually, I spent most of the day with Gigi, picking her life apart, which was not very much fun for either of us."

"Oh, yeah, I'll bet." Seth thrust a beer in my hand with a scowl.

"Hey, don't be like that."

"How am I supposed to be, Dino? You spent the whole damn day with your ex and then you tried to blow me off."

"Until I saw you," I pointed out. "It only took one look to change my mind."

Seth leaned against the counter and folded his arms over his chest. He didn't say anything.

"Come on," I said, going to him. "She was ten years ago. You can't tell me you're seriously jealous over this."

"You're not over her."

"Yeah, I am."

He glared up at me through his eyelashes. "I saw the way you were with her last night, you still have feelings for her."

"I still care about her," I said. "I also care about the ladies in this building, but that's never seemed to bother you."

"It's not the same thing, Dino."

"I know that. Look, Gigi and I split up because we couldn't live together. We both wanted different things out of life, and none of that has changed. If anything, it's worse."

"Are you kidding? She's gorgeous, classy, Italian, smart, and single. She's everything that's perfect for you, Dino. If anything, ten years has probably given her a lot of time to reconsider. Give me one reason why I shouldn't be a little worried."

"Ah, well your dick is a lot bigger than hers."

Seth rolled his eyes and took a swig of beer.

I was at a loss because insecurity is not a trait Seth Donnelly shows very often, and I wasn't sure how to deal with it. There was only one way I knew to handle that kind of situation, so I pulled him into my arms and kissed his neck.

"I'm serious," I said. "You've got nothing to worry about. I even told her I'm seeing someone."

"Did you tell her who?"

I sighed and rested my forehead against his, then took a deep breath. "No, I didn't, but that doesn't have anything to do with *you*. You know that."

He relented, finally, and slipped his arms around my waist. "Yeah. I know that. I don't like it, but I know what it's about."

Not surprisingly, we wound up in bed about the same time everyone else was eating dinner. I know it makes me kind of a pig, but I was still at the stage where I could express how I felt about him through sex, easier than any other way.

I had him stripped naked and spread out on my bed, flushed and panting from twenty minutes of intense attention from yours truly that involved a lot of kissing, a lot of petting, and a lot of tongue. We were both halfway there already, and I was getting into position to finish us off when Seth pounced on me. He shoved me to my back and squirmed in between my legs, fitting his groin against mine in a way we had down to a science. His cock was hot and hard, and I moaned with satisfaction.

He'd once told me it was his favorite way to fuck, and then he'd promptly made it mine as well. It was comfortable and easy, and it got me hotter than hell. But more than that, it allowed me to hold him tight against me, absolutely as close as we could get. I'm a sucker for full on, skin-to-skin contact, and I like to wrap my arms around him and practically wallow in the sensation.

That's what I was doing as our bodies slid together, slick with sweat and hot from the effort, when he bit down on the skin of my neck without warning. Sharp pain shot through me, and I swore out loud.

"What the fuck?" I snapped, pulling away as much as I could.

"Sorry," he panted. "I didn't mean to bite so hard. Let me kiss it and make it better."

He rolled his hips just the way I like, and I shuddered with pleasure. I didn't bother to resist when he nuzzled up under my chin and started to lick my throat. He worked his way around to the sore spot and kissed me hotly, then moved a little higher and bit me again. It wasn't nearly so harsh this time, and I didn't push him away.

But I did ask, "What the hell is with you tonight?"

"You just have me really hot right now, Dino."

He braced himself on his elbows and ground down against my cock, hard and rough, pumping his body forcefully.

"Oh my God," I moaned. My breath was thick and heavy, and forming sentences wasn't all that easy. "I'm not really complaining, it's just weird."

"I bite you all the time, Dino," he panted against my neck. Then he sunk his teeth into me again, just to prove his point.

"Shit." I inhaled sharply. "Not like that you don't."

He lapped his tongue over the spot with a ragged moan, and came hard, losing control of his thrusts altogether. I held him tight and drew my knees up to hold him in place while he rode it out. Wet heat flooded my cock, and I groaned as my own orgasm hung just on the tipping point for a few moments before crashing over me. I jerked my hips and clutched Seth as hard as I could.

We both slowed until we were barely moving, and then just went limp. Seth's body was totally relaxed on top of mine, and he was warm and solid. I love that moment and always lie there as long as possible, running my hands slowly over him.

Seth rested his head against my shoulder while he caught his breath, face tucked under my chin. I was so mellow I was starting to fall asleep when he bit me right over the collar bone.

I smacked him in the back of the head. "God damn it, knock that off."

He snickered and said, "I'm sorry. I couldn't resist just once more."

"You are not sorry, you're an evil little shit."

"Well...you knew that before we started dating, so you only have yourself to blame." He rolled off me and said, "Come on, let's get cleaned up and then I'll make it up to you."

I turned to kiss him and get close again. "And how are you gonna do that?"

"I'll take you out and buy you clams and beer, and you can tell me about the case so far."

"Yeah, all right," I said, "that sounds fair."

Chapter 5

The next day I spent a few hours in the morning with my computer again, running background checks on all Gigi's employees. Out of thirty-six employees, three of them had some prior offences. There was nothing especially heinous, a few misdemeanors for things like drunk and rowdy behavior or drug possession. One DUI. The offenders were a waiter, a busboy...and Marco. In fact, Marco had a fairly decent list of the kind of charges that suggest a misspent youth. Thing was, he wasn't really all that old. All the crimes had occurred a few years before he went to work for Gigi, but not so long ago that you could call it ancient history.

I probably should have run a check on Gigi too, but I just couldn't bring myself to do it. I typed up all my notes, printed off the three rap sheets and slid everything into my briefcase.

Out in the hall, I ran into Della who was just coming up from the garden. She wore a big floppy hat and was putting pruning shears and dirty gloves into the small dresser that served as her foyer.

"Oh! Good mornin', darlin'." She beamed at me the same devious way she had before.

"Hi, Della, how are you today?"

"I'm just fine." She eyed me curiously and reached up. "Here, honey, let me fix your collar, it's all crooked."

Having dressed myself effectively for the better part of forty-one years, I didn't think it really was, but she liked to fuss, and quite honestly, I liked to let her.

Her eyes sparkled with glee while she tided me up, and she said, "Are you going out to see that lovely woman again? Let's see...what was her name..."

"Her name is Gigi. Gigi Sapora." Now I knew what she was up to. There was no way she'd forget.

"Oh, yes, that's right. Charming girl. You spent all day yesterday with her too, didn't you?" Della was positively glowing.

I sighed. "I'm working a case for her. I explained this to you."

"Of course you are, sugar," she said with a coquettish grin.

"Have a nice day, Della," I said, shaking my head as I turned and went down the stairs.

* * * *

I drove to Salvatore's, and the Friday afternoon party atmosphere was already getting into full swing even though it was only two-thirty. There were more cars in the lot, and the place was busier than before, but it still had a calm mood which made a nice contrast.

When I walked in, Felix was behind the bar and he lit up when he saw me. "Hey, Dino! Long time, no see."

He came around the end of the bar to give me a hug and handshake. Felix is a big guy with pure white hair that had already turned when I knew him ten years ago. Now there was a little less of it.

"Hi, Felix," I said, patting him on the back. "It's good to see you."

"Good to see you too, kid." He paused and cocked his head at me. "What the hell happened to you? You get attacked by a piranha?"

I frowned. "What are you talkin' about?"

He pointed to my neck and smirked. I leaned over to check myself out in a beer mirror and discovered a string of small bruises that ran from my ear to my collar bone. That's what Seth had been up to. Nice.

Movement in the corner of my eye caught my attention, and I turned to find Gigi looking at me with a mix of amusement and disdain. "That's very charming," she said.

"Ah, yeah," I said, rubbing my neck. "Listen, could we talk in your office, please?"

"Of course. Have you found something?"

"I don't know," I told her, following her down the back hall. "I want to take a look at your personnel files, if you don't mind."

She held the office door for me. "I don't know, Dino. I'm not sure that's legal."

"Don't tell anyone," I said with a shrug. "I'm not going to use the information for nefarious purposes. I just want to check out the staff."

She closed the door and folded her arms over her chest, apparently weighing her options.

"If it helps you make up your mind," I said, "I already ran background checks on everyone."

She raised her eyebrows. "Then why do you need to see the files?"

"There's different information in there. And I want to see who was tellin' the truth on their application and who wasn't."

"Do you find it difficult to have to distrust people for a living?" She wasn't being pissy, she looked genuinely uncomfortable. I supposed that was because I was asking her to question the honesty of her staff. Too close to home.

"No, I don't," I told her. "In the end, I find out a lot of people are actually honest and decent, so it works out all right."

She nodded and said, "All right. But please don't let anyone know I gave you permission. I don't need that kind of reputation right now."

"You have my word, Gigi, I swear it."

She crossed the room and pulled open a drawer, laying her hand on top of the contents. "All the personnel files are in front here. Do you want something to drink while you work?"

"I'd love some coffee if you don't mind."

When she came back with a steaming cup, I took a grateful sip. It was damn good coffee. I was in the process of going through the files in order, rather than just grabbing the three I was most interested in. I didn't want to prejudice myself.

"If you need anything else," she said, "I'll be in the kitchen. I need to meet with Angelo."

"Actually, I do have a question for you." I didn't think she was going to like this.

"Yes?"

"Are you aware that Marco has a criminal record?"

"I... Do you mean recently?" She furrowed her brows and came back to stand in front of the desk where I sat.

"No, not recently. Before you hired him, but he doesn't say so on his paperwork here." I held up the file.

"Well, I know that he went through a phase when he got into a lot of trouble. People can change. Why are you so concerned with Marco?" She sounded irritated.

"Ah, because he's got a record and he lied to you. He's also in a pretty good position to be someone who'd want to see you go down. If the restaurant tanks, and you decide to sell, he'd look like a knight in shining armor if he offered to buy it cheap when no one else will. Why are you so hell bent on defending him?"

"He's been a wonderful employee for a long time. I trust him."

"Did you know about the record?"

She was silent for a minute. Finally she sighed and said, "No."

"Okay, then I think we need to have a little talk with Marco."

A knock at the door interrupted whatever reply she was about to make. She opened the door to find the prep cook standing there in his white coat. "Joe, good, are all the supplies put away?"

He looked ill and licked his lips. "No. That's why I came to find you. The truck hasn't even shown up yet."

"What?"

He winced and held up his hands. "It's not here."

Gigi spun around with fury in her eyes and reached for the phone. "I do not need this today," she said, stabbing at the buttons.

"Is this unusual?" I asked.

"It's not common," she said, "but they've been late before. I told the warehouse manager if it happened again on a Friday, I might start looking for a new food supplier."

"Put it on speaker. I want to hear this."

The phone rang a few times before someone answered. "Five Star Food Service, how can I help you?"

Gigi said, "May I speak to Richard Kemp please?"

"Yeah, just a sec."

After a moment, another voice came on the line. "Richard, here."

"Richard, this is Gigi Sapora, at Salvatore's." She was working to control her voice. "I'm calling because we're still waiting for our delivery, and it's getting very late. You assured me this wasn't going to happen again."

"What the hell are you talking about, lady? You cancelled the order yesterday."

"I most certainly did not. We need that order. We're only a few hours from our weekend dinner rush. There's got to be some kind of mistake."

"Look, I got caller ID and the call definitely came out of Salvatore's. The guy I talked to said you'd hired another food service and didn't need us anymore."

Gigi ran a hand through her hair. "That's...that's not true. I never authorized anything like that."

She turned and gave me a 'what am I gonna do' face.

I leaned toward the phone. "Who made the call?" I asked.

"I don't know, the guy didn't leave a name."

"A restaurant calls to cancel their business with you, and you don't even ask?" I shook my head.

"Hey, no offense, pal, but restaurants are a dime a dozen around here. We lose one, and two more pop up."

"That doesn't matter," Gigi said. "This is all just a mix up. Could you fill the order and put a rush on it. Late food is better than no food."

"Sorry, lady, all my drivers are gone for the day. I got no one to make the delivery."

I snatched up the phone and spoke to the guy directly. "Listen, I can come get the order if you're willing to load up a truck. We realize this isn't your fault, we just need to fix it. Cut her a break, will ya?"

"No way, man. There is no way I'm letting someone from your outfit take one of my trucks. Even if I didn't mind, I'm sure my insurance agent would. We're not covered for that."

"I'm a licensed private investigator, and I'm fully bonded. I do vehicle repossessions for Ernie Schmendrick in St. Pete, you can call him and check me out."

"I don't really—"

"I'll pay you a hundred bucks cash to use the truck."

"Two hundred."

"Deal. You just get the truck ready."

I hung up the phone and turned to Gigi. "I'm gonna get Seth and we'll go pick up the truck. You carry on here and when I get back, I'm going to have a chat with Marco."

She huffed and said, "He didn't do this, Dino."

"Was he here yesterday?"

"Yes, but—"

"Then I want to talk to him. I'll be back as soon as I can, all right?"

"All right," she said. "Thanks, Dino."

Chapter 6

I was in the car and heading back north before I took out my phone and dialed Seth. He answered on the fourth ring and sounded preoccupied, which probably meant I had pulled him out from underneath a car. Tough.

"Dino, hi, what's going on?"

"You really *are* an evil little shit, and now you're gonna do me a favor and you don't get to say no."

"Oh?"

"Yeah. We need to go pick up a truck, and you have the license for it. I'm assuming you can drive a refrigerated panel truck?"

"I can drive anything, Dino," he said smugly.

"Great. I'll be there in fifteen minutes, be ready. We're in a hurry here."

"Okay. Dino, wait. Why am I an evil shit?"

"You know the answer to that. So does everyone else who's gotten a look at me today. Including Gigi, so I think you made your point."

I snapped the phone shut and threw it on the seat, because I was no mood to listen to him gloat. I know a lot of people think leaving bruises like that is pretty hot, but I prefer not to advertise. Something Seth knows very well.

I turned on the causeway, and when I pulled up in front of the auto shop, Seth already had the place closed up and was standing on the curb waiting for me. I suspected his extreme willingness to cooperate was something of an apology.

He jumped over the door and slid into the passenger seat, leaning over to plant a kiss on my jaw.

I gave him a sharp look and said, "You bite me again and I will knock you flat on your ass, you got that?"

He bit his lip to suppress a smirk. I was wrong. He wasn't sorry at all. I suppose I could have worse problems in life.

"Where are we going?" he asked as I pulled back into traffic.

"We've gotta' run and get a shipment of supplies for Gigi. The saboteur struck again and cancelled their order. If they don't get stocked up for the weekend, they're screwed, and the warehouse doesn't have anyone to drive the truck."

"You have any leads yet?" he asked.

"I have one, but Gigi's not buying it. She swears the guy is legit."

"I bet she's sleeping with him," Seth said.

I glanced at him out of the corner of my eye. "How in the hell can someone who sleeps around as much as you do have such a catty jealous streak? If anything, I should be the one who gets to act this way."

"*Slept* around."

"What?"

"Slept around. Past tense. You don't think I still do that, do you?" He actually looked kind of hurt.

I sighed. "No. That's not what I meant. I'm just sayin', I've got one ex, and you have like thousands."

"That's not true on either count," Seth pointed out, "and I don't have anyone that serious in my past. You're it, dude. You're *the one*."

"So, what, you're making up for lost time?" Admittedly, I liked hearing that, and I was willing to put up with a fair amount of his crap. I suppose in some twisted way, you could call it romantic.

* * * *

We got to the warehouse by four-thirty to find one lone guy with a pallet jack, loading up the most pathetic, run-down truck I've ever seen. It didn't look like it would make it out of the alley, let alone halfway down the coast.

I climbed out of the car and walked across the lot, Seth right behind me. "Hey!" I said to the guy. "I'm not paying you two hundred for a truck I have to push."

"She'll run," he said, giving me a weary look. "She may not look like much, but she runs fine. You the guy from Salvatore's?"

"Yeah." I took out my wallet and showed him my both my driver's license and my P.I. license.

He looked them over and nodded at Seth. "Who's this?"

"Seth Donnelly. He's gonna help, and he's a mechanic, thank God."

Seth pulled out his wallet as well, and the guy chuckled as he peered at it. "The truck is fine. You're not going to have any trouble. Listen, if you guys want to help me finish loading it, you can get out of here that much faster."

"Sure." I draped my jacket over the tailgate of a pickup parked nearby and the three of us got to work.

It took about ten minutes to load the truck and pay the guy, and it took another hour to pick our way through St. Petersburg's rush hour traffic. Seth bitched the entire way about teenagers, old people and crazy tourists.

The drive down through the beach towns wasn't much better, and I was glad I didn't have to do that every day. I made a mental note to cut truck drivers more slack in the future. In the meantime, I went over everything I'd learned so far with Seth. He agreed that Marco bore looking at more closely, and wanted to know about the other two employees with rap sheets. Two blocks from Salvatore's, we were sitting at a long light when an idea struck me.

"Get out of the truck," I told Seth, sliding across the seat to take his place.

"What?" He gaped at me. "What do you mean?"

"I mean get out, now, before the light changes. Hurry up." I reached across him and popped the door open.

"Dino..."

"I don't have time to explain right now. Just get out and wait for me right over there." I pointed to a bus stop bench on the corner. "I'll pick you up again after we get the truck unloaded. Go."

"You are such an ass," he muttered, but he jumped out of the truck and darted across the street just before traffic began to move. I looked in the side view mirror as I drove away and he flipped me off. I rolled down the window and waved.

When I got to the restaurant, I did my best to back the truck into their loading dock. It wasn't a stellar job, but it would do. A band of cooks and busboys rushed out and started hauling food at a frantic pace.

I went inside to find Gigi. She was in the kitchen with Angelo, Marco and the senior line cook, making hasty rewrites to the menu of specials for the night, and planning out how they'd work around the late delivery.

She looked up at me and smiled. "Dino, you're a lifesaver. I can't thank you enough."

Activity in the kitchen picked up as food was brought in, and I drew her out into the hallway for a few seconds of privacy.

"Listen," I said, "I know you'll have to work late tonight, but do you think you could swing by my apartment when you're done? I want to talk to you about our next step here."

She nodded. "Sure, I can do that. I'll give you a call when I'm leaving."

"Great. Oh, and ah, if you have any real good leftovers of anything, pack that up and bring it with you, we're gonna need it."

"Need it? Won't that be kind of late for dinner?"

"Just do it," I said, pressing up against the wall as a guy rushed through with a flat of tomatoes. "I gotta' go, I have someone waiting for me. I'll see you later."

She only had a moment to look confused before the greater concerns of dinner rush grabbed her attention, and I slipped out to go pick up Seth.

Chapter 7

In order to stall Seth's curiosity, I dropped him off at the shop to finish the car he was working on and drove the truck back myself. With the pressure off, I could take my time and the traffic didn't pose as much of a problem.

The guy was pleased to see me return with it in one piece, and before I left I gave him some bull about Salvatore's having a disgruntled employee and got him to agree to call back and check any unusual instructions directly with Gigi until further notice.

Matilda was no worse for wear, and all's well that ends well, I guess. Since I was already in that part of town, I thought I'd make a run past the construction company where Frank worked. I checked my notes against a city map and headed north. JH Construction was owned and run by John Holcomb. Hence the clever name. What little information I'd dug up on them was pretty run-of-the-mill. Small time operation, a few complaints and disputes from unhappy customers, and a pretty steady rate of turnover in employees. I was willing to bet the books were a testament to creative financing.

I pulled into the parking lot of a florist across the street and parked facing JH. From the outside, it looked pretty shoddy, but most of these places do. A painted sign propped up on the roof advertised: *Kitchen Remodel; Bathroom Remodel; Interior Construction; Concrete, Fence & Yard Construction.* Behind the main office stood a larger building for tools and supplies, the garage door open. In the parking lot there was a motley assortment of vans and trucks.

I didn't see anything matching the description of Frank's truck, so I got out of my car and trotted across the street. I wasn't exactly sure what I planned to do, but sometimes you just have to dive in and get a feel for a situation.

Inside, the place was a little nicer. The walls were all brown paneling with carpet to match, and the furniture had obviously been around a long time. None of it matched anything, but it was clean. A window air conditioning unit cranked away feebly next to the desk of a woman in her late fifties, who appeared to be serving as both bookkeeper and receptionist.

"Can I help you?" she asked. Polite, but not what I would call friendly.

"Ah, yeah." I stalled for a minute to assemble a game plan. More often than not, the truth works just fine. "I'm in the middle of remodeling my office, and I'm not getting very far with it. I'm thinking it's time to throw in the towel and see about having it done. You guys handle something like that?"

"We could probably help you." The voice was not the lady at the desk, but a large, bear-shaped man who'd appeared from out of the tiny hallway. The offices must have been close enough for him to keep tabs on anything going on. "How big a job is it?"

"Not too big. Just a few walls, really. I'm creating an office out of an old store front. Two rooms and an entryway, nothing fancy."

"Yeah, that sounds fine. We'll need to have someone come over and take a look to give you a proper quote." He held a hand out to me. "I'm John Holcomb."

I shook it and said, "That'll be great."

"What's your schedule look like?" He moved over near the desk and waved hastily to the receptionist, who turned and flipped open a large calendar book.

"I'm pretty flexible. Say, I know a guy who works here, Frank Novak." He glanced up at me. "You're friends with Frank?"

"More like friend of a friend. I like to try and help out people I know." John scoffed. "He needs all the help he can get."

"Ah. Like that, huh? Can't say I'm all that surprised."

"I do most of the quotes myself, but if you want Frank, I'll see to it he's assigned to the job. How big a hurry are you in?"

"I suppose sooner rather than later," I told him, "but I don't have any particular deadline."

"That's good," John said flatly. He didn't elaborate.

We scheduled an appointment for the following week and I left, not much more enlightened than I was before. It didn't take any leaps of imagination to guess that Frank had a pretty spotty record on the job, or that he wasn't especially well liked by his boss. The prospect of Frank working on my office didn't bother me. Honestly, I didn't think it was going to happen, but if it did, I couldn't see a problem there. He already knew who I was, so it made sense that I would choose his company for a remodeling job, and it might offer me another angle to work on Seth's case.

I drove home and put in a little time on a standard info search I was doing for a law office, and then stretched out on the couch for a while, just to rest. Seth showed up at ten and joined me, flopping onto my chest and falling into a light snooze.

At eleven o'clock, Gigi called to say she was on her way. I woke Seth and we both started moving so we'd be alert when she got there. I put a pot of coffee on, and was pouring it when she knocked on the door. I let her in, and she set two plastic bags full of takeout containers on the counter. Seth raised an eyebrow and took an immediate interest.

"You want a cup of coffee?" I asked her. I unpacked the food and took out some plates.

"Yes, please," she said, watching me quizzically. "This was all about bringing you a free dinner?"

"No, this is about your case. I just asked you to bring the food because Seth did most of the driving today and had to work late because of it."

"Oh," she said. "Well, thank you, Seth."

"Sure, no problem." He loaded a plate with a slab of lasagna, three kinds of pasta, a piece of fish, and two hunks of garlic bread, which he took to the table. "I would have helped unload it too, but Dino wouldn't let me."

"There's a reason for that," I said. I picked up a carton with the remains of some glorious smelling puttanesca and grabbed a fork. I pulled out a chair for Gigi and we joined Seth.

"Dino, what is going on?" she asked. "You're being very cagey."

I took a deep breath, because I had a great plan, but I knew it wasn't going to be well received by at least one, if not both of them.

"All right," I said, "today's little incident makes it pretty clear that whatever's going on, they have someone on the inside."

"They?" Gigi asked, eyes wide.

"Well, it still could be one person, but if so, he's still there, because that's where the call came from to cancel the shipment. And it had to be someone who knew there was going to be a shipment in the first place."

Gigi said, "Maybe the guy at the warehouse was lying to us. Maybe he's the one."

I shook my head. "When I went back, he showed me the caller ID memory. The call really did come from Salvatore's. I don't think he would have gone to that much trouble to fake it, and I don't see much of a motive there, anyway."

"You're just convinced it's Marco," she said, crossing her arms.

"Oh, don't start with that. I have very good reason to suspect him, but I haven't made up my mind about anything. We're just getting started here."

"But you're not willing to consider any other options."

"The hell I'm not," I said. "I've spent the last two days considering all kinds of options, but the one that has someone working on the inside covers all the events better than anything else."

Seth sighed and pushed noodles around on his plate. "I hate it when mom and dad fight."

Gigi started to say something, but snapped her mouth shut.

"Look, I'm sorry," I said. "I'm not just targeting Marco here. At the moment, I suspect everyone there but you. That's why I want *us* to have someone on the inside too. That way we stand a better chance of figuring out what's going on."

"What are you talking about, Dino?" Gigi sat up straight.

Seth froze with his fork halfway to his plate. He spoke through a mouthful of pasta. "This is bribery food, isn't it?"

"Yes it is, busboy, eat up."

Understanding dawned on Gigi's face. "You want me to hire Seth at the restaurant to spy on the staff."

"That's why you didn't want me in the truck," Seth said, leaning back in his chair. "You didn't want anyone there to know I was with you."

"Yes, and yes. We get Seth in there to find out who's the one pullin' strings from the inside and then we can find out what the story is."

Gigi nodded slowly. "Okay. Yes, I think that would work. I'm willing to do it."

Seth didn't look so certain. "I'd love to help, but come on, Dino, I already have a pretty full workload at the shop."

"Yeah, I thought about that," I told him. "I can come over in the mornings and give you a hand, so you're free to go to the restaurant."

"I would put you on the payroll, of course," Gigi said.

Seth made a few faces, and I said, "It's not gonna be more than about a week, I don't think."

"You know, I'm not very good with authority," he said, working hard to come up with excuses.

Gigi is a shrewd woman, however, and she leaned forward, resting her chin in her hand and grinning at him. "I'll feed you. Every night. All you want."

He smirked and said, "Yeah, yeah, all right. I'll do it."

"Thank you," she said. "I know it's asking a lot."

Seth scooped more spaghetti into his mouth and gulped it down. "I'm really *not* good with a boss, though. I'll try, but I can't make any promises."

"Actually," I said, "that's not gonna be a problem. We don't want you to come across like Gigi's pet project or no one will talk to you. Without causing any actual trouble, the bigger a jerk you are, the more likely it is you're gonna get along with whoever doesn't have Gigi's best interests at heart."

Seth considered that, and Gigi said, "Hmm. This might be kind of fun. Well, if the stakes weren't so high."

I felt bad for her, with that cloud hanging over her head. I hoped we'd solve the case quickly, and I hoped for her sake it really wasn't Marco. Whatever her relationship with him, it was clear she'd be devastated if he turned out to be the one screwing with her.

"Gigi," I said, "do you think you can get Seth in there tomorrow night without causing a lot of suspicion?"

"Sure. I have people putting in for vacation all the time, and one of our servers just told me she's pregnant. We can always use people. I can also say that I hired him as a favor to someone, which really isn't even a lie. We do that a lot anyway, since bussing doesn't require much training." She turned to Seth. "When you come in tomorrow, just act like we've already had an interview, and I called you up to hire you. Everyone will think you were around on their day off. As far as most of the staff is concerned, new people just show up all the time."

"Yeah, okay. What time should I be there?"

"Four or five is fine. If you want to really hear anything interesting, you should probably plan to work until close."

"Deal."

"You're a good man, Seth," I said.

"Don't you forget it, either."

"I don't plan to," I told him. There was another subject I wanted to touch base with Gigi on, and I asked her, "Have you noticed that car following you in the past couple of days?"

She shook her head. "No, not lately. I still get that feeling like I'm being watched, but maybe that's coming from someone at the restaurant."

"Maybe," I said. "I just want you to watch your back. Are you safe when you're at home?"

"I think so. I live in a secure building, and I'm on the second floor."

"All right," I said, "but make sure you have my number and you give me a call if anything strange happens. I mean anything. And don't get real nervous if you see me hanging around. I'm gonna be keeping an eye on you, and want to try to catch that guy in the act."

She nodded and stood up. "I'll be careful."

After she left, Seth and I ate a little more and cleaned up the mess. Then I took him to bed and thanked him properly for putting his neck on the line.

Chapter 8

While Seth was learning the ropes at Salvatore's, I opted to spend the weekend tailing Gigi to see if I could catch whoever might be following her. Even if I only got a look at the guy, it would confirm she *was* being shadowed and I'd have a place to work from. If not, we weren't any worse off.

After Seth went home Saturday morning, I got Ruth to loan me her car and drove out to Gigi's apartment building. I parked across the street and down a ways, where I had a good view of the front door and the parking lot. If anyone pulled out after Gigi, there's no way I'd miss it.

I checked my watch. It was just after ten, and Gigi said she didn't usually leave for the restaurant until about ten-thirty unless something was going on. Otherwise, she worked at home in the mornings.

I had a hot cup of coffee in the console, and binoculars and my camera on the seat next to me. My gun was stashed under the seat just in case. I was all set. I considered calling Gigi to let her know I was there so she wouldn't get freaked out if she noticed, but thought better of it. For one thing, I didn't want her acting strange if someone else was watching, and for another, there was always the off chance she hadn't been completely up front with me. If I was going to do surveillance, I may as well do it on everybody.

Several people left, and a few arrived in the time I sat there. Nothing noteworthy that I saw. About a half hour later, Gigi finally came out and went to her car, carrying a briefcase and an armload of three-ring binders. I watched her pull out and turn down the street away from me, and then waited. No one followed her, so after a couple minutes, I started the car and headed off in the direction Gigi had gone.

I caught up to her two blocks away at the stoplight and tailed her all the way to work. I hung back a few cars and kept my eye on the traffic to see if anyone else took the same route we did. As far as I could tell, she and I were the only ones who drove to Salvatore's.

She pulled into the parking lot and took her usual space at the back. I waited on the corner until she was safely inside, and then went home to get some sleep before the night shift.

The drive to Gigi's that night didn't net us anything either, and after hanging around until midnight, I called it off and went home.

Sunday, she only spent part of the day at the restaurant. After a few hours, she left and I followed her while she ran a few errands and went to the grocery store. A block away from her apartment, she stopped to put gas in her car, so I went ahead and got into position outside her building. It would look kind of suspicious if I drifted in right after her anyway, and if I was there and waiting, I'd be able to see if anyone else was following her.

A few other cars were parked along the street, and I examined those. The one that caught my attention was a hunter green sedan. Not only did it fit the description of the one Gigi'd mentioned, it had a guy sitting in it.

When he was still waiting there a few minutes later, I started to get a prickle at the back of my neck. I picked up my camera and focused on the back end of the car, zooming in to snap a picture of his license plate. I also used it to get a better look at the guy. He was in his late thirties, maybe. Younger than me, but not by much. He had longish brown hair which was tucked behind his ears and mussed salon style. I would call him average looking, and he appeared to be wearing some kind of non-descript pullover jersey. I couldn't see the rest.

I put the camera in its bag and reached under the seat for my gun, clipping the holster to the back of my waistband. Hopefully, there'd be no need for it and the evening would end with both of us driving away, and me running down the plate number so I could nail the bastard.

I kept my eye on the end of the block, and when Gigi's car came into view, I checked out the sedan. He had noticed, too, and was watching intently. Gigi parked her car and got out, then went to the back to take out a bag of groceries. When she turned and headed for the front door, he opened his. That was the less desirable end to our evening, and it was my cue to move.

He was a lot closer, and he got to Gigi before I was halfway across the street. She stopped short when she saw him, and it was clear she was startled by him. He said something I couldn't make out, and she responded by making excuses.

"...really isn't the best time. I just got home, and I've had a long day. I'm sorry."

"You just need to hear me out," he said. "Give me a chance."

I had been planning to act like I just ran into Gigi by chance, and play the friendly neighbor routine, but when he grabbed her elbow, I rushed forward and tackled him.

He went down like a house of cards. I got him pinned and wrenched an arm up behind his back. "You got about three seconds to explain yourself, asshole."

"What the hell, man?"

Gigi gasped with surprise and then said, "Dino, what are you doing?"

"Ah. My job..." I looked up at her and frowned. "Some guy stakes out your apartment and hassles you, I figure he's a pretty good candidate."

"Candidate for what?" The guy struggled beneath me. "What's he talking about, Gigi?"

"Shut up," I said, pushing him flat. "You know this guy?"

"Yes. Dino, let him up." She looked confused and obviously rattled. And it wasn't just by me.

"Are you gonna stand there and tell me you weren't bothered when you saw this guy? Because that's what it looked like to me."

"Well, yes, but not like that." She shifted the grocery bag in her arms and avoided my gaze. "I dated him a few months ago, but we split up. His name is Derek."

I tightened my grip on his arm. "So, what, Derek? She dumped you and you decided to make her life a living hell?"

"What? No!" He twisted to look at Gigi. "Who is this guy? What the hell is going on?"

"Drop the act, asshole. We know you've been following her. She saw your car. As far as I'm concerned, that makes you look good for everything else."

"Dino, stop it," she said. "People are going to start to notice you kneeling on a man in my front yard. Let him up and we'll talk."

She had a point, and by then I *was* the reason she was upset, so I stood up and hauled Derek to his feet by the back of his shirt. I didn't let go. I steered him over to a garden bench and shoved him into it. "All right, talk. You can start by explaining why you've been following her."

Gigi came to stand next to me, and he looked nervously between us. "I haven't been following her, exactly. I did try to catch up to her a couple times, but it didn't work out. That's why I came here and waited." He turned to Gigi. "I just wanted to ask you out again."

"Ever heard of a phone, jackass?"

Gigi sighed. "I've been ignoring his messages."

"So clearly, he can't take a hint. I'm not hearin' anything that says he's not our guy."

"What guy? Could someone fill me in, please?"

"I'm sorry, Derek." She sat on the bench and set the bag in the grass. "Someone's been sabotaging the restaurant, and I've just been too worried and preoccupied to deal with anything else. I should have at least called you back."

"Holy shit, are you all right?" He seemed genuinely shocked, but I've seen some pretty good actors in my day.

"I've been better." She pointed at me. "This is Dino. He's a private detective I hired to investigate the situation."

His eyes got big. "And you think I would do something like that?"

"She may not, but I sure as hell do," I cut in. "Give me one good reason why I shouldn't."

"I like Gigi, I would never hurt her."

"Who broke it off?"

"Neither one of us, really. We both got busy and decided to take a break. I play in a band, and we had a bunch of out-of-town gigs lined up. I wasn't going to be around for a while."

Gigi nodded. "That's true. There weren't any hard feelings. I really don't think he's involved."

"Then why the unhappy face when you saw him?"

"Because I've been avoiding him, and I still don't want to deal with it." She gave Derek an apologetic look and put a hand on his shoulder. "I'm sorry. I don't mean to be so blunt. I'm just tired."

"No sweat. You're a straight shooter. I've always liked that."

I rubbed the back of my neck and sighed. He was still on my short list of suspects, but there wasn't a lot more I could do at the moment. "All right then, I guess. Derek, I think you should beat it."

"Dino," Gigi scolded.

"Hey, I'm a straight shooter too."

Derek stood up and said, "It's okay. I didn't mean to give you a hard time. Maybe when this is all over we can get a drink sometime."

She nodded and stood up.

To me, he said, "Good luck finding the guy. I hope you solve it real soon."

"Oh, you can count on that, Derek." I gave him a hard look and kept it up until he was in his car and leaving.

When I turned back, Gigi had her groceries and was flipping through her key ring for the house key. "Did you really have to be so hard on him?"

"Well, if he's the guy, yes. And if he's not, I don't really give a rat's ass."

"He's not the guy."

"You know, this is going to be a very difficult case if you keep trying to defend all my potential suspects."

"I'm just trying to save you some time and trouble." She went up to the front door and unlocked it. "I know these people."

"Sometimes you don't know 'em as well as you think. Just be careful, all right?"

"I will be. Thanks, Dino, and good night."

She went inside and I walked back to the car. I made a few notes, and then sat there and read the sports section, in case Derek decided to come back. An hour later, when the coast was still clear, I called it a night and drove home.

Chapter 9

I was sitting on the patio with Ruth, drinking iced tea and sharing a newspaper. It was Monday afternoon, and I'd just gotten back from helping Seth fix cars. Two days of bussing tables hadn't produced anything in the way of leads, but we hadn't really expected it to. It was too soon after the cancelled shipment for them to try anything, which was fine because Seth needed time to get known among the staff before he was likely to make any progress.

That morning I'd run Derek's license plate and didn't find anything to suggest he wasn't telling the truth. He actually had been out of town more often than not in the past two months. Including, I noticed, the date when someone had been checking out Salvatore's at County Records. It was looking far less likely that he was involved.

I'd put off questioning Marco, partly because I didn't think Gigi needed her feathers ruffled any more than they already were, and partly because we had Seth in there. I wanted to give him some time to observe Marco before I tipped my hand. However, in the absence of any other good leads, I planned to do it that evening.

"Oh, for heaven's sake," Ruth muttered, shaking her head. She was frowning at her newspaper.

"What's the matter?" I asked.

"It's all these greedy land developers. They're not going to stop until the entire Gulf coast is nothing but a bunch of high-rise hotels and condominiums. The sun won't even be able to shine on the beach half the day."

"What's going on?" I put down the sports section and took a sip of iced tea.

"Sunset Hotel Corp just got city council approval to build three brand new luxury hotels. The county is going to rezone those neighborhoods from residential to commercial for them."

"Does it say which ones?"

"Paradise Island, Crystal Island, and Vina del Mar. Frankly, I'm a little shocked that they went ahead with it. I've been following this story, and I really thought they would vote it down."

That caught my attention. I leaned forward. "How long have you been following this?"

"Oh, a couple of months, I suppose. I mostly know what they report from the city council meetings. Why?"

"Because Vina del Mar is across the bridge from Gigi's restaurant. The only way to get there is right past Salvatore's."

Ruth raised her eyebrows. "Mmm. I'd imagine that's going to be a pretty hot property when the hotel plans are finalized."

"You and me both," I said. "And whatever jackass has been targeting her. So, how common is this knowledge? I had no idea this was going on, but you did..."

"I have no idea how long ago these deals started, but at a certain point, it needs to be brought before the city council and once that happens it's a matter of public record. Anyone who takes the time to read the council reports could know about it. I don't gather very many people bother, however."

I gave her a wide smile. "You have no idea how glad I am that you bother. You just gave me a hell of a leg up on this guy."

She seemed pleased, and said, "Anything I can do to help. Gigi seemed like quite a nice woman, and I'd like to see you solve her case."

"Yeah. So would I."

"Has it been very difficult? Working with someone you used to be involved with?" She looked at me in a kind of a maternal way, and I wondered what was up.

"Ah. Not too bad, really. I mean, it's a little weird, but you expect that, you know?"

"That's good to hear," she said. "Maybe ten years has made a difference in the two of you."

I nodded and licked my lip. "Okay, yeah. You sound like Della now, you know that?"

"Oh, I'm not that bad, am I?" She smiled and shook her head. "We're fond of you, Dino, we'd just like to see you be happy. It seems a shame for such a sweet man to be alone, that's all."

"Well, I'm not...like other guys. I'm fine."

I'd started to say I wasn't alone, but couldn't quite do it. That would have required explanations I wasn't planning to give. I was glad Seth wasn't around to hear me, but she might not think I was so sweet if she knew.

"I'm sorry, Dino, I shouldn't be prying."

"Hey, it's all right, Ruth. It's nice to be cared about. But you can sure as hell bet I'm never gonna introduce you ladies to my mother. I'd be sunk."

She laughed and poured herself more iced tea.

"Listen, I have to get going," I said. "Do you mind if I hang on to that article?"

"Of course not." She folded up her section of the newspaper and handed it to me.

Upstairs at my desk, I got online and looked up everything I could on the Sunset Hotel deal. There wasn't a whole lot available. What there was consisted mostly of council reports like the ones Ruth had told me about, but I printed them off anyway and added them to the file of information I was building.

I pulled out the list of records accessed at the same time Salvatore's was, and sure enough, I found several with the same timestamp that had to do with Sunset, council reports, and Vina del Mar. There wasn't anything that pointed me in a new direction, but at least it confirmed the hotel deal as a likely motive.

Then it occurred to me that at some point all the houses on Vina del Mar would have to be bought and demolished. You hear all the time about guys who are the last hold-out in a neighborhood like that and get paid a mint just to get them out of there. I scanned the list and found reports for a whole slew of residential listings in Pass-a-Grille. It could be coincidence, of course, but I didn't think so. Somebody was covering all his angles.

Now that I had a motive, it was time to have a talk with Marco.

Chapter 10

I arrived at Salvatore's around six; right about the time dinner rush picked up, but on a Monday night that wasn't a big deal. Instead of getting right down to business, I took at seat at the bar and asked for a menu. I figured I could have dinner, check out the scene for a while, and then take care of business.

The bartender brought me the menu and an amaretto on the rocks. I turned sideways and studied the room. The tables were maybe half full, but the room was lively, and the staff was hopping. One gregarious waiter was charming the pants off a table of coeds. I didn't see Marco anywhere, but Seth was across the room cleaning off a table. When he hauled his pan of dirty dishes through to the kitchen, he met my eye and smirked, but didn't show any other sign of knowing me. I allowed myself a moment to admire his strong arms, then went back to actual detective work.

I ordered spinach ravioli and some garlic bread, and after a while, Gigi herself brought it out to me. "Good evening, Dino. How are you tonight?"

"I'm good. New kid working out all right?"

"Well, he gets the tables clean." She threw a little exasperation in her voice for the benefit of anyone who might happen to be listening.

I swallowed a bite of ravioli and said, "So, is Marco working tonight?"

This time the exasperation was entirely for me. "Yes, he is. Do we really have to do this?"

"You know we do. I've explained this more than once. If he's everything you say he is, then there's no harm done."

"Except that he'll think I don't trust him."

"No," I said, "he'll think *I* don't trust him. You can hate me as much as you want to in there. He'll think you're his fairy godmother."

She sighed. "I don't hate you, Dino. This whole mess is just getting to be too much for me."

"You're tough, you'll get through this."

"Thanks. When do you want to talk to him?" She ran a hand through her hair and glanced over at Marco, who was showing an elderly couple to a table by the window.

"You tell me," I said. "I've got all evening. Just let me know when there's a break where you two are free for about half an hour."

"All right. Enjoy your dinner."

She left and I finished eating in between chatting up the bartender and casually watching the interactions of the staff in the large bar mirror. Two waitresses and a flamingly gay waiter were gathered near the server's station engaged in the latest gossip. From what I made out, it was more of the dating and parties variety than anything really pertaining to the restaurant. Seth passed by them with a saucy grin, and all three responded warmly. If there was anything useful in their conversation, I'd hear about it later.

It was past seven when Gigi finally came to get me and led me to the office. Marco was already there, sorting through a pile of invoices. He looked up when we walked in, but didn't seem too concerned with us.

"Marco, do you have a minute?" Gigi asked.

"Of course."

"This is Mr. Martini. He'd like to talk to you."

Marco's gaze turned to me. He looked curious, but calm. Gigi folded her arms over her chest and faded back into the corner of the office. Clearly, I was on my own.

"What do you know about the problems the restaurant's been having?"

"Well, it's been pretty bad. I mean, every time we turn around there's something else going on. We can hardly keep up with it." He glanced at Gigi and back to me. "I'm sure Gigi's explained everything to you."

I nodded and stared him down until he started to squirm a little. "What if I said I think you know more than you're lettin' on?"

He looked confused for a moment, and then his eyes widened. "You... think I have something to do with it?" He turned to Gigi. "Do you think I'm behind all this?"

She was silent, but shook her head almost imperceptibly.

"I don't know, Marco," I said, leaning heavily on my accent. Sounding like a wise guy can be very useful sometimes. "You had opportunity for all of it, you know what kind of things could really hurt this restaurant, and you're privy to the necessary details like the timing of shipments and what's coming up on the menu for the week. A guy like you could stand to be in a pretty good position if this place starts to go down."

"How can you say that? If Salvatore's goes under, I'm out of a damn good job." He appealed to Gigi. "I swear I don't have anything to do with what's going on. I love this job. You must know you can trust me."

"Yeah?" I said. "Then why did you lie on your application? Doesn't sound like the work of a trustworthy guy to me."

He looked pale. "I... What do you mean?"

"Come off it, kid. You got a rap sheet as long as my arm, but you neglected to mention any of that on your paperwork here."

"That was a really long time ago." He slumped in the chair.

"It wasn't so long ago when you were applying here."

"I know that." He spoke to Gigi. "You know I had kind of rough patch for a while. I just never told you how rough. I got into a lot of trouble, drugs, arrests, the whole deal. Thing is, I woke up one day and realized that if I didn't change my ways, I wasn't going to live too long. I got scared. So, I did my time, I paid off my fines and I moved away from all that." He ran a hand through his hair. "I tried playing it straight for a while, but when you tell the truth, no one wants to hire you. I was getting desperate. So, I lied to get the job. I knew once I got hired on somewhere, I could prove myself. I just had to convince someone to give me a chance."

The guy was so earnest it was pitiful. Every gut instinct I had told me he was being straight with us. I still planned on keeping an eye on him, but I no longer considered him our best lead. Which sucked, since I didn't have any second best lead.

"Marco, I'm sorry," Gigi said. "We had to ask about it. I *do* trust you. I couldn't run the restaurant without you. You've been a huge help through all of this."

He smiled, relieved. "Thank you. I'm just glad you're not going to fire me. You're not, are you?"

"No, I'm not."

Business in the dining room was starting to pick up again, and Marco was needed out on the floor, so that pretty much put an end to our meeting.

He left, and as we followed him out into the hall, Gigi gave me a snooty little smirk and said, "I told you so."

I sighed. "Yep, you did. Although, I would like to point out that until we actually know who's guilty, we still can't completely rule him out. Or anyone else."

She stopped dead and turned to face me. "You *wanted* it to be Marco."

"Well, it sure would have made my job a lot easier," I said with a shrug. Even as I did so, I knew joking about it was a stupid idea.

"*Honestly,* Dino." Gigi huffed and stalked away from me.

Seth was just passing us with another pan of dirty dishes and muttered under his breath at me, "Trouble in paradise?"

I turned to stare after him as he disappeared into the kitchen. "Well, shit."

Chapter 11

I was a week into the case, and not only did I not have a whole hell of a lot to show for it, I'd managed to piss off both my client and boyfriend. Or whatever we were calling it. Gigi was going to be a little harder to placate, but Seth could be bought off with beer, so Tuesday night I picked him up after the restaurant closed and took him out for some.

It was a warm night, and we opted to head further down Pass-a-Grille and sit on the deck of one of the nightspots on the beach. Calypso music drifted out of the bar on one side of us, and the surf rumbled quietly on the other. Seth looked tired and dirty, but relatively content as he slurped the head off a huge mug of pale ale.

"I don't mind helping you out on a case, but man I hope the next time you make me go undercover it's as the towel boy for the Swedish Coed Tanning Team."

"Not having fun at the restaurant?"

"Look at this, Dino, I have dishpan hands." He held one up for me to see.

"At least they're clean for a change."

"All I can say is I hope you get this one solved quickly."

"I talked to Ruth yesterday," I said. "I think we found a possible motive."

"No shit?" He licked foam from his lip and took a deep drink.

"Sounds like Sunset Hotel Corp is looking to put in a new luxury resort on Vina del Mar, which means Salvatore's will be sitting on the corner of High Traffic Boulevard and Exclusive Gateway to Rich People."

"And Gigi didn't know about this?"

"Still doesn't. I haven't had a chance to tell her. The project is so early in the planning stage that most people don't know. Ruth found the info in the city council reports."

Seth stretched his legs out on an empty chair and leaned back with his beer clutched in his lap. "That would certainly be one hell of a motive."

"Yep. I don't want to rule out anything else just yet, but it's my working theory for the moment." I took a sip of my beer. "What about you? Have you learned anything?"

"People are disgusting, Dino, you know that?" He made a face and swallowed more beer. "You should see the kind of messes they make. And I'll tell you what, it doesn't take long for a dumpster of food scraps to start smelling like rotting ass."

I hid a smirk behind my hand. "Let me rephrase that. Have you learned anything useful?"

He shook his head. "Not much. I'm still getting to know everyone. Most of the servers are either college students or singles tryin' to make a living. Three of the busboys are partiers and spend their paychecks as fast as they make them. For the most part, everyone's happy to be there. Gigi's a nice boss, easy to work for."

"Who's not happy?"

"Well, I can't really point to anyone who's clearly got an axe to grind, but I do have a short list of people I'd be more likely to suspect of being our insider."

"Let's have it," I said, pulling a notepad out of my pocket.

He sat up straight and leaned across the table. "There's Karen. She's a server, and she's a Class A bitch. Everything pisses her off, and I've never seen her even crack a smile. She spends most of her time complaining about her husband, and I wouldn't really suspect her, except that she's got a pretty nasty vindictive streak and thinks everyone deserves what they've got coming to them."

"Yeah, I remember her," I said. "She's got a pretty solid work history. Maybe she's sick of the daily grind."

Seth shrugged. "There's Julio, whose English is so bad I can't understand most of what he says. He could be plotting to overthrow the government for all I know."

I jotted that down, but he didn't seem too likely as a suspect.

"Oh, there's this dude named Lester, who's about as swift as a box of hair."

"And you suspect him why?" I asked.

"He's got beady eyes."

"Beady eyes." I regarded him flatly while I took a sip of beer.

"I am not shittin' you, man. This kid is creepy as hell. He's got this lizard stare, and he skulks around all the time. I would not be surprised to find him in the kitchen eating bugs."

"There aren't any bugs in Gigi's kitchen, are there?"

Seth seemed to realize what he was saying and shook his head. "No. No, there's not, but they ride in on the produce sometimes. We kill 'em in the freezer and dump them."

"Okay," I said, adding Lester to the list. "Who else?"

"Chad. He's one of the servers, gayer than hell. He also works at a bar and a dance club, because he wants to learn the business. He'd like to open his own place someday. I'd probably put him at the top of my list, although he's a pretty decent guy. That's about it for now, but I'll keep paying attention to everyone."

I put away the notebook and settled back in my chair. "Have you been able to hear or see anything incriminating on any of these people?"

"Sorry, dude. It took a couple days just to get the hang of things and figure out who everyone was."

"Don't worry about it," I said. "Cases are usually slow at the start. Look how far I am."

"I take it Marco didn't pan out?"

"No, not really. I'm not takin' him off the list just yet, but he sounded pretty sincere to me. What's your take on the guy?"

Seth thought about it a minute. "He seems okay. He's always doing eight things at once, but doesn't lose his temper with people. Most of the time he has the restaurant's best interests at heart. He's been giving out free food and drinks right and left to keep people happy. Some lady was bitching about the latest review that said they used old seafood, so he brought out a sample for her to taste before she ordered."

"Yeah," I mused. "That doesn't sound like someone who wants to see Salvatore's reputation go down the toilet."

"I don't think so, but I'll keep an eye on him anyway." He drained the last of his beer and set the mug on the table, stretching and trying to stifle a yawn. His eyes were half-closed, but he still managed to give me a flirty leer. "You wanna take me home and put me to bed?"

"Sure," I said, finishing my drink.

"Are you going to stay in it with me?"

"In *your* bed?"

"Yes, because then I can sleep until the very last possible minute before I have to go down and get to work. I don't want to have to schlep over from your place in the morning."

"How bad is it?" I asked, following when he got up and headed for the steps to the parking lot.

"How much do you love me?"

"Oh, jeez...that bad?" I cringed at the thought of what I'd be facing up there. It was tragic even on a good day, and he sure as hell hadn't had any time for cleaning in the last week. Of course, it was my doing that he was so damn busy. "Yeah, yeah. I'll stay. You manage to survive somehow, so I suppose I can too."

"You're all heart," he said wryly.

We got in the car, and I swung out, crossing back over to the main street and heading north. Traffic was heavier than before, since all the bars and clubs were closing down, but it was still manageable. Seth was slouched in the passenger seat, and we weren't especially in a hurry.

"So tell me how you're making out with my sister's case," he said.

"I ran a background check on Frank and a credit report on Molly."

He sat up straighter and eyed me. "You what?"

"That's the way I start most cases," I told him. "I run the names through a few databases and agencies, see what I can turn up."

"Yeah, for *Frank*. You're not supposed to be digging up dirt on my *sister*."

I rolled my eyes. "I was not digging up dirt, I was gathering information. You want me to come up with enough stuff so you could convince Molly to kick this guy to the curb, right?"

"Yeah..." He was wound up tight, and if I didn't have sisters myself, I would have found it amusing. As it was, I knew he was entirely likely to take my head off if I crossed the line. After the sex, of course.

"So, I think being able to tell her this guy is starting to take her down with him will go a long way toward that, don't you?"

He shrugged and nodded reluctantly. "What else have you done?"

"I scoped out the place he supposedly works. They admit to having him on the roster, but they didn't seem too impressed with him. I doubt he's going to have that job for long. I also made an appointment to have them look at my office and give me a quote. I figure that gives me a reason to be around asking questions without anyone getting suspicious."

"Okay, good. What else?"

"Nothing else. I'm just getting started here, what do you expect?"

"I expect you to give my case at least as much attention as you're giving Gigi's." He folded his arms over his chest and I half expected him to stamp his foot.

I sighed. "You're not serious..."

The look he gave me was equal parts pissed and incredulous. "Why the fuck not? You think my case isn't as important?"

"I'm not talking about the cases. I can't believe you're getting jealous over this and accusing me of playing favorites here."

"No, Dino, the problem is that you're *not* playing favorites."

"I…" It took me a minute to work that one out, and I turned to stare at him. "Who the hell are you and where did the obnoxious mechanic go?"

Seth looked embarrassed, his mouth working silently while he fished around for some kind of response. Finally, he sputtered, "I told you when we got together this was a new thing for me and I might possibly freak out a little. You got to have your freak out, now it's my turn." He slumped back into the seat and furrowed his brow.

"Okay, settle down, sparky. I get it." I reached over and patted him on the leg. Irrational behavior is often a lot easier to deal with when everyone knows it's irrational.

As we approached Salvatore's, I saw someone dart across the parking lot and jump into a waiting car which took off.

"Hey," I said, rapping Seth on the shoulder. "I thought you were part of the closing crew tonight."

He sat up and peered out the windshield. "I was. I have no idea who the fuck that is, but I can pretty much guarantee they shouldn't be there."

I slowed and said, "Am I supposed to ignore this, or can I work on Gigi's case without you imploding?"

He made a rude sound. "Yes, of course. Get going."

I stomped on the gas and set my sights on the guy. "Gotcha, asshole," I muttered as I watched the tail lights ahead of me. I ran the red light and tried to catch them. Unfortunately, it was single lane traffic in tight, narrow streets. Not much room to maneuver.

"Move it, Dino," Seth snapped, gripping the dashboard. "I can still see him, but he's gettin' away."

"I'm doing the best I can." I caught a break and was able to pass the slowpoke ahead of us, but it was close. I got a blast of truck horn in my ear, and I suspected there was a finger involved, but didn't bother to look. "This is not good territory for a car chase, you know."

We kept on him all the way to St. Pete Beach, but there the traffic is heavier, and the roads fan out into several blocks in each direction. I stayed on the main drag for a few blocks, thinking it was his most likely route. Unfortunately, we'd lost sight of him at the intersection. I tried a few of the side streets. We cruised slowly and looked down each crossing.

There were too many places for him to go, and not enough light to see by. We'd lost him.

"Damn it." I slammed my hand on the steering wheel and pulled over when we finally admitted defeat. "Son of a bitch."

"Did you get anything?" Seth asked. "Plate? A good look at the guy gettin' in?"

I sighed. "No. We were too far away. I saw a dark colored sedan, that's the best I can do."

"That is not a fat lot of help, sadly."

"Yeah, I know." I pulled into a gas station to turn around. "We better go take a look at what they were up to back there."

Everything seemed quiet and normal when we drove into the lot. I shut the car off. If I hadn't seen someone messing around there, we'd have just driven past assuming things were okay. I got out and walked toward the side lot, where I'd seen the figure running from. It made sense, that's where the back door was, along with the dumpsters and all the restaurant machinery.

Seth fell in step beside me, and we walked carefully along the side of the building, looking for signs of vandalism. The seals on all the electrical panels were still intact, and I didn't see any broken windows, or damage that suggested anyone had broken in.

"It's quiet," I said. "If anyone had gotten inside, the alarm should have gone off."

Seth stood still and cocked his head, glancing at me.

"You got something?" I asked him.

He held up a hand for moment. Finally, he said, "It's too quiet." He paced along the side of the building, scrutinizing all the equipment. He looked up at the roof and muttered, "Oh, shit."

"What?"

"The compressor's not running. They knocked out the refrigerator." He reached for the gutter of the roofline. "Give me boost."

The building was only a single story, with a roof that sloped sharply off the sides, so it wasn't very high to get up to. I stood behind him and laced my fingers to give him something to step on, then pushed him the rest of the way up.

He leaned over and said, "You have a flashlight you can toss me?"

"Yeah, hang on." I ran back to the car and got my tool kit out of the trunk. Seth was out of sight when I returned, and I whistled up to him.

"Toss up a screwdriver too," he said when he reached for the flashlight.

I handed up both, and then stepped back a few feet to see what he was doing. He crouched down next to the large gray compressor and pried a side panel off, casting around with the flashlight.

"Actually," he said, "this isn't so bad. He cut the electrical wires to knock out power to the compressor."

"Sounds like a pretty big problem to me."

He shook his head. "No, if he'd pulled the hoses, then we'd be fucked, because the Freon would all leak out in just a couple of minutes. Both the freezer and the refrigerator would be dead, and we'd have to call someone in right away. This, I can fix this right now if you have some electrical tape."

I dug in the kit and found a roll, which I threw up to him.

While he worked, I pulled out my cellphone and dialed Gigi's number.

"Dino?" She sounded groggy when she answered. "It's two-thirty in the morning, what's going on?"

"Well, I'm standing in the parking lot of Salvatore's, listening to your freezer not running."

"Oh my God, what happened?" she yelped, sounding significantly more alert.

"It's okay," I said. "We caught it right away, and Seth's fixing it as we speak. Nothing had a chance to even think about thawing out. Your saboteur struck again, and this time we almost caught him in the act." I explained about the car and the cut wires.

"I'll be there as soon as I can," she said.

"I don't think you need to come down here in the middle of the night. Seth's just about done splicing the wires, and that will keep it running tonight. You'll want to get someone in here tomorrow to get them replaced, but you may as well get your sleep."

"If you think it's all right." She sounded deflated, and the fatigue crept back into her voice.

"Yeah, I think so. We never even got close enough to the guy for him to realize he was being followed. As far as he's concerned you've already got fish puddles forming in your kitchen."

"Ugh, you really like to paint a colorful picture, don't you?"

"I'm tryin' to lighten the mood here. Maybe you can get back to sleep. I'll touch base with you tomorrow."

"Okay. I hope you'll have some good news soon."

"I might have a motive," I said. "I'll tell you about it when I see you. Get some sleep, okay?"

"Thanks, Dino."

I hung up and found Seth sitting on the edge of the roof, waiting patiently. His legs hung over the side, and he swung them like a little kid.

"You get it fixed?" I asked.

"Humming like a battleship," he said, banging the side of the compressor. "Come get me down."

"Are you tellin' me you can't jump that? It's barely more than seven feet." I planted my hands on my hips and stared up at him.

"I don't wanna jump. I want to get my jollies sliding down your body. Now get your ass over here."

I chuckled and went to stand beneath him while he turned and lowered himself backward over the side. When I could reach, I wrapped my arms around his waist and he let go. Instead of letting him slip to the ground, however, I hoisted him over my shoulder and carried him toward Matilda.

"Oh, you asshole," he groaned, huffing against my back.

I dumped him into the backseat and smirked at him. "You wanted me to take you home and put you to bed, right?"

"Yes, but I suddenly feel the need to make it clear that I want you to have sex with me in the bed before anyone does any sleeping in it."

"You think I wasn't aware of that?"

"I don't know, dude." Seth stretched out and got comfortable. "Anything's possible with you."

I grinned and went back for the tool kit, stashing it in the trunk before I got in the car and started up the engine. "You coming up front or what?" I asked.

"Hell, no. This is pretty great. Wake me when we get there."

"You are a sad little man, you know that?"

* * * *

I drove up the coast with Seth half asleep in the backseat of the car and the oldies station playing on the radio. I should have been bothered by the latest attempt on the restaurant, but we'd caught it in time, so no real harm was done, and I had a gut instinct things were about to start going our way. There's always a point in a case where I can feel the tide shift, and I knew that time was coming soon.

When I shut the car off outside the garage, Seth didn't stir.

"Hey Red, we're home." I reached back to give him a shake.

He groaned, but said nothing.

"Don't make me come back there," I said, angling the rearview mirror so I could see him.

A faint smile crossed his lips, but his eyes remained resolutely shut.

"Fine," I grumbled, getting out of the car. "Have it your way."

I went around to the passenger side and reached in to grab his arm, hauling him up to sitting. I've gotten more cooperation from a bowl of spaghetti. Seth flopped forward, and I caught him under the armpits and dragged him out of the car. When his feet hit the ground, he did manage to support himself enough to fall heavily against me. Big surprise there.

"You're too tired to stand, but you have enough energy to play grab ass?"

I felt more than heard him snicker against my shirt.

"I am not carrying you up those stairs, I'm tellin' you that right now." I took a step back and held him out at arm's length until he straightened up and eyed me through the slits of his eyelids. "There ya go."

I got behind him and steered him toward the stairs to his apartment. He climbed them slowly, but with little nudging, and when he got to the top, he just sagged against the rail. "Keys are in my pocket, man."

I hooked a finger on the edge of his jeans and slid my hand in the pocket, rubbing along his thigh as I reached for his key ring. He hummed and smiled softly. It didn't take a genius to see that behind the goofing, he really was exhausted, and I felt bad for him. I work some long and weird hours, but most of the time, I can't say I work especially hard. Not physically, like he'd been doing for four straight days with damn little sleep.

"Come on, let's get you inside," I said, pulling the keys out. I unlocked his door and ushered him through it.

The place was a disaster as usual, punctuated by an astounding number of takeout food containers, all bearing Salvatore's logo. At that rate, I sincerely hoped Gigi could afford him.

Seth stumbled through the mess into his bedroom and dropped onto the bed like a ton of bricks. Then he didn't move at all. I followed him and stood at the foot of the bed, watching him. He didn't say anything, either. He lay flat on his back, one hand resting on his chest, and his eyes closed. His mouth was relaxed, and his stomach rose and fell with each smooth, deep breath. He looked peaceful and so disgustingly comfortable he was making *me* tired.

I pulled his shoes and socks off and tossed them into the corner, then climbed onto the bed and knelt over him, supporting my weight on my hands while I studied his face. There was no hint of a smirk, not even a flutter of eyelash.

I bent and kissed along the edge of his jaw. "You're not asleep already, are you?" I murmured when I reached his ear.

"Nnnn..."

"That is not an especially convincing answer." I sat up and popped open the buttons of his jeans, then tried to pull them off. Wrestle them off was more like it, because he didn't offer the slightest bit of help.

I wasn't about to repeat that process with his shirt, so I got on the bed and lay down beside him, pressing up close. He didn't stir, but my weight on the mattress caused him to roll closer to me. There was no break in the gentle swell of his stomach. I slid a hand up under his shirt and flicked my thumbnail across a nipple.

Seth snorted once and blinked. "I'm awake," he blurted, sucking air. He looked up at me, but before he could hit a full leer, his eyes drifted closed again.

"Oh, you are not," I said with a shake of my head. "You're beat, and you know it. Get some sleep."

"No, 's okay. All I gotta' do is lie here and take it, anyway."

"Ah, no thanks."

"What'sa matter? Remind you too much of Gigi?"

"All right, that's it," I said, sitting up. The digs were starting to get old, and Seth wasn't the only one who was tired.

"Aw, come on," he said, flailing around with one hand until he clamped onto my shoulder. "Stay here. 'M sorry..."

I let him pull me down but rolled onto my back, staring up at the ceiling. He was fast asleep long before I considered saying anything.

Chapter 12

I woke early the next morning due to the unfamiliar surroundings and the redhead snoring on my right shoulder. I shifted so we fit closer together and settled against his warm body for a while. There was too much on my mind for me to go back to sleep. The case had grown all sorts of interesting new angles, and there was Seth's unusual jealous streak to contend with.

I supposed I couldn't exactly blame him for that. There were still a lot of things I hadn't said, and bumps we were trying to iron out. I'm not good at that stuff on the best of days, but trying to do it while working a case involving an old girlfriend was clearly getting the better of me.

About ten minutes before Seth's alarm was due to ring, I turned it off and got out of bed as quietly as I could, closing the bedroom door behind me. I found a trash bag and started collecting food containers and empty beer cans. There were dirty clothes everywhere, and I piled those in one corner, straightening up as I went. I finished by piling dishes in the sink and wiping down the counter with a wet rag. It wasn't perfect, but it was far better than it had been, and I thought Seth could use a break.

Around eight, I went down to the shop and started a pot of coffee, then went into the office and looked at Seth's desk calendar. There was an appointment for a tune-up at eight-thirty, and there was one car already in the shop, its fenders draped with blankets where Seth leaned in to work on the engine.

I picked up the phone and dialed the number written on the blotter. When a woman answered, I said, "This is Ed's Garage, ma'am, we have you down for an eight-thirty appointment."

"Yes? That's right."

"I was wondering if it would be a great inconvenience if we rescheduled that for later in the week? We're a little backed up here." I scanned the calendar, looking for a good slot.

"I think that would be all right, a few more days won't matter. When should I bring it in?"

"How about Friday at nine?"

"I can do that."

"Thank you so much, we really appreciate it."

She hung up and I went through the shop to pour a cup of coffee. From the looks of the other car, no one would be coming to get that for quite a while. I taped a sign to the front door that said *Open at Ten Today* and went back upstairs.

Seth was just starting to wake up when I went into the bedroom, and he blinked at me, looking me over before his gaze settled on my coffee cup. "What time is it?"

"It's eight o'clock, and I just rescheduled your eight-thirty. I thought you could stand to sleep in a little."

A sleepy smile brightened his face, and he stretched luxuriously. "*Nice.* So, what are you doing still dressed?"

"I thought I'd run you a hot bath. You've been complaining about bein' stiff and sore."

He patted the mattress. "Sex first, bath later. You owe me after last night."

"Excuse me? Who owes who?"

"Yeah, yeah, whatever. Get in bed, jackass. We can settle this the old-fashioned way." He raised up to pull his t-shirt over his head and turned to lean on one elbow, watching me with glittering eyes.

The bed was disheveled and Seth looked half ravaged already, with his sleep-mussed hair and his skin pink where it had been pressed into the pillow. My dick sprang to attention, and I thought about how good he'd felt that morning. I set down my coffee and stripped out of my pants, pulling my shirt off as I climbed in to join him.

He pulled me down and wrapped around me, kissing my neck with hot, wet strokes of his mouth. His hands were everywhere, palming my skin firmly, grasping and kneading. He was nearly overwhelming, and then as soon as it started, he pushed me away again and got out of bed.

Before I could say anything, he held out a hand and said, "Hold that thought. I'll be right back." Then he disappeared into the bathroom.

When he returned, he straddled my body and eased down on top of me, rocking his hips slowly in anticipation. We kissed and fell into a messy tangle of arms and legs. There were still times when Seth was so intense with his need I wasn't sure I could keep up, that I would be enough for him. He and I operate on very different wavelengths sometimes, and I still didn't know how to handle that. At the same time I was trying to be calming and sensual, he was already reaching for the condoms and lube.

"So much for being exhausted," I said.

"I slept, I'm good. Besides, you're gonna do all the work." He sat back and tore open a condom with his teeth, spitting the corner onto the bed next to me.

"Classy."

"This is a Wednesday morning mercy fuck. You want classy, you're gonna have to warn me ahead of time, so I can practice."

"I'll keep that in mind."

He stroked my dick with a strong, practiced hand, getting me ready so he could roll the condom onto it. I could have told him that wasn't necessary, that I could do it, but then I'd miss out on the single bit of tenderness I was likely to get this time around. He didn't know it yet, but he was going to owe me for this.

I enjoyed the determined look on his face, and was thinking he was one of those guys who look damn good after a couple days without a shave, when he grabbed my hand and squirted a gob of lube into it.

"Gee, thanks," I said. I sat up and watched while he got himself into position on his knees and elbows. That meant a wild ride, and my skin went hot with desire.

"I don't think you're gonna be complaining about much of anything in about thirty seconds, dude. Come on."

"Right. Okay." I was breathless and scrambled to get behind him, steadying his hip with one hand, while I slicked him up with the other. I slid a finger inside, marveling at the heat and the illicit thrill that was so new to me. Seth squirmed, and his breath came thick and heavy. He was a study in carefully measured impatience as I explored.

He blew out a sigh. "Any *time*, grandma..."

"Geez, will you cool it already? This is not at all attractive." My raging hard-on gave the lie to that, and it agreed with Seth, urging me to just drive into him.

"Seriously, man, you are the only person I know who actually *could* fuck me into next Tuesday. Sadly, we don't have that kind of time."

"Yeah, yeah..." I continued to finger him, and I took my time about it. "When we're both good and ready."

"Oh, for fuck's sake." In a flash, he sat up and spun around, shoving me onto my back and pinning me there while he climbed over me. "Do I have to show you how to do everything?"

"You might." I stretched out my legs and ran my hands up his torso, sighing as he started to ease down on my cock. "I do like to watch."

"Oh shit, I'm surprised you can handle it with the lights on." His chest flushed pink and his eyes were shut tight, face set with concentration as he took me deeper.

"You're cute as hell when you get all pissy like this."

"Fuck off."

"Kiss me."

"Go to hell."

"Come on...kiss me." I spread my palm out over his chest and rubbed slow circles, watching as the lines of tension gradually faded from his face, and he relaxed with a blissful smile.

He sat forward carefully and braced himself on his hands, leaning down to plant a quick peck on my lips.

"I hope you're planning to do better than that," I said.

"I will if you will."

"I always planned to."

Seth hummed his appreciation and kissed me again, hot and eager. I slid my hands over his hips and pulled down, burying my cock as deep as it would go. He groaned and shuddered. "Fuck, yeah...now you're getting the idea."

"You know damn well I can do you just fine. I think you just like to bitch about it."

"I think you like hearing me bitch."

"As a matter of fact, I do." I gave myself away with a smug grin. It was true. One of Seth's most interesting personality traits is his spitfire temper, and I discovered early on I got a real charge out of seeing him riled up.

He stretched to lick my ear and whispered, "You are such an asshole."

Desire took over and we dropped the banter in favor of the main attraction, falling into a needy rhythm with Seth in the lead. He planted his hands on my chest and gripped my sides with his knees, working himself on my cock with wild abandon. I moaned and held tight to him, meeting him thrust for thrust. Before long, we were deep in the throes of passion, the heavy rush of Seth's breath cooling the sheen of sweat on my skin. I shivered and grasped his thighs, and drove deep inside him again.

"Son of a bitch," he gasped. He grabbed my hand and pulled it to his dick, jerking his hips when I wrapped my fingers around it tightly.

I was so close to the edge, I could barely control my strokes, but I still had him moaning within seconds. One more strong stroke and he swore loudly, shooting thick come onto my hand and belly. That was one hell of a sight and he took me right along with him. I came hard, shoving my head back into the pillow and bucking my hips. It took me several seconds to regain control of my body, and when I did, I could only wilt on the bed.

Seth planted his hands on my chest and hung there, eyes closed, panting. There was the ghost of a smile on his face. Finally, he said, "You can plan my schedule any day, dude."

"Yeah, I wasn't really expecting an argument from you on this." I slid my hands up his arms and helped steady him as he eased off me and dropped onto his back.

He rolled his head toward me and said, "The only real problem with morning sex is that all I want to do afterward is go back to sleep."

"You probably could catch another hour and still be downstairs in time."

"Maybe half an hour and a shower."

"I think I like that plan better," I said. "You could use it."

Chapter 13

Feeling like I'd squared away things with Seth, at least for the time being, I went home to clean up and put on fresh clothes. It was still too early to check in with Gigi, so I went downstairs and let myself into the old store front.

John Holcomb was due at ten for our appointment, and I wanted to check things out and make a game plan. I still wasn't sure what good this would do me, but it did give me a reason to poke around, and if Holcomb's price was good, I might get my office done before I died.

My design divided the room in half, leaving the back area for tenant storage and turning the front into a set of offices for myself. Unfortunately, things were moving at a much slower pace than I'd hoped. In the past month or so, Seth and I had only gotten as far as framing in the dividing wall.

The morning sun streamed brightly through the windows, and I propped the front door open to catch a little breeze before it really heated up in there. Behind the open framework of the stud wall lay piles of boxes and old furniture, covered in a protective layer of plastic. In front of it stood a gray metal office desk covered in sawdust, paper and empty beer cans. This was command central. We'd hauled it from the depths of the storage heap, with Adele's permission, of course, and were using it as a makeshift workbench.

I sat down with my cup of freshly brewed coffee and pulled the sketched plans in front of me. The next step in the process was to wall off what would be my private office, and then to create a small entryway at the side door that connected the store with the apartment hallway. This would allow the ladies to get to their storage space without intruding on my client area, and still give me inside access to the offices.

On the likely chance that hiring the job done would prove too rich for my blood, I got up to check a few of the measurements, and then went back to the desk to make a supply list. I wasn't entirely sure when we'd get the chance to work on it, but I wanted to be ready when we did. Even an hour here and there would get the place built and then I'd finally have an office again. I was getting a little tired of meeting clients in bars and feeling like some kind of thug for hire.

A gentle knock on the glass caught my attention, and I looked up to find Ruth standing in the open doorway. "Hey, good morning," I said.

"Good morning, Dino. I hope I'm not disturbing you."

"No, I'm just making some notes so I know what materials to buy. What's up?"

"I wanted to ask if you'd seen this morning's newspaper yet? There's an article on the proposed hotel development plan I thought you'd be interested in."

That caught my attention. "Yeah, definitely."

She handed me a section of newspaper, folded open to the story in question. It was the usual quotes from the locals, half of them for and half against the new development, along with some comments from the city commissioners about tourism and the revenue the hotel would bring in. There was an entire sidebar devoted to discussion of the residents who would be bought out, and that interested me most.

"Thanks, Ruth, I appreciate this."

"I don't know if there's really anything there that will help you with your case, but at least it's some background material."

"Hey," I said with a shrug, "you never know what's gonna be useful until it is, right?"

She smiled at me, and turned to leave. "I'll keep my eyes open for anything else then."

"That would be great."

About three minutes later, Holcomb pulled up in a battered Ford pickup outfitted with built-in tool boxes and equipped to haul lumber. He got out and mopped the sweat from his brow with a wrinkled bandana, then grabbed an old clipboard.

"Gonna be a hot one," he said as he entered.

"Hey there." I shook hands with him and pointed to my wall. "This is the job. You can see how far we've gotten. If I keep going at this pace, the building's going to crumble from old age before I'm finished."

He nodded and took an appraising look around. I showed him what I had in mind and explained about the storage and the hallway access. He took a lot of notes, asked several questions, and then set about measuring everything for himself.

"So, you want Frank working on this job, eh?" He strung his tape measure across the doorway and wrote down the information.

"Yeah, well, not 'want' so much as feel like I ought to." I rubbed a hand over the back of my neck. "You know how it is. I'm kind of a friend of the family, and if I got the work, I might as well toss it his way."

"Thing is, he's not the most reliable guy, and if you're bent on having him do the job, I don't think I can guarantee when it will be done."

"Hey, I completely understand that," I assured him. "Even if he only shows up half the time, he's bound to get it done faster than I will."

Holcomb nodded. "I wouldn't normally be so candid, but since you know the guy I guess you already know what he's like. I have a hunch he's been doing jobs on the side for cash, which I don't normally approve of, but I know what it's like to have a wife and kid to support, and I don't think he's hurting my business."

"Wife and kid," I said wryly, "absolutely. I'm not a family man myself, but I can imagine the pressure that puts on a guy." I wouldn't be the least bit surprised that Frank had spawned a kid or two in his time, but it sure as hell wasn't with Molly.

"Anyway—" Holcomb headed for the door. "I'll take this back to the office and work up some figures for you. Got a number you want me to call?"

I gave him a card from my wallet and thanked him for his time, then locked the door behind him. My hunch was the kid and wife story was just an outright lie Frank told to explain away his absences, but I thought I'd dig a little deeper anyway.

* * * *

My next step was to head down to Salvatore's and fill Gigi in on the incident with the compressor, and tell her about the hotel. She wasn't there when I went inside, but Felix was working the bar, so I pulled up a stool and ordered a beer.

He brought it to me along with a lunch menu and said, "It's good seeing you around here again. Just like old times."

"Not exactly like old times," I pointed out.

"Sure, I know. But it could be, if you get my drift." He gave me a lighthearted leer and ambled down to help a pair of sunburned tourists who'd just come in.

I shook my head and flipped open the menu. Seemed like everyone but me and Gigi thought we should be together. We'd gotten a pretty high approval rating when we were together too. People always commented on what a good looking couple we made. Part of me kind of missed that.

It gave me that classy man-about-town feeling that folks of my parents' generation always seemed to have. For all its other benefits, that was certainly one thing I didn't get from dating a scruffy mechanic. Not that anyone actually knew I was, which was another thing I was never going to get being with Seth. I'm a fairly private person in general, so most of the time keeping our relationship under wraps didn't bother me, but there was that part of me that missed being able to take my date to a fancy restaurant and make a decent showing of it.

Felix came back to take my order and handed it off to one of the busboys, then leaned on the bar and took a drink of his water. "I always thought you and Gigi were going to be running this place until long after I was gone."

"Some things just don't work out the way you expect them to, I guess."

"That is true enough. Doesn't always make sense, though. What happened with you two, if you don't mind me asking?"

I took a swallow of beer. "You know what happened. My job didn't fit with her lifestyle, and neither one of us wanted to change."

He eyed me critically. "If you don't mind my saying, you passed up a pretty good life, Dino. Why you want to risk always getting your head shot off when you could be here all the time, working in style?"

It occurred to me this was another thing I'd never get from dating Seth, and I noted that in the plus column of the mental tally I'd been keeping. "If you don't mind *my* saying, I actually have a pretty good life, and very little of it involves anything getting shot off. Don't get me wrong, I still think Gigi is a great lady. She deserves a lot better than me."

"Oh, shit," Felix scoffed. There was a fatherly tone to his voice. "Don't sell yourself short."

"Fine. Just take my word for it, we're both better off now."

Whether or not he was convinced, I couldn't tell, but he seemed to be content to let the subject drop, and for that I was grateful. A waiter brought me a plate of rigatoni, and Felix and I spent the rest of my meal reminiscing about old times. By the end of it, I wasn't sure he didn't have a point about Gigi and me, but I didn't tell him that.

Instead, I changed the subject and tried to earn my pay. "Felix, what's your take on this trouble Gigi's been having?"

He scowled. "This is bad business, Dino. I don't like the direction it's heading. Someone's going to get hurt. I'm glad you're on the case."

"Got any idea who might be responsible? You hear stuff. You remember anyone hanging around asking a lot of questions about Gigi or the restaurant?"

"Not off the top of my head, but I'll keep it in mind."

"What about the staff?" I asked. "Is there anyone who gives you a bad feeling, or you think might be up to something?"

"Oh shit, they're all just kids. Most of them don't know the meaning of an honest day's work. It's a shame what the world is coming to."

I laughed and gave him a grudging nod. "Okay, what about Marco?"

"Marco's a good kid," Felix said. He wiped off a glass and put it away, then reached for another. "He's done a real good job here. Since he came on, Gigi's been able to finally take a little time off and not have to worry about the restaurant. It's about time."

"That's good. I'm glad to hear that."

At that moment Gigi breezed in the front door looking windblown, and gorgeous as ever. My heart did a little flip for old times' sake, and I turned back to my beer before I got myself in trouble.

"Oh, Dino," she said, folding her sunglasses and tucking them in her purse. "I'm glad you're here. Can we talk in my office?"

I gave Felix a little salute and followed her down the hall. She waited until I closed the door and said, "Thank you for taking care of things last night. Everything was fine when I got here this morning, and I have an electrician lined up to come out and fix it tomorrow."

"I'm glad to hear it."

"Tell me what happened," she said as she sat down.

"There's not really much more to it than what I told you last night. We were driving past on our way home, I spotted the guy taking off out of your parking lot and we chased him, but couldn't catch him. Seth figured out what he'd done and was able to patch it."

She looked agitated, and I knew she wanted more, but that's often the way it goes. "Well, what should I do now? Should I hire a security service to patrol the parking lot at night? Will that do any good?"

"You could," I said. "That would protect the restaurant, which is what you want. On the other hand, it limits the opportunity for them to try anything else, which will make it harder to catch them."

"So I should do nothing, and just let someone attack me?"

"No, I'm not saying that. I'm just pointing out all the angles here. You should do whatever makes you feel most comfortable. I'm gonna catch these guys no matter what."

"What makes you so sure?"

I leveled my gaze on her. "Thanks for the vote of confidence."

"You know what I mean."

"Yeah, I do. And I know I'm gonna catch them because this is what I do. I know it takes time, and it seems like we're not getting anywhere, but we are. That's one of the reasons I'm here."

She sat up straighter. "You found something?"

"Yup. Two somethings, actually." I sat down across from her. "First of all, Seth has been watching the staff, and he's got a couple of possible candidates picked out for the insider."

"Who?"

I hesitated. "Look, don't get mad, but I don't want to tell you right now—"

"I think I have a right to know."

"You do, but I'm asking you to wait a couple days, okay? If I tell you now, you might accidentally tip them off, and we really don't want that."

"Oh, well, thank *you* for the vote of confidence." She sighed and sat back in her chair. "I'm sorry. That was cheap. I'm just...edgy. We'll do it your way, of course. What's the other thing?"

"I have the motive."

"Oh?" Any irritation with me was gone.

"There are plans in the works for a big hotel development right out there." I pointed toward the back of the restaurant.

"Out..." She turned to look, and then comprehension dawned on her face. "You mean...on the island?"

"You are sitting on a piece of land that's about to become very valuable, my dear. If that hotel goes in on Vina del Mar, you'll be in prime position to gain a lot of well-heeled business."

It took her a few moments to process that. Then she took a deep breath. "So...it's not me that's the target, it really is Salvatore's."

"Yes. But that doesn't mean you should let your guard down. It just means this has a solid, non-creepy basis behind it."

"Well, I guess that's something." She ran a hand over her face and the relief was apparent. "I can deal with this."

"I knew you could," I told her. "Go ahead and hire your security. Maybe they'll catch the guys red-handed and we can all get back to normal."

"What about you?"

For a minute, I thought she was asking if I'd get back to normal and I flashed on the conversation with Felix. My breath stuck in my throat until I realized she meant what was I going to do. I gave myself a shake and said, "I'm gonna keep picking at the edges until something comes loose. It'll happen. It always does."

Chapter 14

As I was leaving, I noticed Chad in the side parking lot, climbing into his car. He was college age, or a little older. Average height, average weight, soft looking, but always stylish. Although Seth didn't really think he was the kind of guy who'd use dirty tactics to get ahead, his extreme interest in the service industry, along with his ambitions made him a possible candidate. I had no plans for the evening, and when an opportunity presents itself, you go with it.

I got into my car and ducked down to hide my face as he pulled out, then drove out after him. We were headed north, which stood to reason, since his address and both his other jobs were in Tampa. The fact that he was willing to drive so far to work at Salvatore's was curious, and it might have made me suspicious, but he'd been doing it for almost two years. That didn't clear him, but it did mean if he was behind the sabotage it was an opportunity that dropped in his lap.

He led me into one of the college neighborhoods down around the University of Tampa, where he had the lower left corner of a four-plex. It was a busy street, with people out doing all kinds of things. This was bad for me, because Matilda sticks out and I couldn't really just sit there and wait.

Chad parked and went inside, so I figured I had a few minutes at least, if he was going out again. If he wasn't, I was screwed anyway, since I wasn't likely to learn anything staring at his front door. I backtracked to a gas station we'd passed so I could fill up the tank and use the bathroom. I stocked up on snacks and a couple cans of pop, and grabbed a cup of coffee.

When I got back, Chad's car was still where he'd left it. I circled the block once, to kill more time, and then parked where I had a good view and unfolded a map across my steering wheel. I didn't belong there, and this way anyone who noticed would think I was lost.

After twenty minutes, I was beginning to push it with the lost tourist bit and was about to leave again when Chad came out and locked his front door. He was dressed like the guys in the kind of clubs Seth likes to hang out in, and his hair looked freshly washed and expertly messed. He had a cellphone tucked against his shoulder, and he talked the whole time it took him to get his car started, buckle up and drive away.

I followed at a discreet distance, and we went further into Tampa, into the section called Ybor City, which is one of the areas known for nightclubs. Seth was going to be pissed when he found out I was there without him. We wound up at a place called Eagle Jack's. It looked like an old warehouse, but smaller, and it had a flag pole next to the front door with an eagle at the top and a rainbow flag.

I was lucky to snag a parking spot with a good view, and watched Chad walk up to the place. He was greeted by a group of guys who all looked about the same, dressed in varying colors of skintight clothes. There was a lot of hugging and squealing, which made me think this was a night out rather than the second or third job. They all crowded inside, and I had a choice to make—follow, or let it go.

Before I made up my mind, I pulled out my cellphone and dialed Seth. He answered on the fourth ring and spoke in a hushed voice. "I'm at the restaurant, man, make it quick."

"I followed Chad to a club in Tampa called Eagle Jack's. I gather it's trendy. How big an ass am I gonna look like if I go in there?"

"What are you wearing?"

"Orange and black button-down shirt and a suit coat."

"That silk shirt?"

"Yeah."

"Ditch the jacket and take smokes if you got 'em. Sit at the bar and check out every young guy that passes by you. Blatantly."

"Are you tryin' to make me look like a lecher?"

"It's a college hang out, Dino. You're going to look like you're trolling no matter what you do."

"That's great."

"I wish I could be there to see it. Have fun, gotta' go."

He hung up and I was still stuck with my decision. Only now I got to go undercover as a pervert. I sighed and fished in the glove compartment for cigarettes. After I locked up everything that needed to be, I crossed the street and went inside.

The room was large and open, with the bar running down one side, the front half filled with tables and booths, and the back half dominated by a

DJ stand and dance floor. It was early, so the place was half empty and the dance floor was deserted. Chad and his friends were in a booth near the back. They had a variety of drinks in martini glasses and talked excitedly.

The only guys sitting at the bar were older like me, and except for one couple, appeared to be alone. It was creepy. I joined them, choosing a seat that gave me a good view of Chad's table, and ordered an amaretto on the rocks. I lit up a cigarette and turned to stare at the ass of the kid who'd just walked in. Seth would be so proud.

I wasn't close enough to eavesdrop on Chad and his friends, but the occasional word drifted over when they got especially rowdy. I got the impression it was the same kind of talk any group of people has when they're out for the night. How much everyone's jobs suck, who's sleeping with who, and how everyone's planning to get laid. I was coming to the conclusion that Chad wasn't our guy. Seth didn't think so, and everything about him screamed happy-go-lucky and friendly. He wouldn't need to steal the restaurant from Gigi, he could just charm her out of it.

My gut told me I was wasting my time, so I decided to finish my drink and go home. I turned to flick my cigarette off in the ashtray and when I turned back, Chad was right in my face.

"I know you," he said cheerfully. He had a cock-eyed grin that suggested he was extremely pleased with himself.

"I think you got me confused with someone else. I have no idea who you are."

"No, you probably don't. I'm not confused about you, though. You're Gigi's friend, from Salvatore's."

I took a deep breath. There was no point in denying it. Just because he recognized me from there, didn't mean anything. "So? What about it?"

"I think it's interesting that you just recently showed up there, and now you're here for what has to be the first or second time, because I've never seen you before. Not to mention that your boyfriend just started working at Salvatore's. Lot of firsts there, you know?"

"I don't have a boyfriend," I said. I was busted and I knew it, but I had to try. "Maybe I'm dating Gigi."

He clapped a hand to his chest and laughed out loud.

"Darling." He composed himself and stared at me. "My gaydar is infallible, and I had you pegged the first time you walked in. Also..." He leaned in close and used a stage whisper. "You're sitting in a gay bar."

"Fine. I'm gay. So are you. We should both get gold stars." I crushed out my cigarette and picked up my drink.

"Ooo, you're spicier than you look. Now I know how you handle that little firecracker you're dating."

This kid was unnerving. "What makes you think I'm dating anyone?" He gave me that pleased grin again. "I've seen how you look at each other. You're trying to pretend you don't know each other, but I make a habit of knowing who's doing who, and you are definitely doing him."

"Are you goin' somewhere with this?" I finished my drink, and before I could stand up, he was waving to get another round for both of us. "You're a pushy little shit, you know that?"

"Yes, I am." He beamed at me. "You and Seth both showed up after all the trouble started at the restaurant, and I want to know if you're there to stop it."

"Why don't you tell me?" I didn't really think he could answer that, because I didn't think he was our guy, but he seemed to know everything else.

"Tell—" He clutched his shirt and put a hand over his mouth, then clapped with glee. "You think I'm doing it? That is so *cute*. Oh my God, did you follow me here? Are you tailing me?"

"As a matter of fact, I am. And if you're the one who's fuckin' over Gigi, and you're sitting here bullshitting me about it, I'm gonna find out."

His eyes went wide and he shivered. "That is so *sexy*. Do you want to frisk me?"

"Do you think all this is funny?"

"No! Oh my God." He looked so stricken, I felt bad. "I adore Gigi. I think it's horrible what's going on. Really. I've learned so much from her, I would never do anything like that."

"Who do you think is?"

"I don't know. I've been trying to figure it out, but I can't. I try to watch people at work, but it's busy and I just can't see everything."

"You managed to see plenty about me and Seth."

"Well, darling—" He put a hand on my arm. "When gorgeous men are involved I don't miss a trick."

I smiled and shook my head. "I bet you don't."

He leaned on the bar and put his chin in his hand, looking smug. The kid was cute, no doubt about it. Like all the other dead ends, I'd keep my eye on him, but he wasn't the one.

I took a sip of my drink, then asked, "Have you talked to anyone else about me, or Seth, or what's going on at the restaurant?"

"No. I didn't know who I could trust. It's all very film noir."

"Well, you still don't, so I'd appreciate it if you kept your mouth shut about it, got that?"

He nodded. "Can I ask you a question?"

"Shoot."

"What made you think it might be me? Gigi doesn't think so, does she?"

"No, she doesn't. And Seth doesn't either, for what it's worth. I just had to check you out because you've got jobs in two other bars, and Seth said you talk about wanting your own place someday."

"Oh, I do," he gushed. "It'll be fabulous. But it would never be in Pass-a-Grille. There's no clientele for me there. I want a club like this one or even better. I need to be in the city for that."

"You ever get it, let me know." I took out my wallet and gave him one of my cards. "If you see anything at the restaurant, please give me a call."

"Sure." For a minute he looked earnest, then he smirked and said, "And you can check me out anytime, darling."

I thanked him for the drink and he hopped back to his friends, waving my card like a trophy. I hoped that wasn't a mistake.

Outside, I got into the car and flipped open my cellphone. This time I dialed Gigi. When she answered, I said, "Hey, it's Dino. I got a name to run past you."

"Who?"

"Chad Lundgren."

"Oh, Dino, no. There's no way Chad could hurt Salvatore's. I know I keep defending everyone you mention, but he's a sweetheart. It's not him."

"I didn't think so. You have a great night."

Chapter 15

Thursday brought us an interesting twist in Seth's case. It became Molly's case.

Seth had the day off from Salvatore's and I'd been at the garage helping him catch up. I don't do too badly if I do say so myself, and sometimes it's good to get your hands dirty. We were sitting at the workbench enjoying a well earned pizza and a few bottles of beer.

"If it's Chad," I said, "my faith in humanity will be completely shot."

"I know. It would be like watching Peter Pan shoot heroin and blow Hook."

I set my pizza down and reached for my beer. "I think you just ruined my appetite."

Seth's cellphone rang, and he wiped his hands off on his coveralls before fishing in to get it. I was impressed he made the effort to keep it clean. When he glanced at it, his expression became a mix of confusion and wariness.

"It's Molly," he said to me. Into the phone, he said, "Hey, ugly. What's up?"

I assumed the wariness was due to his fear of getting caught meddling in her life. As he spoke to her, both of those faded, to be replaced by concern and then anger.

"I told you that asshole was gonna get you into trouble." A pause, a look of horrified pissiness, then, "Are you serious? How can that *not* have something to do with him? You don't really think this is totally a coincidence do you?"

There was more silence while he nodded, shook his head, then pointed to his phone and mouthed 'What the fuck?' to me. This was a prime example of why it was best he wasn't dating women. I could easily picture him in a stained wife-beater, with a beer, standing on his front stoop and screaming obscenities at his old lady. I've seen what that does to women, so it was just as well I was in line for that role.

"Look, Mol...*Mol*, Dino's right here, would you just talk to him, please? This is what he does." He glanced up at me like he was asking if I would, so I nodded, and he handed the phone over.

"Hi, Molly. You got some kinda' trouble?"

"I don't know," she said. "It's just something weird, which might be nothing at all, but I wanted to get a second opinion. Seth seemed like a good choice, which just goes to show I'm getting old and senile already. Now, he's blowing it all out of proportion."

"Well, why don't you let me give you a third opinion? I'm well known for not flying off the handle."

Seth muttered, "Oh, bullshit."

"All right." Molly sighed. "There's been this guy, sitting out in his car. He doesn't really do anything, except maybe read a newspaper once in a while. I wouldn't even have noticed, probably, but he's right in front of the house, across the street, which is between houses on that side, so it's not like he's visiting someone. Maybe. It's stupid, I know."

"Molly, that doesn't sound stupid to me. Is the guy there now?"

"Yeah."

"Is Frank?"

"No." There was another pause and then she said, "There might be something else."

"What's that?"

"The last time the guy was sitting out there, Frank *was* here and he got pretty pissed off when he saw him. He swore and charged out the back door. I thought he was going to go tell the guy to get lost, or find out what was going on. But he just took off. It took me a while to realize it actually. I kept watching for him to cross the street, but he never did."

"As a friend of Seth's, and a representative of decent guys everywhere, I feel obligated to point out that was crappy behavior on Frank's part."

"Don't you start too."

"I'm just sayin'." Pointed silence was her response, so I went on. "Look, lock your doors and go back to doing whatever it is you do at this hour, and we'll be right over."

"You really think that's necessary?"

"It can't hurt. Besides, I haven't taken Seth out for his walk yet and he's gettin' antsy."

Molly laughed, and Seth flipped me off.

"Okay," she said. "Thanks, I appreciate it."

"No problem." I hung up and handed the phone back to Seth. "I assume you're up for a ride?"

"Yeah. I don't like this at all, Dino. What do you think's going on?"

I closed the pizza box and wadded up used napkins. "Well, there's a pretty short list of reasons to camp out in front of someone's house. Intimidation, surveillance, or to catch someone coming or going."

"Is that it?" he asked as he crammed the leftovers into the battered old fridge in the corner.

"There's also unrequited love. Maybe this guy's got a thing for your sister."

We shut the lights off and headed for the door. Ahead of me, Seth was snickering to himself.

"What?" I asked. "You don't think someone could be pining for Molly."

"It's not that."

"What then?"

"You forgot one." He grinned broadly.

"Which is…"

"Drunken moping."

"Yeah, all right, you can shut the fuck up now." I pushed him out the door. "If I remember correctly, that turned out to be a very effective tactic."

"I'm surprised you can remember it at all."

"Nice. Get in the car, asshole."

We took my car and drove into Tampa, where Molly lived. They grew up in St. Petersburg, and although they both claimed to hate it, neither one ever got very far from home. Molly headed for Tampa where the good jobs were, and worked as a senior lab tech at Tampa General Hospital, in a field I can't spell *or* pronounce. Seth went the opposite direction, where the beach and the mostly naked people were.

It was dusk before we left, and by the time we hit Tampa, night had officially fallen. This was good for my purposes, because it would make checking out the guy in the car much easier. But I was glad we were nearly there, since it would give him the exact same advantage, and we still didn't know what he was planning.

Seth was wound like a top and fidgeting so much that if I didn't know him, I'd think he was on something. I'd have to keep an eye on him or he was liable to become the point where things got out of hand.

"Would you cool it?" I said. "The last thing we need in a situation like this is for you to go off half-cocked."

"I'm fine." He stared straight ahead.

"Sure, and I'm Princess Leia."

That he turned for, and said, "Hey, would you wear that metal bikini for me?"

"Ah, no I would not."

If he could joke, he wasn't as bad as I thought, which was good. I pulled onto Molly's street and cruised down it so we could get a quick look at this guy. Her house was third from the end, and sure enough, right across the street was a dark colored sedan. I didn't want to attract his attention, so I couldn't go too slowly, but I was able to make out enough to see that he was still in the car.

"What's the plan, Dino?" Seth asked. He was gripping the seat in an effort not to turn around and look at the guy, and I appreciated his restraint.

"First we're gonna go in and talk to Molly, make sure she's all right. Then we'll figure out what to do from there."

I already knew what I was going to do, but I didn't intend to tell Seth about it until I had to. I turned the corner and drove about halfway down the block before pulling over and shutting off the car. Seth hopped out immediately and started around the car to cross the street. I hung back and reached under the seat to grab my gun and holster, which I'd been keeping there since the business with Gigi started. When I carry a gun, which is only when necessary, I carry a Baby Glock, clipped in its holster in the waistband of my pants, right at the back. Easy to get to if I need it, but stays hidden until I do.

"What'cha doing?" Seth had turned back and was standing near my side of the car.

"Nothing," I said. I got out and straightened my jacket, then closed the car door quietly.

"Bullshit." He eyed me in the dim light of the streetlamp. "You're *actually* gonna stand there and lie right to my face?"

"Well...if you can tell I'm lying, then it's not really a lie, is it?" I nudged him in the direction of the sidewalk. "Let's go."

"You think this is that serious?"

"I don't know. But the kind of guys who sit in cars to intimidate nice women usually speak 'gun' very fluently and conversations tend to go better."

"Yeah, all right," he said, but I could tell he didn't like it.

Seth took the lead, and we picked our way silently through the backyards of Molly's neighbors. It was a nice thing no one had any jumpy dogs, because most people don't like to discover a couple of strange men sneaking around out back, but I didn't want to tip off our guy by going up the front way.

We got to Molly's and went up to the back door. Seth knocked lightly and peered through the glass. Within a minute, the lock clicked and Molly opened the door.

"Thanks for coming, guys." She held it open for us and stepped back. "I tried calling Frank, but couldn't get a hold of him."

"There's a big surprise," Seth muttered.

Molly rolled her eyes, but let it go, and we ducked into the kitchen where we couldn't be seen through the front windows.

"Any change out there?" I asked her.

"Nope. At least, not that I can tell. It's too dark to see very clearly now." She wrapped her arms around herself and shivered. "This guy gives me the creeps."

"He should," I said. "He's not out there writin' up orders for Girl Scout cookies."

"Why do you think he is there?" Molly's eyes were wide, and I felt bad for scaring her, but I thought she should know.

"If we're assuming Frank is involved—"

"Which we are," Seth tossed in, and Molly whacked him square in the chest with her forearm.

"—then the most likely explanations are either someone's watching him, or someone's trying to intimidate him."

"But why?"

I shook my head. "I don't know. Don't hit me, but I'm with Seth on this one. Frank is in some kind of trouble, and now it's sittin' on your doorstep. He probably bailed out of here last time because he knows exactly who's out there."

Molly's cheeks turned pink, and she avoided my gaze. "So what are you going to do?"

"You two are gonna go in the living room and watch some TV." I steeled myself for an argument. "And I'm going to go out and introduce myself to Mr. Creepy."

"The fuck I am," Seth snapped, right on cue. "I'm going out there with you and give this fucker a piece of my mind."

He was actually starting to get up in my face, and I put my hands on his shoulders. "No...you're going to stay in here with Molly in case something goes wrong. If that guy decides to come make trouble, I want you here."

He fumed in silence for a moment, but I thought playing the chivalry card would get him. Strong family loyalty was one of the things I liked about him. "Fine."

Molly tugged on his sleeve, and he turned to go in the other room.

"Oh, and Seth?" He turned to look at me. "If I see you come out that front door, I will shoot you, got it?"

He made a face. "You would not."

"Don't try me."

They went and settled in to make a showing of life as usual, and I slipped out the back door again. I circled around, crossed the street at the far end, and approached the car from the rear. It was the long way, but I wanted to be sure I had the element of surprise. I stuck to the shadows as much as possible, and when I got close, I pulled out my gun, keeping it low.

The radio was on softly, and the window was rolled all the way down. There were a couple of cigarette butts on the ground. I stopped for a minute to take a good look at the situation and to plan my move, because once I started, I had to be fast.

After one more deep breath, I got up close to the car and darted along the side. When I came up to the driver's door, I reached around inside and grabbed the guy by the front of the shirt, pulling his head out the window while I shoved the gun in his face at the same time. Close enough to be frightening, but far enough away he would see exactly what it was.

"Put your hands out here on the door, right now," I snapped, keeping my voice low, but hard. "I don't want to make a scene and neither do you."

His eyes were wide, and his breath came in short little gasps. He was more likely scared shitless by the surprise than actually afraid of me, but I'd take what I could get. At the moment, it was enough, because he rested his hands on the edge of the door and wiggled his fingers.

"That's good," I said. "I guessed you were a smart guy."

He was a garden variety thug. Big arms, thick chest. Thick head. He had blond hair, and looked like the hulk who lifts weights on the beach and kicks sand in the little guy's face.

"Now, seeing as how you *are* so smart, I know you're gonna be able to answer all my questions. Starting with why the fuck are you out here scaring the shit out of a nice lady who's so clean she frets about getting her library books back on time?"

"It ain't her, it's her old man."

"He's not here, which I'm sure you know, but you still are, so let's try that again."

"No, seriously. It's Frank Novak we want. I'm supposed to wait for him."

"Who's 'we' and what do you want him for?"

His gaze slid off to the side and he licked his lips, reluctant to answer that one. I tapped him on the jaw with the barrel of my gun, and he focused on me again. "Look, the guy owes someone a bunch of money. What's it to you?"

"That nice lady in there is special to a very good friend of mine which makes it my business. She doesn't have anything to do with this."

"I told you, it's Frank—"

"Frank isn't home, and you know damn well he's not coming back as long as you're parked out here. Your intelligence seems to be slipping."

He sighed. "My boss wanted me to lean on her a little bit, get her rattled so she'd do whatever it took to bail Frank out."

Loan sharking, that was just great.

"That's disgusting." I wanted to deck the jerk, but that would mean letting go of him or the gun, and my whole advantage at that moment depended on keeping both in my grasp. "Who's your boss? What kind of money are we talkin' about?"

"Guliano," he said. "And I don't know how much. I'm just paid to lean on people."

"Tony G? That's who you work for?" Tony G was a fairly notorious loan shark. At least in circles of people who have a reason to be talking about loan sharks. Word had it he was not someone you wanted to cross. He also had a reputation for appreciating the finer things in life. Good cigars, expensive liquor, fancy food. Supposedly, he lived in some kind of fancy villa on the waterfront.

"Yeah. Tony G. And I don't think he's gonna like it much that you're messing in his business."

"You let me worry about that." I kept my gun trained on him, but let go of his shirt and reached into my back pocket for my wallet. Honestly, by this time the guy looked more bored than anything, and I was pretty sure he wasn't going to waste the energy to jump me. I slid a card out of it and handed it over. "Give him that and tell him Dino Martini wants to meet with him."

This amused him, judging by the way he was trying not to grin. "You think Tony G's gonna be scared of a pipe cleaner like you?"

"No, I do not. But from what I hear, business comes first with him. You tell him I want to deal."

"Sure, what's it to me," he said with a shrug. "You gonna shoot me now, or can I go? I assume that's what's next, right? You tell me to get the hell out of here?"

Yeah, he was shaking in his shoes. "You assume correctly. And don't let me catch you around here anymore, or I'll let her brother be the one to come out here."

"And he is somehow worse than you?"

"You ever see a rat terrier attack a chew toy?"

He looked mildly perplexed and put the car in gear. "I'll give Tony G your message," he said, and drove away.

I slid my gun into my holster and straightened my jacket as I walked back across the street. As I came up the walk, the front door opened and Seth stepped out to look down the block. Molly hovered behind him in the entryway.

"I see you scared him away," Seth said, turning to me.

"Oh, yeah. I put the fear of God in him," I deadpanned. "He's running home to Mommy as we speak."

Seth snorted. "Did you at least find out what's going on?"

"Who was he?" Molly asked as we went inside.

"It seems Frank owes someone a little money and the guy's just trying to catch up with him to collect. That's why Frank took off the other night." It wasn't a lie, and I didn't see any need to scare her with the truth if I didn't have to. With any luck, I'd work a deal with Tony G and she'd never have to know.

The look of relief on her face was worth it, and when she offered me a beer, I accepted. The three of us sat in the kitchen, and she put out a bowl of pretzels and some dip. Seth and Molly did most of the talking, which was fine with me, because I had to figure out what the hell I could offer Tony G that would carry any weight.

We stayed for about half an hour and then called it a night. "If you have any more trouble," I said, "give me a call, or let Seth know, all right?"

"I will. Thanks, guys. I appreciate it."

Molly locked the front door behind us, and Seth and I took the easy way back to the car. On the drive home, he said, "You were kinda' quiet in there. What really happened outside?"

"You ever hear of a guy named Tony G?"

Seth stiffened up. "Isn't he some kind of Mafia bad ass? Are we talkin' like The Godfather here? What the fuck has Frank dragged my sister into?"

"Settle down, Rover." I reached out and put a hand on his chest. "Tony G is a loan shark with a pretty bad reputation, but I don't think he's gonna bring the whole weight of the Mafia down on your sister's head."

"Then what? What do we do?"

"I'm going to meet with him and see if we can't work something out."

"Work something out? What the fuck does that mean?" He twisted in the seat to face me. "If this guy is such bad news, I don't want *you* messing with him either."

"As much as I appreciate your concern, I don't think you need to worry. I know how to handle guys like this."

"Oh yeah, that's very reassuring."

"I'm always careful. You know that."

"Fine." He slumped back into the seat. After a pause, he said, "Rover?"

"Sometimes I compare you to a rat terrier to scare bad guys."

"Oh, nice. You are such an asshole."

"And yet you still hang out with me."

"You don't know this, but your mother mails me five dollars a week to be your friend."

"You're cheap. I would have held out for ten."

Chapter 16

Late on Friday, after Seth had helped close down Salvatore's and I'd given up on yet another unsuccessful watch, we met up at my place to commiserate over a couple beers. One thing led to another, as it often does with Seth, and we ended up in bed.

"Fuck yeah, Dino, you are finally getting the hang of this." He clenched his fingers in the hair at the back of my neck. "I was really beginning to worry."

He'd coaxed me into bed with promises of a blow job, and I figured it was only right to return the favor. As best I could, anyway. I paused to glance up at him. "Do you really think it's a good idea to antagonize the guy who's got your finer assets in his teeth?"

"Finer ass—" he scoffed. "And here I thought you wanted me for my brains."

"I do. Why do you think I'm down *here*?"

"Funny man," he said, and pushed my head back down.

When I went back to sucking him, he moaned loudly and swore. I had a sneaking suspicion he was playing it up for my benefit, and I stopped again to shush him. "You wanna keep it down a little? Ruth and Della live right on the other side of this wall, and I'd just as soon not advertise what we're doing if that's all right with you."

"Dude. It's not like Della ever worries about the noise."

"Yeah, well, sometimes I wish she would."

"See, this is why I like it better when I can get you to come to my apartment. You are not this uptight over there."

"Sure," I said, fisting his cock slowly. "There's no one around there. We can just be ourselves."

He pushed up onto his elbows and gave me a hard look. "And doesn't it bother you that we can only be ourselves when no one else is around?"

I fought the urge to sigh, because we'd been down this road before. "You know…if you were female, I'd still be shushing you."

The best way out was distraction, and I bent my head and sucked him off with all the fledgling skills I possessed. Happily, he abandoned the gay rights lecture in favor of more moaning and swearing. At top volume too, but that just served to motivate me to get him there that much faster. I like it when he comes, and he's right—when we're at the garage, I don't care how much noise he makes. He's hot as hell when he cuts loose.

This time was no different, and for a few minutes I forgot who might be listening and just focused on him and his pleasure. He rewarded me with a stellar performance and then pounced on me for about ten minutes of solid necking, which I took to be a thank you. Then as quick as he was on me, he was gone again, padding off to the kitchen stark naked.

He came back with a beer and twisted the cap off. "There's only one left. You want to share it?"

"It's three o'clock in the morning, and has anyone ever told you getting into bed with you is like fucking a tornado?"

He stretched out next to me on the bed and braced himself on one elbow. "Now, that's a new one. But I think I like it." He took a swig of beer and handed it over. "It's not bedtime yet, though, I have interesting news to report."

I swallowed. "You what? Since when?"

"Since tonight."

"You holding out on me now? When were you gonna bring this up?"

"Right now." He tapped a finger on my chest. "You tend to get a little single-minded when you're on a case sometimes, and I wanted to get my rocks off before I lost your attention."

"You realize that speaks to a certain single-mindedness on your part, right?"

"You wanna hear this or not?" He pulled the bottle out of my hand.

"Spill it then."

"All right. Since you've ruled out nearly everyone else, I've been keeping an eye on Lester, right? Which you and Gigi owe me big time for, because that kid is nine kinds of creepy, and if I never had to look at his freakishly large head again, I could die in peace."

"I keep telling you detective work is no walk in the park."

"Tonight, while I was on my break, I took a little tour of the dude's car. You're never going to guess what I found…"

I waited to hear what this amazing thing was, but he just stared at me expectantly. Finally it dawned on me. "It's three AM, jackass, I'm not playin' twenty questions with you."

"Rats."

"Oh, come off it, would you? It's late and I'm tired—"

"No. *Rats.* That's what I found in the car. A cage full of rats. What do you want to bet he was going to smuggle them into the restaurant?"

"Are you serious? What is this, *The Three Stooges*? That's veering completely into the realm of farce."

"No shit, man. Makes me think maybe this turkey is working alone after all."

I smirked and rolled onto my back. "Yeah, somehow I don't think the same mastermind that came up with a cage full of rats is running this whole show. There's someone a lot more dangerous behind this."

I lay there fitting this new piece into the puzzle for a while, and tried to make sense of it all. Seth swallowed the last of the beer and settled in next to me after he chucked the bottle at the trashcan. A thought struck me and I asked, "You didn't let him get the rats inside, right?"

"Of course not," he said with a yawn. "I let them loose in his car."

"Nice."

"I also hung around until he left, just to be sure. I work tomorrow too, so I'll keep an eye out for any refugees who might have managed to escape."

"Thanks, I appreciate that."

"You should. And I'll expect to be well compensated too."

"Yeah? What kind of sexual favors are an appropriate reward for rat patrol?"

"Mmm... I'm thinking something involving implements."

"Right. So back to the case—"

"Chicken."

"—I think this pretty much proves Lester *is* the inside man."

"Yup, now Gigi can fire his ass and get him out of there. Maybe then we can all get back to life as usual."

"No, not yet, and I'd appreciate it if you didn't tell Gigi about this for a while. Lester's only a flunky. There's a much bigger fish behind this, and we still don't have a clue who that is. I want to watch Lester for a while and see if he can't lead me to the real threat."

"Why don't we just beat it out of him?"

"Because we'd tip our hand. Right now, we have the advantage over them. If Lester gets a sniff that we're on to him, he'll go running to his boss and we'll be screwed. I don't want you treating him any different than you have been, all right?"

"It won't be easy…"

"I have faith in you," I said, reaching out to pat his stomach.

"Can I beat him when this is all over?"

"We'll see. Depends on how it plays out."

"Man, you are tough," he said, as he rolled over to go to sleep.

"I don't want you getting spoiled, is all."

* * * *

I woke up around nine, when the sun hit the right angle to shine in my face. Seth probably had a least a half an hour before it reached him, so I let him sleep and went out to the kitchen to make a pot of coffee.

My mind was on Lester and his rats. It was remotely possible that he just liked to take his pets for a ride once in a while, but I doubted it. I had that exciting tingle I got in my spine when a case seemed like it was about to break. It wasn't going to take much more for this one.

I also thought about Molly's situation and wondered if Frank's loan shark would bother to give me a call. It was a long shot, but you never know. Not too many people like to find out there's a private eye messing in their business.

Since there wasn't a lot I could do for Molly at the moment, I turned my attention back to the restaurant. I took a cup of coffee and went to my desk in the corner of the living room. I fired up the computer and pulled out the file of notes I'd made on Salvatore's personnel. Now that we knew exactly who to look at, we could dig a little deeper and hopefully find the connection that would lead us to whoever was really behind all this.

As I searched, I found that Lester didn't actually have much of a history, since he hadn't done much with his life. I knew what school he went to and where he grew up. There were a couple of traffic tickets on his record, but nothing else. I had a feeling he was the kind of guy who faded into the background and never got noticed. If he was at a party that got busted, he'd be the type who just slipped off to the side and walked home while the cops rounded up the other kids who drew more attention. It made him perfect for the gig he was messed up in now.

Noise from the hallway signaled that Seth was up and moving, and after a minute he came shuffling out barefoot in nothing but a pair of jeans. He looked pretty good, in spite of the zombie pace and the messed up hair. I actually liked the messed up hair.

He went straight to the fridge and pulled it open, staring inside for a long time. "Dude, don't you have any Monster or Rock Star?"

"I don't even know what that is," I said.

"It's lifeblood, man."

"Ah. Around here, we call that coffee. Help yourself."

He poured himself a cup and added a horrendous amount of sugar, then came over by me, snagging a dining chair as he passed. He sat down on it backward, leaned on it heavily, and took a sip of coffee. "What are you doing?"

"I'm diggin' up as much as I can on your friend Lester."

"He not *my* friend," he scoffed.

"Well, he's gonna be."

"What?" He leveled a weary stare at me, and I felt bad for putting him through so much.

"I want you to try to get close to him. Maybe he'll let something slip."

"Shit. I thought I could be done now."

"Almost." I leaned over and gave him a kiss on the neck. "I don't think this will take a whole lot longer."

"What are you going to do?"

I showed him the page with Lester's job history. "I'm gonna check out the other places he's worked, see if anything strikes me."

"That ought to take the better part of an hour," he said, reading the painfully short list.

Lester's work history was as sparse as the rest of his record. He'd worked three jobs in his life. McDonald's, a place called The Sandwich Shack, and Mickey's Bar & Grill, where he was listed as a busboy. Salvatore's made four.

"I don't know whether this'll pay off or not," I told him. "The connection is just as likely to be somewhere in his private life, if not more so. That's why I need you to talk to him. Find out who he hangs out with, and where. That kind of stuff."

"Yeah, okay. What about Frank?"

"I'm waiting to see if that loan shark gives me a call."

"That's it?"

The edge in his voice told me I needed to tread lightly. "If I have time tonight, I'll take a drive by there, see if I can't catch Frank and find out what he's been up to."

"Oh, great," he said, nodding. He took a sip of coffee. "If you have time."

"Come on, don't be like that."

"What am I supposed to be like, Dino?"

"Look. I gotta' focus on Gigi's case because I think there's a real chance the next time they try something, someone's gonna get hurt. This is a serious situation."

"And Molly's isn't? You don't seem to be too worried about her." He pressed his mouth into a thin, irritated line.

"I'm concerned about her, you know that. I just don't think she's in much danger. That guy the other night was just meant to be intimidating. I don't think anyone's gonna try to hurt her."

"But you don't know…"

I put a hand on his shoulder and tried to jostle the scowl off his face. "Let me talk to this Tony G guy and find out what's really going on. I swear, if I thought there was gonna be trouble, I would be all over it." Which was the truth. If Tony G got my message, he was unlikely to do anything until he found out what kind of threat I was.

"All right, all right." Seth rolled his eyes and looked at me almost apologetically. "It's just frustrating to not be able to do anything, you know?"

"Yes, I do know." It wasn't too awfully long ago I was in the same spot and Seth was the one in danger. "We'll get it all taken care of."

I slid my hand up to the back of his neck and pulled him in to a long kiss. He relented by degrees, until he was nipping my lip in his usual enthusiastic style.

When we broke, I said, "Why don't we get showered, and I'll take you out to lunch before you have to work."

"The Blue Bottle? Or how about Elmo's? I could eat a Shipwreck Burger."

"I was thinking The Sandwich Shack."

He frowned and said, "Where the fuck is that?"

"In St. Pete. It's one of the places Lester used to work. I thought we could check it out and get a bite to eat at the same time."

"That doesn't sound very promising."

"No, it doesn't. Sorry about that."

"Well," he said, standing up, "you're just gonna have to suck me off in the shower then." He grabbed my hand and pulled me along in his wake.

I have to admit, I couldn't really see the connection there, but I wasn't inclined to argue, either.

Chapter 17

"I stand by what I said." Seth pushed his sunglasses up his nose and leaned over the door of my car. We were parked across the street from The Sandwich Shack. "That doesn't look very promising."

I had to agree with him. It was a dumpy place in the middle of a strip mall full of other dumpy and depressing shops. "No argument from me. But duty calls. This place might be the key to cracking Gigi's case."

"I highly doubt that."

I climbed out of the car and went around the front end. Seth still hadn't moved. "Come on, will ya. Where's your sense of adventure?"

"Cowering behind my instinctive drive to avoid food poisoning."

I walked down and yanked open the door. "If this is that bad, we can always get a better lunch someplace else."

"Promise?"

"Do I *ever* deny you food?"

"Ugh." Seth made a face and got out. "This damn well better turn up something."

We crossed the street and went inside. It turned out to be one of those places that's run pretty much like a fast food joint, only you get better food. Usually. There was a big counter at the back of the shop, with a disinterested looking girl behind it. On the wall were a couple of those black felt signs with the white letters you push in individually. This displayed the menu. In front were a bunch of small round tables with wire chairs.

Seth leaned close and whispered. "I wouldn't order anything with seafood in it. Or meat." A fly buzzed past and he added, "Or…produce."

I walked up to the counter. "Hey there."

The girl, who had a variety of black make-up and a nose ring, just stared at me like she was trying to kill me mentally.

"What do you have that's good here?" I asked.

"It's all good. What do you want?"

"I guess I'll take the ham and cheese wrap."

She turned her attention to Seth, who said, "You got like a cheese wrap or something?"

"I could do a cheese only pressed grill sandwich."

"Pressed grill. That sounds appetizing." He gave me a sidelong glance, and I resisted the urge to remind him that I've seen him eat all kinds of horrendous crap in the many years I've known him.

I pulled out my wallet. "Why don't you give us a couple bags of chips and some Cokes with that."

She rang up the order, and we took our drinks and went to sit down. The only other person in the place was a woman roughly my age absorbed in a paperback book.

When she brought the tray out with our food, I said, "Hey, we're lookin' for a friend of ours. Skinny kid with brown hair."

"Big head," Seth interjected.

"His name is Lester, hangs out here a lot. You know him?"

"No." She set the tray down. "I've never seen anyone like that around here."

Before I could ask her anything else, she turned her back on me and returned to whatever she'd been doing before we rudely interrupted her.

"What makes you think he hangs out here?" Seth asked while he carefully examined his sandwich. It must have looked okay because he took a large bite.

"I don't know if he does or not. I figure if he's workin' with someone here, it would be likely, but who knows. They could just as easily meet in a bar, or someone's house."

"You're saying this is really just a giant waste of time."

"Probably." I peeled back the paper on my wrap. "A lot of my work is, but you have to keep doin' it until you hit the part that's not."

"That's very philosophical. You think there's anything here?"

I swallowed and took a sip of Coke. "Honestly, no. I don't think there's any connection here. There's probably not any point in checking out the McDonald's he worked at either."

"What about the other place? Mickey's?"

"That place is as good as any. I'll give it a shot, but I don't know."

"So, really, we're nowhere." Seth scowled and took another bite of grilled cheese.

"Well, not exactly. Ruling stuff out *is* progress."

"Not the fun kind."

Elle Parker

"I'm sorry. I'll try to arrange another car chase for you as soon as possible."

He flicked a chip at me and went back to his lunch. The food wasn't nearly as bad as we'd feared, but the atmosphere was depressing, prompting us to finish quickly and get the hell out of there. We were a little early for his shift at Salvatore's. To kill time, I bought him a beer at one of the nicer touristy places, where we could shake off the gloom and enjoy the beach mentality again.

When we finished, I dropped him off a block away so no one would see us together. When he got out I smiled and said, "Go make a new friend, sweetheart."

He gave me the finger. "You ever call me sweetheart again, and I'll beat the crap out of you."

I laughed and drove away.

With the dinner shift starting at the restaurant, I knew Lester wouldn't be at home, so I dropped by his apartment building in St. Pete. It was a dismal place, but large, so there were a lot of people around. If I wanted to do any serious snooping I'd have to go back at night, and even then I doubted if there'd be enough privacy to try it without being better prepared. I asked around about him, but no one seemed to know who I was talking about. The kid was a fucking ghost.

Since I was halfway there, I drove over to Molly's house to make sure everything was okay. The house was dark, and neither of their cars was there. The thug was gone too, but then, it's hard to be intimidating when no one's home.

Just to be safe, I pulled out my cellphone and dialed Molly's number.

"Hello?" She sounded hesitant, and I realized she wouldn't recognize my number.

"It's Dino. I just wanted to check in."

"Oh, hi," she said, much more brightly. "I'm fine. That guy hasn't been around the house at all, that I've seen. I really want to thank you for that."

"That's good," I told her. "I'm on your street here and everything looks normal. Are you at work today?"

"I'm at Mom and Dad's. Mom decided to cook a big dinner and invited me over. I'll probably drink a whole lot of wine and sleep on their couch."

"Sounds like a good plan. Is Frank there?"

"No," she said. "He always goes out on Saturday nights. It's his chance to unwind."

As opposed to every other night of the week, I could hear Seth saying. "Okay, have a good time. I'll tell Seth things are cool."

We hung up and I turned toward home without a clue as to what to do next. Options were slim, and if Seth didn't get anything out of Lester in the next day or two, I'd have to risk tailing him.

* * * *

I went home, spread all the notes and printouts I had on the kitchen counter, and cracked open a beer to study them. For all the progress I'd made, I still wasn't getting any closer to solving Gigi's problem. I could tell her why, and I could tell her at least part of who, but I didn't have the final piece to be able to make it stop. Until I figured out the brains behind the operation, the sabotage was going to keep happening.

About ten o'clock, my phone rang. It wasn't a number I knew. "Dino Martini."

"Is this the Martini that's a private eye?"

"Yes, it is. Who's this?" I folded my arms and leaned back against the counter.

"I have a call here from Tony G, hold on a minute."

That got my attention, but I wasn't surprised. I'd been expecting a call soon. When Molly told me the thug never came back, I knew I'd made an impression.

"Mr. Martini?" Another voice came on the line and I thought I detected a Jersey accent. "My name is Anthony Guliano. People call me Tony G."

"I've heard of you."

"Good, good. That always helps. I understand you crossed paths with an associate of mine the other night, and that you have some business you'd like to discuss."

"That's right. Do you think we could meet? Maybe tomorrow?"

"Oh, no, no, I never work on Sundays. Let's make it Monday. Evening."

"That sounds fine," I said. "Where?"

He gave me an address, which I wrote down, and told me to be there at seven.

"Oh, and Mr. Martini? I don't recommend you come armed. My boys don't like that."

"Yeah, I can probably do that. I look forward to meeting you."

"Likewise," he said, and hung up.

Okay then. Now I had two things I could report to Seth on Molly's case, which I hoped would get me out of the doghouse on that one.

If something would only move on Gigi's case, I could call it a full weekend.

Seth phoned late, almost at the end of his shift. "You don't have to come pick me up, dude. Apparently my charm is irresistible to one and all, and I convinced Lester to give me a ride home."

"Wow, you work fast."

"Hey, you can count on me to get the job done," he said. "Plus, it's right on his way, so it's not exactly like it's a big deal. I'm exhausted, so I think I'm just gonna crash. Can I catch up with you tomorrow?"

"Of course. Come on over whenever you get up. We can trade notes then."

"Thanks, dude. See you later."

I didn't know if I could call that progress just yet, but at least it was something.

Chapter 18

By noon on Sunday, I still hadn't heard a word from Seth, but that wasn't all that strange. Ordinarily, it would barely catch my attention, but I was getting antsy to trade notes. He'd had a good twenty minutes or so in a car with Lester, and possibly significantly more if they opted to have a beer or whatever.

Since I also had gotten no word from John Holcomb on the price of an office, I decided to work on that until Seth rose from the dead. I took a cup of coffee and went downstairs.

There was enough lumber for me to finish hammering studs into the framework for the back wall. It was a warm day, without much wind, and the sun beating through the plate glass windows turned my office into a sauna in pretty short order. I stripped down to my undershirt and wiped the sweat off my brow, wishing I'd brought beer rather than coffee, and thinking I might head out to get some, Seth or no Seth.

"God damn, wife-beaters and old jeans look good on you." I turned to see Seth leaning against the door frame with a paper bag in his arms. "Wish I got to see that more often."

"You get to see plenty. I don't think you're hurting in that department." Even so, I didn't exactly resist the urge to put a little extra sex appeal into my body language. "If you have beer in that bag, I'll love you forever."

"You're supposed to do that anyway, but as it happens, I do." He crossed over to the desk and set the bag down. First, he pulled out a beer for me, and one for himself, then he unpacked a pile of sandwiches and a large bag of potato chips.

When I took the beer from him, I realized he was acting cagey, keeping his back to me or his face turned away. Something was up, and the less subtle I got about trying to get a look at him, the more ridiculous his evasion became. I finally just grabbed him by the elbow and spun him to face me.

He was sporting a fresh shiner and a fat lip. "What the hell happened to you?" I asked, touching the side of his face. "Things go bad with Lester last night?"

It wasn't that unusual to see him wearing the evidence of his latest bar fight. Seth was never slow to throw the first punch. Didn't mean I liked it any. One of these days he was going to find out the hard way he wasn't a kid anymore.

"No, that went fine." He swatted my hand away and opened his beer. "How 'bout we just say I walked into a door."

"How 'bout we don't," I said, scowling. "I want to know what's going on."

After a long swallow of beer, he sighed heavily and stared up at the ceiling. "I got into it with Frank this morning."

"You *what?*" I crossed my arms over my chest. "What the hell were you doing over there? I told you I was taking care of it."

"Except that you're not," he snapped.

"The hell I'm not. I have a meeting with Tony G tomorrow, which you would know if you had come over here instead of charging off to play The Enforcer when Molly's not home."

"Fuck you, Dino." He was geared up for a fight and it took a moment for that to sink in. "Wait. How did you know Molly wasn't home?"

"Because I spoke to her last night. You know, when I wasn't working her case at all?" I sat on the edge of the desk and took a sip of beer.

"So I probably could have spared myself the black eye."

I raised an eyebrow. "I have never known you to do so before."

The fire drained out of him and he looked sheepish. "Oh. Well. Good thing I bought lunch today, eh?"

"And beer. That's what's really saving your ass right now."

"I'll remember that."

"Come 'ere," I said, spreading my knees and holding a hand out to him.

He took it and I pulled him against me to kiss his neck and run a hand along his back. "You hurt?"

"No." He looped his arms around my shoulders and leaned in.

"Is Frank?"

"Not much. Molly's gonna kill me as it is."

"It's been nice knowin' ya."

He smirked and kissed me in a way that promised an active and sweaty afternoon. Can't say that I minded.

We eventually broke it up and settled in to eat lunch. I unwrapped my sandwich and put a pile of chips next to it. "So, did you learn anything from Lester?"

"Amazingly, he's not even as swift as we gave him credit for. I'm impressed he manages to survive."

"He's got enough brains to be sabotaging Salvatore's from the inside," I pointed out.

"Yeah, well, he's getting a *lot* of help. But he's perfect for the job. He's got just enough upstairs to be able to do what he's told, but there's no danger of him ever getting any ideas on his own, so he's a safe bet. Whoever's pulling the strings doesn't have to worry about him going rogue."

I took a swallow of beer and shook my head. "Guys like that are bad news. They're dangerous."

"Oh, and here's something fun," he said, wiping mayonnaise off the corner of his mouth. "He thinks you're Gigi's new boyfriend." The disgusted expression on his face told me exactly what he thought about that.

"Yeah, well…" I sidestepped the issue. "That means he's not too likely to realize anyone's onto him."

"Yes, that's the important thing."

"Oh, come off it—"

"Tell me about this meeting with Tony G," he interrupted. Which was fine with me. A change of subject was exactly what we needed at the moment.

"He called me last night. Wants me to go see him at his villa. He sounded reasonably amiable, but he told me to come unarmed."

Seth looked up at me. "And are you?"

"I'll certainly have the gun in the car, but I don't think I have much choice otherwise."

"Do you think that's smart, Dino?"

I shrugged. "They'll frisk me for sure, and if I tried to sneak something in, I can promise that would get me into a hell of a lot of trouble. Right now, I'm just business to him. If I don't give him any reason to think different, there shouldn't be a problem."

"So…no chance of me going as backup, then?"

"Nope. If you got caught it would be the same thing, and if you didn't, there's no way you'd get past his security if I was in danger. Don't worry, it'll be fine."

Seth wadded up his sandwich wrappers and tossed them into the bag along with his empty beer bottle. Then he came to stand in front of me, where I still sat on the edge of the desk. He took my face in his hands and kissed me hard and dirty. This was one of those kisses with a lot of tongue and a lot of heavy breathing. It was enough to make me forget what planet I was on.

He practically tried to climb into my lap, and ended up half straddling me and half perched precariously on the edge of the desk. I wrapped my arms around him and hauled his body tight against mine. It certainly wasn't the most graceful make-out session I'd ever had, but at that moment I didn't care. Seth was hot and smelled earthy and raw. He had his hands tangled in my hair, and he was rocking his hips against me.

When he stopped for a moment to catch his breath, I said, "I take it this means you'll worry about me while I'm there?"

"Just don't get your dick shot off." Then he bit my lip and caught my mouth in another raunchy kiss.

I moaned and shoved a hand up under his shirt to press against his back. He was damp with sweat, but warm, and felt damn good. Maybe it's because he seems so much like a teenager a lot of the time, but he often ended up making me feel like one. I was hard as a rock and panting heavily, and all I could really focus on was his mouth.

Seth snaked a hand between us and popped open the button of my jeans, and I started to think about taking the party upstairs.

"Dino, sugar, I couldn't stand to think about you working so hard in this heat for one more second and I just had to— Oh, my goodness."

Della's voice preceded her by a few seconds, and my blood ran ice cold. I switched gears so fast I probably broke something in my head. Without thinking, I let go of Seth and was off that desk and on my feet like a shot. He landed flat on his ass, with a smack and a lot of foul language. It was not one of my finer moments. Della stopped dead in the middle of the room with a pitcher of lemonade and dumbfounded expression on her face.

"This is not what it looks like," I blurted out. Although, what I thought I was going to try to convince her it *was*, I had no idea.

"Oh, honey," she said, slightly breathless. "There's nothing else that looks like that." She was pale and put a hand over her mouth, glancing between me and the desk with worried eyes. She looked down at my pants, and I hastily buttoned them up.

"Look, Della, I know this is kind of shocking and all that. I never meant for anyone to find out, I just—"

"Darlin', I don't care about that any, you should know better." She still looked pretty shaken, though, and I was at a loss until she explained. "You *know* I can't keep a secret to save my life. It doesn't matter how hard I try, sooner or later it just…slips out."

She looked genuinely distressed, and I was touched she'd worry about me that way. I put my hands on her shoulders. "Don't worry about it, that's not your problem. I'll cross that bridge when I come to it. I could never hold anything against you anyway."

"Thank you, sugar." The relief was evident in her voice, and she clasped her hand to her chest. "I'll do my best. We can talk later on, all right?"

She was already hedging out the door, and as soon as she finished speaking, she darted out the side door, taking her lemonade with her.

When I turned around, I realized the reason for her hasty departure.

Seth was still on the floor, staring up at me with an expression so livid it made me want to run and hide in Della's apartment too. He was practically shaking, he was so angry.

"Ah. Jeez, I'm…sorry," I offered. I knew it was weak, but my mind was still struggling to process everything that had just happened.

If possible, that only made him madder. He finally ground out, "You dumped me on the *floor*, you…you…son of a *bitch*."

"Shit, I know. I'm sorry. I just wasn't thinking."

I rushed forward to help him up, but he shouted, "Don't," and stopped me in my tracks. "Don't come any closer, Dino, or I swear I'll kick the shit out of you."

There was not a doubt in my mind he'd do exactly that, and I stood stock still. I'd only ever seen him that mad at me once before, and it damn near cost our friendship. I swallowed hard. "Seth, come on…I'm sorry."

"Shut up." He got up off the floor and dusted himself off. "Just shut the hell up."

"I was just shocked, that's all. Della scared the crap out of me, and I stood up without thinking."

"You don't get it, do you?" he seethed. "You have no idea why I'm pissed off."

"Well, you said…" I gestured toward the floor, helpless. I felt short of breath, and a sick sense of dread was creeping over me. "You seemed pretty pissed off about that."

"I am!" he shouted. "I'm pissed about that, and I'm pissed that you have such a deep-seated fucking fear of anyone finding out about us. Jesus, I have to sit here and listen to you trying to explain me away, like you have some kind of fucking disease. 'I'll cross that bridge when I come to it'? Fuck you! Why don't you save us both the trouble and take a flying leap off that fucking bridge."

"You know, it's not as simple as you make it sound. People lose their homes and their jobs for being gay. People get hurt all the time. I could lose my apartment over this."

"Oh, cut the bullshit. You're not gonna lose your apartment. You heard Della, she doesn't care. Ruth won't care, and Adele's not gonna give a rat's ass what you do as long as you pay your rent on time."

"Fern might have something to say about it."

He narrowed his eyes, but ignored my comment. "You sure as fuck aren't going to lose your job unless you're so self-loathing you fire yourself for being gay."

"I am not self-lo—"

"The fuck you're not," he snapped. "You've been bi the whole fucking time I've known you, and I'm sure long before that, and it took until you were forty-*one* for you to even *consider* acknowledging that part of yourself."

"That doesn't mean I hate myself. It just means I never met a guy I was that interested in until you."

"Meanwhile, you're so fucking afraid for anyone to know about us. You're ashamed of me, and yourself, and our relationship. Yeah, I feel real special." He turned and stalked toward the door.

"Seth, wait. Come on, don't leave."

"I have to leave right now, because if I don't, I will almost certainly deck you as hard as possible."

I knew from experience that's pretty hard. "I'm sorry, Seth. I'll…call you later."

"Don't bother," he said and stormed out to his truck.

I watched him get in and drive off, tires squealing, and it felt like someone had kicked me in the gut. I'd fucked up in a major way, and it was going to take a whole hell of a lot to fix it. If it could be fixed at all. This was a fight that was a long time coming, and there were some seriously deep issues at stake.

I didn't know what to do with myself, so I fished a pack of cigarettes out of the desk drawer, sat down on the floor and lit one up. I leaned back against the desk and tried to think, but I was numb. Maybe in shock.

I don't know what time it was when Seth left, but it was dark when I finally dragged myself upstairs to my apartment. I tried calling Seth, in spite of what he'd said, but he didn't answer, and I guess I didn't really expect him to. After that, I just got drunk and went to bed.

Chapter 19

I didn't crawl out of bed until ten o'clock the next morning. For one thing, I couldn't see any reason I should get up, and for another, I had a splitting headache. I probably had a hangover too, but if I stayed very, very still I might not wake it up.

Unfortunately, there's only so long you can stay in bed before certain matters become too pressing to ignore. So, I got up, said hello to my hangover, and trudged toward the bathroom. I made some coffee and got dressed in the softest, quietest clothes I could find. I thought about calling Seth, but knew damn well there was plenty more ignoring in my future before I had any hope of making things right.

There is no rest for the wicked, the hungover, or those of us with our heads up our asses, so like it or not, I had to get to work. Without Seth, I needed someone to go with me to check out Mickey's Bar & Grill. A guy alone is more likely to attract attention than a couple of buddies or someone out to lunch with family. I took my coffee and went downstairs.

Ruth and Della were sitting outside on the patio with coffee of their own and a newspaper they were sharing. I sat down carefully and stretched my legs out under the table.

"Good morning, Dino," Ruth said.

Della gave me a once over and smiled coyly. "My goodness, honey, you look just *plum* tuckered out."

I sighed and closed my eyes. "I'm not tuckered out. I'm hungover."

Ruth glanced at me over the top of her paper. "I have to admit, Dino, you do look it."

"Thank you. I worked very hard on this."

She looked bemused. "I hope it was worth it."

"It served its purpose," I said, and sipped my coffee. "I came down to ask you ladies a favor."

"Of course, darlin', whatever we can do to help." Della seemed concerned, and I hoped she wasn't speculating too hard on my state of affairs. I wasn't prepared to deal with that.

"I think this should be pretty easy for you. I'd like to take you both out to lunch tomorrow."

Della lit right up, and I was glad for the distraction. Ruth set down her paper and straightened her glasses. "We'd love to, certainly, but why would it be a favor?"

"Because it's for a job. I need to check the place out, and I'll blend in better if I have some company."

"You mean we'd be working undercover?" Della's eyes positively gleamed, and if I hadn't felt so lousy I would have thought it was cute.

"Not exactly," I told her. "But if anyone asks you can tell them you're my aunt."

"Oh, this is so excitin'. What should we wear? Is it a fancy place?"

"No, I'm pretty sure it's not. We're going to Mickey's Bar and Grill in Treasure Island. I won't be at all surprised if it's a complete dump, so be prepared."

"What is it you're hoping to find there?" Ruth asked.

I rubbed the back of my neck. "I have no idea. We've traced one guy in Gigi's case back to Mickey's and with any luck that will lead us to the real criminal. I need to find a connection I can use."

Della fanned herself. "Oh my. Will it be dangerous?"

"I doubt it. I wouldn't mention Salvatore's while we're there. And I'd appreciate it if you didn't shout my name either. Otherwise, just enjoy a meal on me."

"Now, *that* sounds like the way to spend an afternoon, sugar."

I really had to learn to stop setting her up like that.

Ruth clucked her tongue and said, "We'd love to, Dino. What time would you like to go?"

"Let's aim to get there about one o'clock. Things'll be starting to pick up by then. Want to meet out here at twelve-thirty?"

"It's a date," Della said, clapping her hands. "Oh, this is going to be so much *fun*."

"Thank you, both. Now, if you'll excuse me, this sun is killing my eyes."

I got up and went back inside where I felt less like my head was going to explode. I decided that I wouldn't be doing myself any favors if I showed up at Tony G's in substandard condition, so I drank a large glass of water, took three aspirin and went back to bed.

* * * *

When I woke up again, it was nearly five, which was kind of alarming. Usually, though, if I sleep that long it's because I needed it, and in this case it did the trick. I felt significantly more human and far more ready to face a notorious gangster.

Since I had a little time, I made some eggs and sat down to watch the news. Then I showered and got dressed. Florida casual, jacket, but no tie. I grabbed my cellphone and keys. I had my gun on the desk and I checked to make sure it was loaded. I had no intention of violating Tony G's rules, but I wanted to keep it as close as possible.

Then I needed to figure out where I was going. The address he'd given me was still on the notepad, and I took out my county map and looked it up. I had to double check, because it wasn't in an area I expected it to be. It was on the Waterway, as rumored, but nowhere near the ritzy inlets of St. Pete Beach or Pass-a-Grille. Still, there's no accounting for taste.

I checked my watch. I was still running a little early, which was good because that would give me a chance to do a drive-by and see what I was dealing with. I wanted to call Seth and let him know I was on my way, but that seemed pointless at best, and kind of pathetic under the circumstances. Besides, he was probably currently hoping I got shot, and that was something I didn't want confirmed.

I went downstairs, got in the car and stuffed my gun under the seat. It was a nice evening. Late slanting sun, not too bright, and a crisp Gulf breeze. I backed out of the parking lot and headed toward Tony G's.

The drive was pleasant and it relaxed me, so when I turned onto his street, I felt calm and ready to face him. The neighborhood was on the plain side, and the houses were small, though most of them were cute, and all had trees in the yards. I started checking house numbers as I rounded a sweeping curve. There on the edge of the Marina was Tony G's villa. I know because it said so.

I parked Matilda at the curb out front and sat staring at it in disbelief. The supposed magnificent palace of the badass loan shark was a two-story house with a deck around the top level and a garage underneath. The yard was neatly kept, with a fringe of leafy trees, an assortment of palms, and a hedge along the front. The grass, however, was scrubby and brown. A low fence circled the property and the driveway was gated. Two rock pillars stood one on either side of it. The pillar on the left said *Villa* and the one on the right said *Tony G*. Both were topped with cement lions. No mistaking that.

Up on the main level, I saw a face peering out through a lighted window, and when I got out of the car, the front door opened up. The blond thug from the other night came down the wooden staircase and crossed the driveway to the gate. I met him there.

"Oh, hello," I said. "Nice meeting you again."

"Yeah, charmed." He was a complete deadpan as he opened the gate to let me in. "I know you got a gun. I hope you were smart enough to leave it at home."

"Close enough."

I held my arms out while he frisked me quickly and efficiently. There wasn't really a direct view from any of the nearby houses, and a curious neighbor would have had to be looking pretty closely to catch it. He didn't find anything, of course, and jerked his head toward the house before turning to lead the way.

The stairs formed an L at the front of the house, leading to the deck on the upper level. There was a table and some chairs in a nice arrangement, framed by flowered plants hanging from the roof overhead.

The thug ushered me through the front door into a small but richly decorated foyer. In contrast to the fairly ordinary exterior, there was slate tile, a fancy rug, wood furniture and a large, gold-framed mirror.

"Wait here," he said, and disappeared deeper into the house.

I peeked into the living room which was more of the same. It looked like a magazine spread, but pushed to the point of being overdone. Everything looked real, and expensive. The carpet was so thick, I thought I might need snowshoes to get across it safely.

"Tony G will see you now." He stepped into the living room and motioned for me to follow him back.

He led me through a large kitchen to another deck out back facing the marina. So yeah, Tony G's villa was on the water, but it had a view of some junky sailboats and the condos on the other side. Not exactly the high life. The deck was standard issue green-treat, painted to match the house, but the furnishings were like the inside of the house. Plush and opulent. Gazebo roofing provided shade for a low table made of highly polished wood surrounded by leather chairs. Tucked in the corner was a matching wooden hutch that served as a bar for a collection of seriously top shelf booze. The whole arrangement sat on a large oriental rug, and Tony G sat in the middle of it all, smoking a cigar.

"So, you're the guy that wants to deal, huh?" He was a large man, built like a barrel with meaty arms and hands. His black hair was slicked back, but didn't seem to want to stay in place, and he was probably in his mid-fifties or so. He flicked ash into a huge crystal ashtray.

"That's right. I'd like to give it a try anyway."

He considered that and nodded. "So, sit."

I pulled out one of the leather chairs and sat down opposite him. The thug took up a post at the other end of the deck. A discreet distance for privacy, but handy if I needed any roughing up.

Tony G had a bottle of scotch and a glass on the table. He reached behind him for another one. "You drink?"

"Of course." I crossed my legs and got comfortable. The villa may have earned a mythical status, but the rumors about the man himself were proving to be true. "Thanks."

He poured me a glass and got settled again. "Johnny tells me you want us to leave Frank Novak alone?"

"Not exactly," I said. "It's the girlfriend, Molly, that I'm acting for."

"What's your angle on all this?"

"Her brother is a good friend of mine. He'd like to see Frank gone, and asked me to help out. See, Molly's a really nice woman and Frank's a dirt bag, and no one can understand what she sees in him, but she is apparently blind to his faults. In the meantime, he's bringin' her down with him."

"You have an interesting idea of what's a really nice woman, Mr. Martini." He swirled the liquor in his glass and took a sip.

"Excuse me?"

"Well, I'm not exactly high society, but even I don't think a stripper with a pot habit and tattoos from top to bottom is a nice lady."

That caught me up short. "I don't think we're on the same page here. She's not anything like that."

"Frank's girlfriend, right?" He regarded me like I was a little slow and needed to have things explained carefully.

"Yeah. Molly Donnelly."

"Well, I don't know about the name, but we got pictures of him at a couple of clubs with her and either they are an item, or he was providing free medical exams. If you get my drift." He stuck a hand in the air and snapped his fingers. "Hey, Johnny. Get the file on Frank Novak. And bring out some of that smoked salmon while you're at it."

Johnny got up and went inside, and I struggled to get the image of Frank pawing anyone out of my head.

"Listen," I said, "I don't think you have your facts straight. Maybe they were havin' a hot night out, but Molly's a lab technician, she's not a stripper."

"Sure she is. She works down at The Mermaid. That's one of the clubs we picked 'em up at. I can personally vouch for the fact that not only is she a professional, but she looks pretty fuckin' good in nothing but a g-string." He took another sip of scotch and pointed at me. "Which is why I also know about the tattoos."

I was extremely glad Seth wasn't there, because the result would not have been pretty. "I can't really say one way or another about tattoos. Except for the skin you can usually see, and there aren't any."

Johnny returned with a folder, which he handed to Tony G, and a platter with a block of smoked salmon surrounded by thin crackers and slices of Swiss cheese. Then he returned to his post at the other end of the deck. Tony G rifled through the folder and pulled out a stack of medium-sized color photographs, which he dropped on the table in front of me.

I spread them out with one hand and could easily see why Tony G was insisting this was Frank's girlfriend. Every single one of them featured him doing something lewd to a woman with short brown hair, heavy make-up, and a lot of tattoos. Even on the places you can usually see.

"That is not Molly," I said, pushing the photos back at Tony G. "Which doesn't really matter. I'm not especially surprised Frank is two-timin' her, but my business here is the same. I want you to leave Molly Donnelly alone."

"This is what I'm telling you," he said, gesturing with a knife in one hand and cracker in the other. "The woman in the pictures is the girlfriend, and it's the girlfriend we're puttin' the screws to. I happen to know she pulls down pretty good money from that club."

"Last Thursday, I had to go chase Johnny off Molly's street because he was scarin' the crap out of her, and she says it's not the first time he's been parked out there. You may think you're putting the screws to this girl…" I tapped a finger on the photos. "But it's Molly Donnelly's house you've been staking out."

Tony G stared at me and chewed thoughtfully. He washed it down with scotch, and then leaned to look around me again. "Johnny. Come over here and take a seat."

Johnny came and sat with his back to the water. He rested his elbows on the table and gave me a look of mild irritation. Obviously, I wasn't worth getting worked up over, but I was ruining an evening that could have been better spent doing push-ups or shining his brass knuckles.

Tony G swiveled to face him. "How is that you came to be staking out that house?"

"I followed Frank home from work. He lives there. And so does the stripper, I've seen her through the windows."

I shook my head slowly. "No, you've seen a *redhead* with short hair, which probably doesn't look all that different from a distance when you're peeping in a house."

Johnny scowled and Tony G considered that. He said, "Is that possible? What he said?"

"I don't know, boss. Looked like the stripper to me. I don't know what this Molly chick looks like."

"Hang on a sec." I dug my cellphone out of my pocket and thumbed through the menu. A few months before, Molly and her mom had planted a little garden in front of her house and I'd taken a picture of the two of them standing in it. Right next to the front door. I showed it to them. "This is Molly Donnelly. You can see it's the same house."

"Well, maybe." Johnny leaned in for a better look. "Lots of those places are the same."

"Look her up in the phone book," I said, getting annoyed with the whole thing. "You know what address you were at, look up Molly Donnelly and you'll find that's her place."

Johnny glanced at Tony G, and Tony G just shrugged. "Sure. Go get it, then we'll know if this is on the level and we can figure out what's going on."

It only took a few seconds for Johnny to step inside, grab the phone book and come back, flipping through the white pages. He ran a finger down one page and raised his eyebrows. "He's telling the truth, boss. That's the address, right there." He turned the book and showed Tony G the listing.

Tony G nodded and shrugged. "When you're right, you're right. Which is lucky for you, because I do not appreciate being screwed with."

"I wouldn't dream of it," I said. "If you don't mind my sayin', your research department seems to be severely lacking." I took a sip of my scotch and studied the ice cubes. "Maybe this is where we can strike a deal."

"How so?"

"Research and fact checking is something I happen to be pretty good at. It's what I do. Maybe if you agree to leave Molly alone, completely, I could see my way to helping you out once in a while." I wasn't exactly eager to go into business with a loan shark, but offering my services was the bargaining chip I'd planned to use anyway, and doing a little research was a lot better than actually running jobs for the guy.

"Sure, okay." Tony G leaned back in his chair and poured himself some more scotch.

I watched him for a minute, and when he didn't say anything else, I narrowed my eyes. "That was awfully easy," I pointed out. "Is there something I'm missin' here?"

"Naw." He pushed the tray of salmon in my direction. "I got no interest in hassling some nice lady. I do business with a somewhat lower clientele. Junkies, dealers, gambling buffs. People who basically got what's coming to 'em if I have to collect the hard way. See, they're gonna play their little games one way or another, so I may as well make a good living, and I still get to sleep at night."

"A loan shark with a conscience," I said, helping myself to fish and a cracker. "I like that."

Tony G burst out laughing. A deep raucous laugh that made his face turn pink. "You're all right, Martini." He drank more scotch and said, "Of course...this leaves me with a small problem."

"Oh?"

"Now I don't have the girlfriend anymore."

I chose not to point out that he never did. Instead I said, "Well, here's my chance to make good already. I'm still gonna be workin' to dig up dirt on Frank and now that I know about the stripper, that seems like a good direction to take with my case. I could possibly fill you in on anything I find that might be useful to you."

Tony G had started nodding halfway through my speech, and a broad smile spread across his face. "I think this is going to work out just fine."

Since he seemed to be especially pleased with me at the moment, I decided to press my luck. "Do you think I could take one or two of those photographs? They'd be pretty helpful in finding the stripper, and if I have to in the end, I can show them to Molly to clinch the deal on Frank."

"Sure, take your pick," he told me. "Frank is a slimy fuck, and I would enjoy helping to make his life a little more miserable. Besides, if this Molly is as nice as you say—and she must be for you to be talkin' to me—she sure as hell doesn't deserve a worm like him."

"She is." I pulled the two most vulgar photos out of the pile and tucked them into my breast pocket. "I appreciate this."

We spent another hour chatting about business in general and what I might be able to do for him in the future, then I finally left, full of fish and good scotch. It was about time I made some progress. I tried not to think too hard about the deal I'd just forged with Tony G. I could deal with that in due course. Besides, as much as I hated to admit it, I kind of liked the guy.

Chapter 20

It was only about eight-thirty when I pulled away from the curb in front of Tony G's. Too early to go back to my apartment and rattle around thinking about how badly I'd screwed up with Seth. I needed a distraction. I figured I could go check in with Gigi and kill two birds with one stone, plus get some dinner. I headed out of Tony G's neighborhood and turned south on Gulf Boulevard, my mind on scampi with linguine.

So, now I had good leads on both my main cases. There was a stripper to track down for Tony G, which would ultimately solve the Frank situation. And we knew who was sabotaging Gigi's restaurant. Even if I couldn't track down the brains behind the operation, we still had Lester and if nothing else, we could lean on him and find out what we needed to know. That wasn't my preferred outcome, though, because it left too much potential for the real crook to slither into hiding and take another shot at it when the heat wore off.

About halfway to Salvatore's my cellphone rang, and I was surprised to see it was Seth. "Hey there," I answered cautiously. I wanted to sound pleased to hear from him, but not too eager or desperate.

"Did you go see that loan shark tonight?" His voice was cold and mechanical, but not exactly sharp.

"Yeah, and—"

"Did he kill you?"

"Ah, no, not that I'm aware of."

"Okay then." And he hung up before I could say another word to him. There was something in his voice I couldn't quite place at first. Aside from the extreme dislike of me, of course. Then I realized…he was drunk. That was fine with me. Why should I be the only one nursing a hangover in all this? It was about time he took a turn.

I tried dialing him back, but it went to voicemail. Instead of ignoring it like I usually do, I waited until the beep and said, "I'm sorry, Seth. I really am."

The call put me in a foul mood. I tried telling myself at least he still cared if I was alive or dead, but all I could think about was the fact that he still wasn't talking to me. I sighed and wondered how long it was going to take to fix this one. Assuming it was still possible. That was the story of my life…moving from one doghouse to another.

I came up to Salvatore's and was about to make the turn into the parking lot when a car roared backward out of its spot and squealed out into the street, nearly taking off my front fender in the process. I didn't get a look at the driver, but the car was a dark colored sedan. It was apparently a night for pissed off people.

That was an understatement. After I parked and went inside, I found Gigi fuming by the hostess stand, in the middle of an agitated conversation with Marco. Nearby diners glanced over at them and spoke to each other in hushed tones. Across the dining room, two busboys were cleaning a mess off the floor.

"What's goin' on?" I asked. "I nearly got run over pulling in here."

Gigi turned on me, but immediately softened when she realized who it was. "Oh, Dino. I'm sorry about that. We had a very irate customer who was making one hell of a scene." She ran her hands through her hair. "I finally had to threaten to call the police, and that's when he stormed out of here, swearing a blue streak. I don't know how much more of this I can take."

"So, you're pretty sure this was related to your other problem, and not just a random jerk?" The car that peeled out of there could have been the one, and I wished I followed it. On the other hand, it could have been one of a million other dark sedans.

"Yes. We never have people acting like that in here. Would you be willing to wait for me at the bar? I'd like to check on the customers and apologize, see if I can calm people down."

"Sure. Buy me dinner?"

She nodded. "Just order whatever you like. I'll be over in a minute."

I gave her shoulder a squeeze and left her to her damage control. At the bar, I ordered scotch on the rocks and a plate of linguine with seafood. While I waited, I watched her make the rounds, chatting with people and assuring them that things were fine. She looked happy and calm, as if nothing noteworthy had happened. I knew better, though. I sincerely hoped I was close to bringing her case to an end.

Finally, she joined me at the bar. The happy was replaced with weary resignation, and she ordered a scotch for herself. That was a big clue right there how bad things were. She never drank on the job.

"So, tell me what happened," I said.

She took a deep breath and wrapped her hands around her glass. "This guy came in for dinner alone and at first there was nothing distinctive about him, but then he started to be rude to the servers, talking down to them and questioning everything. He complained about the service, and how long it took to get his food, and then when he got it, he complained about that. He was getting louder and ruder all the time, and he finally demanded to see the manager. I came out and tried to calm him down, reason with him, but he didn't want to hear any of that. He just wanted to yell at me and talk trash about the restaurant. Finally, he stood up and threw his plate on the floor and got very threatening. That's when I told him I was calling the police."

"Wait a minute, he threatened you?" There was no doubt in my mind this was another sabotage attempt.

"Not in words. He was just very physically intimidating. The implied threat was there, but he didn't actually say anything or try to hurt me."

"Yeah, okay. If it's any consolation, I don't think he would actually have done anything. It's pretty clear it was the scene he was after. It was a show for the other customers."

She nodded in agreement. "Dino, please tell me you have something."

"I have something," I said, and took a drink of my scotch.

"Do you plan to share?"

"I still want to keep a lid on it around here. But I can tell you we know who's workin' the inside, and I'm tracking down his connections to figure out who he's taking orders from. I have one more place to check on tomorrow. If that doesn't pan out, we'll lean on him and find out what we need to know. It's a pretty sure bet this will all be over by the end of the week."

There was a hint of relief in her eyes when she looked up at me. "You really think so?"

"If I can't get anything out of him by then, we'll bring the police in on this. I know you'd rather not, but it's starting to get serious. There's enough to make a case now, and when they cut the compressor line, they added property damage which makes it official."

"Okay," she said with a nod of her head. "If that's what it comes to, I'm willing."

"Good girl. It's gonna be all right. You'll see."

"I hope so. Angelo has been talking about finding another job. He's afraid if he waits too long, his reputation will be ruined and no restaurant will have him."

"There's gratitude for you."

"Can you blame him?"

A waitress brought my dinner and set it on the bar with silverware rolled up in a napkin.

Gigi said, "I'm going to go take over at the hostess station and make sure everyone gets a proper goodbye so I can show them this is still a nice place. You enjoy your dinner."

"Hang in there," I told her. "It's almost over."

She left and I turned to focus on my meal. While I ate, I mulled over this new development. In a way, it was promising. Staging a scene like that was a step down from physical sabotage, and seemed to indicate their goal was to simply chip away at Gigi and Salvatore's reputation until it crumbled, rather than continue the escalation.

I kept an eye out for Lester, but never saw him and had to assume he had the night off. Since I had no place better to be, I hung around until late, nursing my drink and watching the comings and goings of the crowd. On the off chance the asshole decided to come back, I wanted to be there.

By eleven, business was pretty much back to normal and they were getting ready to close down. I offered to drive Gigi home and make sure things were okay, but she refused. "I appreciate the thought, Dino, but if I let you do that, it'll feel like I'm letting him win. I'll be fine. Marco and I will help the closing crew, and we'll all leave together. I'm sure I'll be safe."

"All right," I said. "I can understand that. I'll stop by tomorrow after I follow my leads and let you know if I found anything."

I sincerely hoped I would.

Chapter 21

The night air was warm, with the right amount of breeze, so I took my time driving home. The only thing waiting for me there was an empty apartment anyway. I thought about going over to Seth's place, but based on our conversation earlier, I didn't think it was time for that yet. Besides, if Seth was drinking, there would be no reasoning with him. I'd only make things worse.

I pulled up to a stoplight in St. Pete Beach and wondered what to do next. While I waited for the green, I looked around and wished I was one of the tourists whose only dilemma was where to get the next pina colada. That's when I realized I was half a block away from The Mermaid, Frank's stripper's club. It sat there in all its sleazy magnificence, offering exotic dancers and a bar you could actually still smoke in.

It crossed my mind that the stripper might very well be there, and I figured a look around wouldn't hurt. It wasn't like I had anything better to do. When the light changed, I turned the corner and parked Matilda on the street, rather than put her in The Mermaid's parking lot. It wouldn't be dignified for her, and I didn't want the clientele smudging up her wax job.

The club was a low concrete building with nothing much in the way of distinguishing features, except the entire thing was painted lavender. Even in Florida it stuck out. Purple neon trimmed the roof line and advertised the dancers. A red sign over the door read *Smokers Welcome*. One on the roof advertised *Free Drink With Room Key*. Nice.

I paid my cover charge and went inside, where a thin blue haze proved the sign was legit. The interior was lavender too, but it was harder to tell because of the dim lighting. There was a bar in the back corner, and a large stage to the right with two stripper poles and glowing footlights. A girl with long pigtails and white thigh-high boots gyrated for the guys along the rail while they stuffed dollar bills in her g-string. Judging from the amount of green, she was a very popular attraction.

Since I wasn't actually interested in the show, I chose a table at the other end of the room, along the wall. From that vantage point, I had a view of just about everything that went on. I sat down and lit a cigarette from the pack I'd brought from the car. If it worked at Eagle Jack's, it couldn't hurt here.

A well-endowed waitress in shorts and a bikini top came over to take my drink order. "What are you doing way back here, hon? You're not shy, are you?"

I smiled at her and shook my head. "Just came in to get a quiet drink with a nice view." I'd been drinking scotch all night, so I stuck with that.

When she came back, I decided on a proactive approach. "Actually, I need to find out about one of your dancers, and I'm tryin' to figure out how to do that without getting beat up or tossed out."

"Oh, really." She gave me an arch look. "I guess that depends on what you want to know and why."

"Mostly, I just want to find out her name and talk to her for a few minutes."

"That's what lap dances are for. If you have twenty-five bucks you can talk to anyone you want to."

"You got someone here with short brown hair and a lot of tattoos?"

"I'll see what I can do," she said curtly and turned on her heel.

I fully expected her to tell both the bartender and the bouncer to keep an eye on me. I also figured if the girl I wanted was there, she'd have to like the looks of me if I was ever going to find that out. I concentrated on not looking creepy and hoped they'd just assume I was a fan of her work. I also put three twenties on the table so they knew I was serious.

They let me sit there for a good half hour before the waitress came back to bring me another drink. In the meantime, I saw a cowgirl, a biker chick and two party girls strip down to nothing but their boots and a hint of underwear. None of them looked like they enjoyed themselves.

Finally, after another twenty minutes, a different woman came over to me. This one had short brown hair, and what I could see of her shoulders and torso had a decent amount of ink. I recognized an especially creative flaming heart and barbed wire arrangement I'd seen in the photos. This was definitely Frank's stripper. She wore a black lace bra, leather shorts and fishnets that had seen better days.

"You want a lap dance, I hear?" She was playing it tough, and apparently wanted to be sure I got the message I was about as appealing as a cockroach. That was fine by me.

"Sort of. I'll pay you the money, but you don't actually have to do the dance. I just want to talk to you." I held up twenty-five dollars which she snatched from my hand like lightening.

"That's what Sandy said. What for? I already have a boyfriend, I'm not looking for any more company."

"As a matter of fact, I knew that. His name is Frank, and he's an acquaintance of mine."

She narrowed her eyes at me and said, "How in the hell do you know that? I don't know what your game is, buddy, but I'm about two minutes from calling the bouncer."

"Relax," I said. "I just wanted to meet you."

"Bullshit."

I didn't exactly blame her for going on the defensive. I'm sure she dealt with a lot of jerks, working in a club like that. "Okay, I'll level with you. Just sit down and let me buy you a drink or something. I realize this is weird, but I'm just tryin' to get a problem fixed."

"What kind of problem?" She was still on guard, but she slid onto the stool across from me and flagged the bartender. He brought her a tall soda with a long straw in it and she took a drink.

"None of it makes Frank look too good, I'll warn you right now."

"That wouldn't take much," she said with a wry smile. "That's okay, though. I know he's not a saint. I like him anyway."

I wondered what it was about the guy that made women so loyal to him, when he was clearly such a loser. Maybe he was especially good in the sack.

"All right, then. My name's Dino, and I work as a private eye, but I also have a personal interest in this."

"Roxanne," she offered. "And what exactly is 'this'?"

I contemplated which angle to approach her with first. She seemed savvy enough, so I opted to go with what she probably already knew. Or at least wouldn't be as surprised by.

"Frank owes someone a lot of money, and I said I'd try to help collect it."

She sighed and nodded. "Yeah, that makes sense. How much?"

"I don't know. I'm only recently involved in that side of things. Mostly what I said was I'd help find Frank, or where he's living."

"I thought you said you knew him."

"And that brings us to the other side of the problem, the one I was originally brought in for." I took a sip of my drink, and she raised her eyebrows. "See, the way I know him is through a friend of mine whose sister has been dating him for a while. As far as I knew, that's where he lives."

Her expression turned instantly dark, and I prepared myself for a blow up. Instead, she spoke in a voice so low and threatening, it gave me chills. "Well, if that little tramp thinks she can send you over here to get rid of me, she's got another thing coming. You tell her he's mine, and I will take out anyone who gets in my way. She better pray we don't ever cross paths."

"Whoa, take it easy. There's no need to get violent here. First of all, she doesn't know a thing about you, and second, she didn't hire me. Her brother did, and he's got the same idea you do."

"To kick the shit out of his sister?"

"Ah, no. To get rid of Frank. As in, he'd like to break them up, which is what he hired me to do. So, we're on the same page here."

She was skeptical again. "Sounds great to me, but why in the hell would he want to chase off his sister's boyfriend?"

I wanted her on my side, and I figured a little flattery wouldn't hurt. "She can't handle him. She's not like you, she's more naive, kind of a goody-goody, you know?"

"Oh, shit," she said, shaking her head. The storm had passed and she seemed mostly amused. "What in the hell does he think he's doing? You just never know with him. So, what was your plan?"

"Well, I planned to dig up enough dirt on him to convince her he's not the guy she thinks he is. She's expecting to marry him someday."

Roxanne burst out laughing and had to wipe soda off her chin. "Like he'd ever settle down. I can't imagine what he even sees in her."

I shrugged. "Well, they've been together for a couple years, and I think maybe he's changed a lot, but doesn't exactly know how to get out."

"I can give him a few pointers, all right." She sounded irritated, and her far-off expression told me Frank's ass was in the hot seat this time.

"Anyway, that's how I found out about the money, and then about you. Personally, this makes my job a hell of a lot easier."

"Breakin' them up will be my pleasure."

Her tone unsettled me. "You realize I don't need to you actually do anything, right? Just telling her about you should do the trick."

"If you're sure…" She gave me a wicked little grin.

"Oh, I'm sure. Sounds like you got your hands full with Frank and his money problems anyway."

"Yeah, and you can let me worry about that all on my own." She pointed a finger at me. "I hereby excuse you from having anything to do with that. You got what you need to help out your friend, but you can just forget about Frank or me or where we live, got it?"

"I got it," I said.

She slid off the stool and gave me another sharp look. "And don't even think about following me or anything cute like that. I know guys who would tie you in knots if I asked them to."

"You have my word as a gentleman that I will not try to follow you home, or be cute in any way."

She turned on her substantial heels and stalked back to whatever backstage area she'd come from. I smiled at her back and thought about Seth. I hoped what I learned would go a long way toward getting him to forgive me.

I took a sip of my drink and said to myself, "I'll follow Frank home, instead."

Chapter 22

Tuesday morning, my world looked a little brighter. Granted, Seth still wasn't speaking to me, but he did care whether I was alive or dead, and I would be able to report substantial progress on his case. If we ever made up. I was feeling more optimistic about that too. If nothing else, Seth was not the type to keep things bottled up for very long. He'd have to talk to me sooner or later.

I spent an hour or so catching up on neglected mail and paperwork. There were a couple of phone calls to return, and one of them landed me an easy job doing background checks on a few new hires at a big security firm. They were one of my bread-and-butter clients, and it was nice to know I had work to count on after my current cases.

When I felt like I'd done enough to be considered responsible, I cleaned up my desk and got John Holcomb's card out of the drawer. I was on the verge of wrapping that one up, and the sooner the better. I dialed the number and leaned back in my chair.

"JH Construction," answered the woman at the desk. "How may I help you?"

"I had a meeting with John Holcomb last week about a job, and I wanted to see if he had a quote ready for me yet. This is Dino Martini."

"Hold on just a minute, please."

She put me on hold and almost immediately, Holcomb himself picked up. "Hi there. Yeah, I have a quote for you. Sorry about the delay, we had some extra work to do on a site and got behind. If you have time, you can come in to the office here. I'll go over it with you and we can talk about options. How does that sound?"

"Fine with me. Are you gonna be around this afternoon? I have some time then."

"Sure, I usually am. You might want to call right before you come just to be sure, but it shouldn't be a problem."

"Thanks," I said, and hung up.

I already had enough to convince Molly to dump Frank, or at least I hoped I did. If she wanted to try to hang onto him after I showed her the pictures and told her about the stripper who would gladly break her arms, then she was beyond help. What I needed now was something I could give Tony G to seal the deal and be sure Molly was completely in the clear.

I checked my watch and realized I didn't have a lot of time to get ready for my lunch date, so I poured out the last of my coffee and headed for the shower.

At twelve-twenty, I was dressed and ready to go. I trotted downstairs feeling good about the progress I'd made and hopeful that I'd be able to keep my promise to Gigi to have it wrapped up by the end of the week.

Della and Ruth were already waiting for me outside on the patio, and both of them looked sharp. Ruth wore a simple tan sweater with dark trousers, and Della was dressed in a classy pantsuit with a flowered scarf draped around her neck and jewelry sparkling from her hands and ears.

"Dino, darlin', don't you look handsome," she said, getting up to greet me. "I'm so excited to be helping you with a case. This will be just like *Murder, She Wrote*."

"Well, I'd prefer it if no one dropped dead, thanks."

"No, of course not." She giggled and looped her arm through mine. "Shall we go solve a mystery?"

Ruth rolled her eyes. "Should we drive together or would you like us to meet you there?"

"Oh, I planned for us all to go in Matilda."

I like showing off my car, and I was gratified when Della squealed and said, "We get to ride in that beautiful car? This day just keeps gettin' better and better."

"I thought you'd like that."

We all piled into the car, with Ruth in back and Della riding shotgun. She tied her scarf over her hair and I took off. It was a gorgeous day for a drive. We took our time, watching the tourists and talking about our favorite spots.

"I feel just like a movie star," Della exclaimed. Gauze tails whipped around her face and the sun gleamed off her giant sunglasses. She looked like a movie star.

Mickey's Bar & Grill was off the main road a couple blocks, away from the beach. The tourist traffic stayed pretty steady, though. I wound my way into the parking lot and found a good spot. A minor miracle on a day like that.

The bar was something less than impressive, considering it was pretty run down. Paint peeled off the sign, and the roofing curled up around the edges. The building was long and squat, colored pale aqua. People came and went, though, and it seemed to be doing business like everyone else on the block. Honestly, it can't be that hard in a beach town where there are tons of tourists looking for a meal at any given time of the day.

Della came around the end of the car and considered it, lowering her sunglasses to get a clear view. "Well, sugar, you did say it wasn't a fancy place. I guess you didn't lie."

"If you don't want to stay, I'd understand," I told her.

"Oh, nonsense. It'll be an adventure."

Ruth said, "I've eaten in worse places than this. You never can really tell from the outside."

"All right, then. Shall we, ladies?"

We crossed the parking lot and I held the door for them. I was about to follow them inside when something caught my eye. Sticking out from around the corner of the restaurant was the back end of a car that looked a hell of a lot like the one that nearly ran me down leaving Salvatore's the night before.

I caught Ruth by the elbow. "Would you go ahead and get us a table? I'll be right in."

"Is anything wrong?"

"I just want to check something out. It's fine."

She nodded and went in. I walked down to the corner and took a look at the whole car. It still looked like the one from Gigi's, although it was impossible to be sure. Dark sedans are a dime a dozen anywhere you go, and there was nothing especially memorable about this one. What was more interesting was finding it sitting there, when I was working on the same case. I jotted down the license plate number and peered into the windows. There wasn't anything inside that gave me any information. I filed it away for future consideration and went inside.

The inside was as rundown as the outside, but it seemed to work better. There was a bar, a hostess stand and about a dozen tables. It looked like there might be a few more tables around the corner at the end of the bar as well. There were also a couple of video games and a claw machine crammed with cheap stuffed animals.

Della called "Yoo hoo!" and waved to me from a table toward the back. I joined them just as the waitress delivered menus and glasses of water. They had left me a seat with a good view of what was going on, and I sat down.

Ruth took a sip of her water and looked around. "See, now? This isn't bad at all."

"I won't be making my mind up about that until I try the food," Della said. She scanned her menu critically.

When the waitress came back, we all placed our orders. A hamburger for me, and club sandwiches for Della and Ruth. I also asked for a cup of coffee, since the ladies were having iced tea.

After she left, Della leaned toward me and said, "Now what do we do?"

"Just act natural. Talk about whatever it is you usually talk about at lunch. If you happen to notice anything really strange you could mention it, but don't worry too much about that. I'll do most of the surveillance."

Della was just a little too excited to be playing private eye, and I'd have to be careful not to let her blow my cover. Assuming there was anything to worry about in the first place. For all I knew, I was barking up the wrong tree. Maybe no one in the place gave a rat's ass who I was. Until I knew for sure, I got her chatting away on subjects dear to her heart to keep her occupied. That didn't take much. Once she started telling stories of her days in South Carolina, she could go on for hours.

Ruth was a pretty good sport and asked a lot of questions she surely must have heard the answers to a hundred times. I was grateful, though, because it allowed me to watch the staff working. I figured if there was any connection to Salvatore's it was going to be with one of them, rather than a customer. I kept a watch on the crowd too, but only as a formality.

The waitress brought our food, along with a pitcher of iced tea, and we all started eating. The food was average at best, but not really what I would call bad. I asked the ladies how their meal was.

"Well, the lettuce is nothing to write home about," Ruth said with a frown. She pulled it out of her sandwich and dropped it at the edge of her plate. "Otherwise, I suppose it's all right."

Della examined hers. "This bread is soggy. I can get better club sandwiches out of the deli at Winn Dixie. And that's not saying much."

As the ladies bitched about their sandwiches, I became aware of some kind of showdown going on at the bar. Seemed like a waitress had done something against the liking of the guy that apparently ran the place. He stood about six feet tall and used all of it to intimidate. He'd come from somewhere in the back where the offices likely were, and was giving her a ton of grief. There was the kind of body language going on that wasn't all that hard to read. Papers clutched in hands and pointing fingers, accompanied by irate gestures and a lot of looming. I felt bad for the girl.

She wasn't our waitress, but I'd been watching her work and she seemed to be a favorite among the crowd. Probably regulars by the familiar way she had with them.

There was something about the guy that pinged my radar, and I felt the hairs prickle at the back of my neck. On impulse I pulled out my cellphone and said to Ruth, "Why don't you two squeeze closer and let me take your picture, as a memento of the occasion."

Ruth leveled her gaze on me. "You don't really need a memento of this."

"No, I don't. Now get over there and smile."

The smirk she gave me was more shrewd than I think I've ever seen on her, which is saying something. I was going to have to have a few drinks with her sometime.

Della perked right up and slid her chair next to Ruth, fussing with the ends of her hair and acting the perfect debutante. She gave herself away when she whispered, "Oh, this is it, isn't it? You're doing something sneaky, aren't you?"

"I am." I gave her a big grin and focused my phone's camera over Ruth's shoulder to frame Intimidating Guy. I snapped off a couple shots while the ladies gamely hammed it up for the camera, and on the last snap, I got a good view of the guy square on.

Since I was on a roll, and I had a good feeling about the place, I decided to take a few pictures for Seth's reference as well. If this was the source of Gigi's trouble, he might very likely recognize some of these people.

"Okay," I said. "Why don't you two pose by the shark jaw there? That'll be great."

They both laughed, but stood up and arranged themselves by the post it hung from. While I pretended to take pictures of them, I was able to get shots of all three waitresses working the room and one busboy. Since they were being such good sports, I actually took one of Ruth and Della. In spite of what Ruth said, it would be fun to have if this little charade paid off.

We sat down and the waitress came by to see how we were doing. "Would you like me to take a picture of all three of you?"

"Sure," I said, and handed her my phone. Della and Ruth crowded up on either side of me and we all grinned for the camera.

"Are you here on vacation?" she asked as she lined up and took the picture.

"Oh, we're not," I said, pointing between Ruth and me. "But Auntie Della is down here visiting for a week from South Carolina."

"Oh, how nice. And are you enjoying your stay?"

Ruth smirked and Della preened like a diva. "Oh my, yes. I'm just having the most marvelous time. The beaches are quite scenic, and I certainly have gotten an eyeful."

"Do you like picking up seashells?"

"Oh, no, sugar...college boys." She flashed the waitress a hundred watt smile.

"Okay, then." The waitress giggled. "Enjoy your meal, and let me know if you need anything else."

After she left, Della turned to me and said, "How did I do?"

"You were perfect," I told her, which earned me the same smile.

We settled down to eat our food, and they talked about a garden party they were going to later in the week. I half listened, but mostly spent the time watching the staff.

Intimidating Guy drifted in and out, ragging on various servers and generally being an ass. He had a couple of cronies down at the end of the bar that he'd trade wisecracks with once in a while before disappearing into the back to find more infractions to nail employees for. Meanwhile, the pals filled in by making the bartender's life significantly more difficult and harassing waitresses as they passed by. I took an instant dislike to all three of them.

I'd only eaten half my burger and didn't feel like having any more. A devious thought occurred to me, but I dismissed it out of hand. The longer I sat there, however, the more it appealed to me. I suppose it had a lot to do with my rotten week, and the need to do something for Gigi. In the end, I couldn't resist. If this was the guy, he deserved it.

"Are you ladies close to being finished?" I asked quietly, running a finger along the rim of my water glass.

"I think so," Ruth said. "Dino, is there something wrong?"

"No. Everything's fine. I'm just gonna shake them up a little bit to see what happens, and when I'm done we probably won't want to hang around here anymore."

"What are you planning to do?"

"Oh, you'll see."

Della's eyes sparkled and she tucked her sunglasses and scarf into her bag, which she set within easy reach.

I picked up my fork and threw it down on my plate with an obnoxious clatter. "No, I will not settle down, damn it," I said, raising my voice as loud as possible without actually yelling. "If they think I'm gonna pay good money for this kind of crap, they're nuts. If I wanted to eat overcooked meat and soggy bread I could have stayed at home and eaten my wife's cooking. When I come out to a restaurant, I expect to get a decent meal. Even in a cut-rate pit like this!"

Every head in the place turned toward us. Ruth buried her face in her hand and Della pushed her food around on her plate, apparently trying not to burst out laughing.

The waitress came hustling over. "Excuse me, is there some kind of problem?"

"Yeah, I'll say there's a problem. Let me talk to your manager, I'd like to give him a piece of my mind."

She paled and I felt kind of bad. "If there's something I can do—"

"You've done just fine," I said. "It's your manager I want to talk to. Get him out here right now or I'll go back there and find him. If he thinks he can run the place like a school cafeteria, he's got another think coming."

By then, I actually was hollering, because the point was to stage a scene, and if I made enough racket to get the manager out on his own, I might save the waitress some grief.

People all around us were whispering now, and the busboy and two waitresses leaned on the bar watching the show.

"All you hotshots think you can just screw the tourists and it won't make any difference because they'll be gone in a week anyway. But some of us live here, and we are not going away!"

Right on cue, Intimidating Guy blew through the kitchen doors and looked both ways before fixing on me. He came storming over. "What the hell is going on?"

Up close, the guy looked sleazy and mean, and I felt bad for the whole staff. Mostly for having to put up with him in general, but also for the mood I was going to leave him in.

"I'll tell you what's going on," I said, standing up to meet him. I threw my napkin on the floor. "This meal is pig slop. What the hell kind of place do you think you're running? You think people are just gonna shut up and take it because they don't want to mess up their vacations? Well, I'll tell ya, buddy, you can take this lousy excuse for a hamburger and shove it right up your a—"

"Sugar!" Della exclaimed, fanning herself. "There are ladies present."

"Sorry." I nodded at her, then turned back to the manager. "She's too polite to say it, but I can tell you her sandwich wasn't fit for rats to eat, either."

"Yeah, all right, pal," he said. "I don't know who you think you are, but you can just take your attitude and get the hell out of here. We don't need guys like you causing a scene."

"Maybe if more people told you what they really thought, you could find a way to make this place tolerable. I wouldn't bring my dog back here!"

"You got two minutes to pay your bill and get out before I call the cops."

"You can eat my bill, jackass. It would taste better than the food."

He turned beet red and spun on his heels, stalking back in the direction of the bar.

"Okay, girls," I said, "this is the part where we don't wanna hang around anymore."

Ruth and Della got up and hurried for the door. I threw forty bucks on the table, because on the off chance I was wrong, I didn't want to stiff them. I also stuffed a twenty into the waitress's hand as I went past her, and said, "That's for you. You did a great job, thanks."

On my way out the door, I yelled, "And don't think we're ever coming back here again!"

The ladies were waiting for me by Matilda when I came around the side of the building. I gave them a smug grin as I walked up.

Ruth shook her head. "Honestly, Dino. Did that really accomplish anything?"

"It made me feel better," I said with a shrug.

"That was just terribly excitin'," Della said gleefully. She slipped on her sunglasses. "It's been so long since someone threatened to call the police on me."

Ruth rolled her eyes at the both of us and climbed into the backseat. "Dino, would you mind dropping me off at the library on our way back?"

Chapter 23

After we dropped Ruth off at the library, Della and I turned toward home. I wanted to get back and run the plates on that car from the restaurant, and I needed to call Gigi and arrange a time to meet with her so I could fill her in on our progress.

Della chattered happily about her younger days and all the beautiful cars her husband liked to drive. "He always insisted on great big things with all the luxury features. It was like sailing on a cloud. He wouldn't have been caught dead in a convertible. Too noisy."

"Yeah, well, he also had a pretty wife he needed to keep looking nice. Couldn't have the wind blowin' your hair all around, could he?"

"Nonsense," she said with a wave of her hand. "That's why God invented scarves."

"That's good, because you do dress up a convertible. Matilda's gonna get jealous."

She laughed out loud and said, "Oh, honey, you say the cutest things." Then she turned in the seat to face me. "Speaking of cute things...I haven't seen that darling boyfriend of yours around lately. I am terribly sorry about what happened. I hope I didn't offend him."

"Oh, no. I took care of that all by myself."

"Do I sense a little trouble in paradise?" Her tone was sympathetic, but her eyes were bright, and it was clear she was in her element. "Come on, honey, you can tell Auntie Della all about it."

I kept my focus on the road and waffled. "I don't know. I think I'd feel kinda' funny talking to you about this."

"Dino, *honey*, I am an expert when it comes to all things that are matters of the heart. You couldn't do better than to confide in me."

"This is...different. I mean, we're not talking about your usual kind of romance here."

She giggled and lowered her sunglasses to look me in the eye. "Sugar, they had gay people back in my day too, you know. You're not the first one I've ever met."

I felt my cheeks flush. "Yeah, yeah, I get it. You probably know more about it than I do. This is not exactly what I'm used to." She raised an eyebrow at that, and I felt the need to explain. "I like women too, and that's who I've always dated. When I did. Seth is the first guy I've ever gone out with."

"That *is* a little late to the party, isn't it?" she said, musing. "It doesn't really matter that much in the end, though. Romance is romance and deep down it's all pretty much the same."

"Except for the part where most of society can't stand you and people get hurt for doin' what I'm doing."

"First of all, most of society doesn't think about it at all because they're much too concerned with their own tiny little lives, and second, you can't let other people run your life for you. You certainly don't seem like that type."

"You sound like Seth," I said, glancing at her.

She cocked her head. "Is that what the trouble is? You all don't exactly see eye to eye on this subject?"

"You could say that."

"Is this because of what happened the other day?"

"It's because of how I reacted," I told her. "Plus, I, ah…I kind of dropped him on the floor."

"Oh!" She gasped and brought a hand to her mouth. I couldn't tell, but it looked like she might have been trying to hide a smile. "Oh, goodness, I can see how that might complicate matters."

"I helped him up," I protested.

"Yes, well…I would hope so. I can't imagine that went over very well."

"He's still not speaking to me."

She pouted sympathetically and patted my shoulder. "I'm sure he'll forgive you, honey. You would be a hard man to resist for very long."

"I'm not sure I can be what he wants me to be, Della." My gaze was fixed squarely on the road, but even though I was uncomfortable as hell, it did feel good to be talking to someone about it. "He wants me to be all 'out and proud' and 'screw the world' like he is. I'm not sure if I can do that."

She turned serious and considered me for a moment, then tapped a finger on my shoulder. "You know, sugar…sometimes all that matters is that you *could*, more than that you *do*."

I furrowed my brow and looked over at her.

"Honey, if he knows you very well at all, I'm sure he understands who you are. But he wants to know that you care enough not to be ashamed, or to hide all the time." She leveled her gaze on me. "Even to my practiced ear you sound more like someone who's trying to figure out where to hide the body, than a man who's in love."

"That's a little extreme, don't you think?" My face was hot, and I was pretty sure I didn't want to be having the conversation anymore. "I'm not ashamed. What I am is very aware of some of life's harsh realities."

"Well, considering what you do for a living, you ought to be perfectly prepared to deal with them," she said with a challenging smirk.

I took a deep breath and chewed my lip.

She went on. "I think if you just meet him halfway, show him that you could be what he wants, at least part of the time, he might forgive the rest."

"Would you?"

"Of course I would, sugar," she said with a laugh. "You don't think my dear husband was some kind of saint, do you? Hell, I perfected the art of forgiving the rest."

I smiled. "Maybe you can teach Seth a little of that."

She settled back in her seat with a proud air. "Bring him over for dinner some time, and I'll teach you both a thing or two."

"I might just take you up on that, Della. I hope you can cook a big meal."

* * * *

When we got home, Della thanked me for lunch, and I thanked her for the heart-to-heart, and we went our separate ways. I mulled over what she'd told me and filed it away for future consideration. In the meantime, I had some work to do.

Upstairs at my desk, I switched on my laptop and took out my notes from earlier. The first thing I wanted to do was run the plates on the car to see if there was any connection to Salvatore's or to Gigi. It was a long shot, but it was worth looking into. If it didn't pan out, we still had Lester, and I thought it was a pretty good bet we could get something out of him if we leaned on him hard enough. Of course, "we" meant I needed to get back in Seth's good graces, which was next on the agenda.

I entered the license plate number and started the search. In less than a minute, I knew that the car was the property of one Thomas Wallace. The name didn't mean anything to me, but I set to work, running a thorough background check on the guy. In a little over an hour, I knew his name, rank, and serial number, along with a lot of other juicy details. I also learned he was known as Tommy to the bulk of the English speaking world.

The most notable bit of information I found was that he not only ran Mickey's, he owned it. Suddenly, the car outside the restaurant was looking a whole lot less like a long shot, and more like a sure thing. Plus, there was a little thrill running up my spine I usually got when I was onto something good.

Turned out Tommy Wallace was a pretty slimy guy with a history of stirring up city politics, a pattern of run-ins with his business neighbors, and a reputation for wheeling and dealing. He was listed as either the principal or a partner in a long list of real estate dealings, including a lot of what looked like house flipping. Not that there's anything wrong with flipping houses. I knew a guy who made a great living doing that. But it showed that Wallace was well versed in the idea of turning devalued property into something worthwhile. It also suggested that he was in a position to make money at both ends if he started dealing in real estate on Vina del Mar. He had a lot of reasons to want this hotel deal.

He was definitely a prime candidate for asshole of the year in Gigi's life. All I had to do was find some proof. Once we'd built a strong case against him, we could decide on the next step. There were a lot of ways the situation could be handled once we had the advantage, not the least of which as informing the police.

I printed off all the information on Wallace and added it to the folder for Gigi's case. Then I took out my cellphone and pulled the memory card from it to download the photos I'd taken over lunch. I printed off three that managed to show the bulk of the wait staff in various groupings, and a good, clear headshot of Wallace himself. Those went in the folder as well.

The past twenty-four hours had been extremely productive and it seemed like I was on a roll, so I thought it might be a good time to give Seth a call and start trying to patch things up. I reassembled my cellphone and dialed Seth's number.

I was feeling so confident, it took me by surprise when he didn't answer. In all honesty, it wasn't that strange, really. He often let it go to voicemail if he was elbow deep in someone's transmission, or covered in grease and engine oil. But I was so sure things were going my way, I didn't exactly know what to do. Leaving a message felt pathetic, so I just hung up. That part of my plan would have to wait. Maybe that was for the best. It gave me more time to ponder the things Della said.

Next on the agenda was Gigi. I had a lot to fill her in on, and most of it was good news. I figured she'd be thrilled to hear we were close to wrapping up her problem. Turns out, I figured wrong.

"I'm sorry, Dino, there's just no way I can get out of this meeting. It's very important."

"Come on," I said, "I thought you'd want to meet with me as soon as possible. You were the one pushing me to get this done. I've got some solid info here."

"Believe me, I would much rather talk to you than listen to a bunch of association blowhards nitpick a lot of ridiculous bylaws, but I have to be there."

"I bet if you were dying you could get out of it."

She clucked her tongue. "If I was dying, I wouldn't care. What's with the pouting?"

"Now that I'm finally getting somewhere, I'm itching to finish. I want to keep things moving."

"I'm sure at this point, one more day isn't going to make a difference one way or the other. Why don't you come over tomorrow and we can talk about it while we have lunch?"

"Yeah, all right. I'll talk to you then."

"Thanks, Dino."

"Don't mention it."

I set the phone on my desk and slumped in the chair. That was two for two and I was getting nowhere. This is one part of the job that always frustrates me. When I finally get a good lead, I want to follow it right to the end, and a lot of the time that's not possible. Usually, you wind up having to do it in bits and pieces, and in the end the solution is just sitting there waiting for you.

So fine. That left JH Construction to deal with, and although it was the least attractive of my options, it seemed to be the only one I stood a chance of getting in on.

Chapter 24

I was not very thrilled with the plan to go see John Holcomb, so I drove the route that would take me right past Ed's Garage. I'll admit, I would have preferred the safety of a phone call first, to get a feel for where I stood. If he still hated me, I'd rather not have to see that face-to-face. On the other hand, he couldn't hang up on me if I just waltzed in there, and we stood a better chance of clearing things up.

The downward spiral of my day continued when I pulled into the parking lot at Ed's to find the place closed and the tow truck gone. That might explain why he wasn't answering his phone. If he was out helping Ed on a junk run, he turned it off or just left it in his pocket. Ed had a particular hatred of cellphones and would launch into his usual rant whenever he saw Seth using his. Interestingly, that never seemed to stop him from calling Seth on it when he needed something done.

I leaned back in my seat and let my head fall against the headrest. The sun was warm, and there was a nice breeze. It was possible he wouldn't be too long, and I could just wait. But then he'd either be busy with Ed or have a car to unload. If he *was* with Ed, he probably wouldn't be in a very good mood. Ed was a decent guy, and he and Seth liked each other well enough, but they could get on each other's nerves in a hell of a hurry.

The wind was knocked out of my sails any way you looked at it. I actually considered lying down on the seat and taking a nap. Things usually seemed better after a good night's sleep; maybe a catnap would improve my odds. However, getting caught that way would be significantly more pathetic than leaving a message, so I started the car and pulled back onto the causeway.

I got to JH around four, and the place was pretty quiet. Again, I parked across the street and walked over, mostly out of habit. When I went in, the lady at the desk greeted me and took me back to Holcomb's office. It was what you'd expect, dumpy and brown paneled like the rest of the building, cramped, and featuring a desk piled with a mess of papers, binders and envelopes. I promised myself when I finally did get an office, I'd treat it with more respect.

"Hi there, Dino." Holcomb stood up and we shook hands. "Good to see you again. Have a seat."

I looked around for an unoccupied chair.

"You can just shove those catalogs on the floor," he told me, pointing to a stack directly across from his desk.

I lifted them down, rather than shoving, and sat. "So, what have you got for me?"

He slapped a manila folder on top of the mess and flipped it open, turning it for me to read. There were a handful of pre-printed quote forms, all filled out with information on my specific job. At least his handwriting was neat. The top page was a diagram of the layout with markings for what already existed and ones for the proposed construction.

Holcomb used his pen to lead me through it, explaining what would be done in each section. "Now, the basic structure is pretty much the same regardless of what you do, but then the finishing work gives you some options as far as price goes."

I nodded and he turned the page. The next form had a list of materials with a section at the bottom for options.

He went on. "Then you'll have some choices when it comes to trim, molding, doors and the like."

This was all coming out in practiced speech form, and I imagined he'd recited the spiel hundreds of times. The final page was the nail in the coffin, the pricing.

"This column down the left, here, is what the cost would be for the bare bones, cheap everything, using the wallboard," he explained. "The column on the right is top of the line."

Both of them were pretty staggering if you asked me.

"All right," I said. "Well, I'm gonna have to give this some thought. I assume I can let you know in a few days?" I picked up the folder and looked at the price sheet more closely.

"Oh, yeah. There's no hurry. That quote is good for six months, so you got plenty of time to decide."

"That's great. Thanks very much." I stood up and we shook hands again.

I'd been wracking my brain to think of any way I could use the meeting to gain something on Frank, but came up empty. As far as I could tell, the construction office was a complete blank, and unless I wanted them to actually do the job, I wouldn't have to come back. I was no longer remotely interested in having Frank come anywhere near my office, so the likelihood of hiring them at those prices was slim to none.

Outside, I crossed over to Matilda and sat down in the driver's seat. My options were pretty limited. Gigi didn't want to talk to me, Seth wouldn't talk to me. Since I was already in St. Pete, I thought maybe I'd take a run to Tampa and visit Molly's place. She would probably talk to me.

I was about to start the car when I noticed Frank's truck cruise out from behind the construction offices. He must have been working in one of the other buildings, and I was thankful I'd parked across the street. If I was lucky, he had no idea I was around.

I watched him pull out into traffic and head east. If I was really lucky, he was on his way to his stripper girlfriend's house. Molly could wait. If this paid off, I'd have a lot more to tell her, and I'd have something to insure Tony G would keep his word about leaving her alone.

Traffic was light, so I had no trouble catching up to him. I had to hang back more than I'd like, but Matilda isn't exactly the world's most subtle surveillance car. He didn't appear to be in too big a hurry, and we putzed our way through town at a sedate pace. Maybe he was trying to decide which of his girlfriends to go home to.

It wasn't a straight trip either. We stopped at a BP for gas and a bag of chips, at the video store where I strongly suspected he visited the porn section, and at the liquor store for a case of cheap beer. It wasn't until he passed Riverside that I was sure we weren't headed for Molly's. Finally, things were going my way again.

We ended up in one of those neighborhoods that can't really be called seedy, but sure as hell wouldn't qualify for nice. It was close to downtown and almost entirely apartment buildings. There were a few scrubby looking palms here and there, and a couple of the buildings had some landscaping in front of them, but other than that, it was mostly glass and concrete.

Frank turned in at one of the parking lots and took a spot at the far side. I stayed on the street and watched. He loaded up his porn, his chips and his beer and went inside, presumably for the kind of good time only a guy like Frank could show a girl.

It's entirely possible I was way off base and Frank was just going to hang out with a buddy, but I didn't think so. I don't place a lot of faith in coincidence and even my luck's not so bad that with not one, but two women to go home to, he'd be headed somewhere else the day I tailed him. Besides, he had a key for the front entry.

I waited ten minutes and got out of the car. After a minivan passed, I trotted across the street and went up to the entryway to study the call panel. I didn't know her last name, so I took out my notebook and jotted down all the ones with R as the first initial. I'd try cross-referencing the names to see which one was Roxanne. If that was even necessary. I had an address to give Tony G, and I assumed that would make him happy enough. All his goons really had to do was stake out the parking lot.

Back at the car, I used my phone to take a quick picture of the building and enough of the street to identify it. I wanted to be sure they had the right place so there'd be no reason at all to go back to Molly's.

With that last nail in the coffin, I turned Matilda around and headed for Molly's house myself. If I broke the news to her alone, then Seth wouldn't be as likely to catch the fallout. She didn't mind him horning in when she felt threatened, but I imagined she'd be pretty pissed if she knew the real reason he'd been so willing to get me involved.

It was after six by the time I turned onto her street, but when I came to a stop outside her house, it was clear no one was home. Just to be sure, I went and knocked on the door, but as I thought, there was no response. I can't say I was exactly surprised after the day I'd had.

Molly's situation was a lot less pressing since I'd called Tony G off, so I didn't mind that filling her in would have to wait.

* * * *

Back on the beach side, I cruised past Ed's again, but it was still deserted. That didn't surprise me, either, but it bothered me a whole lot more. I was beyond ready to patch things up with Seth, and I was frustrated at being unable to find him. I'm a detective, for Christ's sake, I should be able to find my own boyfriend. Or whatever we were calling it.

At home, I shut the car off and sat there, planning my next move. Seth's mystery whereabouts were still bothering me and I tried to call him again, but like before, got no answer. I swore and hung up, tapping the phone on the steering wheel. On impulse, I flipped it open and dialed Molly instead. I had to schedule a meeting with her, didn't I?

"Oh, hi, Dino," she said brightly. "What's up?"

"I was trying to catch up with you so I could tell you what I found out."

"About the creepy guy?" There was talking and laughing in the background, and something that sounded like kitchen noises, maybe.

"Yeah. You don't have to worry about him anymore," I told her. "Sounds like you're kind of busy, so we can talk about the rest later."

"Mom's sister just retired, and she's got the whole family over for dinner and a big party. It's been going on all afternoon, so you can guess what it's like around here now."

"I didn't think you sounded entirely sober," I said with a smile.

"I'm gonna hate myself in the morning, but Seth is mixing the wildest martinis and they are so good. He can even make a chocolate one."

There are few things cuter than a straight-laced woman with a buzz on, and I felt good about rousting Frank out of her life. She deserved someone better, and I only wished I didn't have to give her the bad news to do it.

"Tell him I said hi, and have fun. I'll touch base with you later."

"Okie," she said cheerfully, and hung up.

Somehow, knowing where Seth had been all afternoon improved my mood considerably. It didn't completely erase the sting of having my phone calls ignored, but at least I could understand why. I could have been standing right in front of him, but with his whole family there, I still wouldn't have gotten a word in edgewise. The Donnellys are a lot like my family, and I'm pretty sure it's one of the reasons we get along so well. When we're getting along, that is.

I went upstairs to my apartment, downloaded the photo of Roxanne's place and printed it out. Since everyone else was busy, I decided to go officially wrap up that part of Molly's case. Then when I met with her, I'd have everything taken care of.

While the printer clattered away, I dug out Tony G's card and dialed the number, wondering what exactly his protocol was for this kind of thing. One of the goons answered the phone. The same one who called me when we set up the first meeting.

"Yeah, listen," I said, "if someone wants to get in to see Tony G, how does he go about arranging that?"

"Who's asking?"

"Dino Martini. I was over there last night."

"When do you want to see him?"

"I don't know. The sooner the better, I guess. I got somethin' for him, but it's not exactly urgent." Hell if I knew what Tony G considered urgent, but I didn't want to piss him off by exaggerating what I had.

"Got what?"

"Information," I said. "On someone he's looking for."

"Hang on."

Chatty Cathy left me hanging on the line for a while, and when he finally came back he said, "Tony G says you should come at seven-thirty, and you should bring a bottle of wine."

"Wine? What, are we dating now?"

"You want to see him or not?"

"Yeah, sure." I rolled my eyes. "What kind of wine?"

"White."

"Care to be more specific than that?"

"No."

The line went dead, and I stared at the phone. No one could ever say my life was dull.

I had just enough time to get ready and stop at a liquor store so I could take a flying guess at what kind of wine a guy like Tony G would like. Assuming he intended to drink it. For one wild second I thought maybe he planned to bludgeon me to death with it. I finally settled on an Australian chardonnay I like, so if he did kill me, it would be with something familiar.

It was just after seven-thirty when I pulled up in front of the Villa. This time, the big gate opened as I reached the driveway, and I took that as an invitation to drive in to park. Johnny trotted down the stairs and met me as I was climbing out of the car. He frisked me with his quick style and we went inside.

As soon as he opened the front door, I was met with cooking smells so delicious my stomach started to growl. Instead of leaving me in the foyer, we went straight through to the kitchen. What I saw there damn near made me drop the wine.

At one end of the counter was a cutting board and knife, covered in the remains of chives or green onions. On the stove, two different pots steamed away, giving off the smell that was making me so hungry. At the other end of the counter was a mess of flour and scraps of dough leftover from whatever was now piled on a plate next to the larger of the two pots. In the middle was Tony G, with his sleeves rolled up and a chef's apron tied around his sizable middle. He was swirling something around in the small pot with a whisk.

I just stood there and stared at him open mouthed.

"What's the matter?" he asked. He clearly enjoyed my reaction, and I was willing to bet he liked to spring this gag on people whenever he got the chance. "You never seen a guy who could cook before?"

I shrugged and attempted to recover myself. "Sure. I've just never seen a loan shark that can cook."

He laughed a deep belly laugh and beckoned me into the kitchen. "Come, sit. You can tell me what you got, and then we can eat." He pointed to a row of stools and told Johnny to chill the wine I'd brought.

I took a seat and Tony G poured me some of the scotch he was drinking. "I gotta' say, I wasn't expecting to see you again so soon."

I shrugged. "I had some time on my hands and caught a couple of lucky breaks. Thought I'd come around and finish the job." I took a sip of scotch and pulled the printed photo out of my jacket pocket, sliding it over to Tony G.

He unfolded it and took a look. "And this is?"

"That's the apartment building where Frank's stripper lives. I wrote the address on there. The girl's name is Roxanne, and her last name is one of the four listed on there. I could find out for you, but I don't think you'll need it."

"This is good," he said, nodding. He handed the paper over to Johnny. "As long as we can catch Frank there, it's all right."

"I followed him there tonight. He looked pretty comfortable, and he had a key. I can also tell you he parked in the back of the lot even though there were lots of spaces closer to the door, so I'm guessing that's a habit."

"You're very thorough, I like that." He turned around and gave the pot a stir. "I hope you brought your appetite."

"Even if I hadn't, the smell in here would've taken care of that. What's cookin'?"

He flashed me a proud smile as he turned down the heat under his sauce pan. "Mushroom ravioli with brown butter sauce. It's one of my better dishes."

"This isn't gonna be my last meal, is it?" I was joking, but it had crossed my mind that the downside of getting in good with a notorious loan shark was what might happen if you ever pissed him off.

"Huh, huh. That's a good one. You're a funny man." He paused in his cooking to take a drink of scotch. "This is just good timing. You called, and I was already cooking, and I remembered I liked you, so you got invited."

"Well, I'm honored then." I raised my glass to him and we toasted.

"I like to cook for people," he said as he went to spoon ravioli into the boiling water. "I woulda been a chef, but I didn't like the hours and I make more money my way."

"Hard to argue with that. I couldn't work on someone else's clock."

"Tell me about it. Self-made man is the only way to go."

Johnny was sent in to set the table, and I was given the job of carrying salad and olives into the small dining room, which was just as ornate as the rest of his house, right down to the crystal chandelier. The food tasted better than it smelled, and after the meal there was espresso, then cognac and cigars on the deck out back. I left with assurances that Molly was safe from them forever, and an interesting new ally in my arsenal of contacts and resources.

It occurred to me that Seth would really like the guy, and I hoped he'd get to meet him sometime. Assuming we ever got back together, which wasn't going to happen unless I could get him speaking to me again. I still had the "Frank's Girlfriend" card to play, and I figured that would go a long way. There was, of course, my own natural charm which was often effective on Seth as long as I wasn't making an ass of myself. God, I missed him.

I sighed and made the drive slowly. There wasn't any point in trying to call him, or even in going past the garage again, because it was almost a certainty he'd be spending the night at his folks' house. If Molly was half in the bag by six o'clock, there was no way in hell Seth would be making it anywhere on his own.

Chapter 25

The drive to Salvatore's was cheerier than any drive I'd taken the day before. I was meeting Gigi for a late lunch and planned to give her the good news that I'd more or less solved her case, and we could start taking action to put a stop to her problems.

Afterward, I intended to go to the garage and use whatever means necessary to convince Seth to give me another chance, starting with doughnuts and a case of beer, and ending with something involving jumper cables. I hadn't fully worked that one out yet, but was pretty confident I wouldn't have to go beyond the offer of a blow job. If everything went my way, he and I could go to Molly's and get Frank out of her hair once and for all.

I pulled into the parking lot of Salvatore's feeling optimistic and better than I had all week. The weather was perfect, with amber sunlight that cut sideways across the neighborhood, leaving long shadows. A white ibis picked its way along the edge of the grass. Inside, the crowd was good for late afternoon and there weren't many empty tables. The mood was relaxed, happy.

Gigi and Seth were both in the dining room when I walked in. She was chatting up the patrons and Seth was clearing off a table, white apron tied around his waist. I looked forward to telling him he wouldn't have to do that anymore. Another point in my favor.

Gigi saw me first and came over to give me a hug and a kiss on the cheek. "Dino, I'm so glad to see you. I have a table reserved for us, come and sit down. I'm anxious to hear what you've found out."

Out of the corner of my eye, I caught Seth watching us, and he didn't look any too happy. "I'll be right behind you," I told Gigi. "Go ahead and order me a beer, will you?"

"Sure," she said, following my line of vision. She nodded and headed for a table near the back of the room.

I followed at a slower pace, and when I got to the table he was wiping down, I spoke quietly. "Hey."

"Don't 'hey' me," he muttered, head resolutely down. "I saw you over there with the kissy face."

"You're not starting that shit again," I said. Snarky or not, it felt good to see him again after so long. "If you'd answer your phone once in a while, you'd know I spent most of yesterday trying to track you down. I hope you slept at your mother's, by the way, what with all the martinis you drank."

He glanced up at me through the fringe of his eyelashes, and I caught a glint in his eye that usually meant good things for me. "I did," he said. He gave a subtle nod toward the back. "Go do your job."

I set my briefcase on the table and leaned in. "I'm gonna do this lunch, and you're gonna finish your shift, then I'm coming over to your place. You get me tonight whether you want me or not."

The smirk I got in return told me if things weren't exactly forgiven, they were certainly going to work out. Everything was going according to plan, and I couldn't have been happier.

It must have showed, because when I joined Gigi at the table she smiled at me and said, "Whatever you have, it must be pretty good."

"I have a lot of good things, Gigi. Yesterday was a shitty day, but today is turning out just fine."

"Okay, then." She looked bemused and that was fine with me.

The waitress brought our drinks, and we ordered. Gigi recommended the eggplant parmesan because Angelo was trying out a new recipe, so I asked for that. She went with a simple Caesar salad.

Once we were left to our drinks, I got Gigi's file out of my briefcase and held up the photo I'd taken of Tommy Wallace. "Is this your irate customer?"

Her eyes grew wide and her mouth dropped open slightly. "How on earth… Yes, that's him. Dino, how did you know that?"

I shrugged. "It's what I do."

She gave me flat stare and said, "Dino."

"All right, all right. I ran into the guy yesterday while I was tracking down one of the other leads. His name's Tommy Wallace. He owns a place called Mickey's Bar and Grill up in Treasure Island, and from the looks of things, he could easily be in the market for a nicer establishment if you know what I mean."

"You think he's behind the whole thing?"

"I'm almost certain of it, but I don't have any proof other than a couple of weak connections."

"What are those?"

"This is one," I said, pointing to the photograph. "Now that you've confirmed he's been in here stirrin' up trouble. I returned the favor, by the way, no extra charge."

She arched an eyebrow. "You did what?"

"Stood in the middle of his restaurant during lunch hour and said a lot of really loud things about how his food wasn't fit for rats to eat." She snickered into the palm of her hand. "I'm not welcome there anymore, incidentally."

"I would love to have seen that," she said.

Seth tromped past us with a bin of dishes he wasn't treating any too kindly, and dumped them off at a server station around the corner. He came back with an empty tub and this time he eyed me, and then Gigi, and then me again. I gave him a quizzical look, and he scowled at me. I couldn't tell if he was serious, or giving me shit.

I let it go and turned my attention back to Gigi, who asked, "What are the other connections? How did you even know about this guy?"

The waitress brought our food, and we took a minute to arrange things and give it a try. I swallowed a second bite of eggplant and nodded. "This is very good. I don't know how it compared to the other version, but this one I like."

"Good. Make sure you let Angelo know. Now tell me how you knew about Tommy Wallace."

"Okay, you remember when I said we had some ideas of who the inside man was?"

She paused with a forkful of salad over her plate. "Yes. Are you going to tell me who that is, finally?"

"Lester."

"Skinny busboy Lester?" She leaned forward and spoke in hushed tones.

"You got a lot of Lesters working here?"

"Well, no, but he doesn't really seem capable of something like this."

I wasn't sure if she meant he wasn't smart enough or if she thought he was too nice a kid, but I said, "We have some proof he's the one. Seth found a cage of rats in his car last week. We're reasonably sure they were destined for your kitchen."

Gigi shuddered. "How did he manage to prevent that without giving himself away?"

Elle Parker

"They accidently got loose. Damn shame."

Her mouth turned up at the corners. "I don't remember you having nearly this much fun on the job."

"I did sometimes, but I had a lot more to prove then."

"Mmm. I suppose you did." She was getting nostalgic and had a kind of dreamy look on her face as she studied me. "I'm glad you've moved past that, though."

I opened my mouth to point out that I could make the same comparisons between her and the Gigi I knew ten years ago, but the atmosphere was shattered with the crash of a coffee cup bouncing off a plate and onto the table directly behind me. "Oops," came Seth's voice, "sorry about that. Nothing broken."

Gigi gave him a little wave that said it was all right and turned her attention back on me. "Lester's working right now. I suppose I should fire him, but do you think that will make things worse?"

Silverware clattered into Seth's bin, on top of plates and glasses. I took a deep breath. "I'm not sure. I don't want him here anymore, either, but if you fire him, that's likely to tip off Wallace. That could go either way. On the one hand, without his inside guy, he might just give up, which I doubt. On the other, you might provoke him into making a bigger move. In that case, you'd really have something you could go to the police with."

She chewed thoughtfully while she mulled that over, and I added, "Now, if you were to let him go real nice, and just say it's seasonal layoffs and you're really sorry or whatever, they might not figure out that you know."

"I could probably do that," she said. "How is he connected to Wallace?"

"He used to work for him. One of Lester's previous employers was Mickey's Bar and Grill, which is owned by Tommy Wallace."

Gigi shook her head and stabbed a crouton. "This all seems so ridiculous. Why would he go to all this trouble to try and put me out of business when he could just use the time and energy fixing up his own?"

"Some people have a different idea of what constitutes success. I guess the challenge of pulling off a crazy deal like this was more interesting than working hard to build a good restaurant."

"Well, I'm glad this is almost over." She dropped her napkin on her plate and pushed it away. "I can't thank you enough, Dino. I knew you'd come through for me."

Behind me, something hit a glass and it rung like a bell, startling the crap out of me. I turned around and fixed my gaze on Seth. "Hey, buddy, you wanna take it easy back there. I imagine the owner of this place would like to have some dishes left at the end of the day."

Seth pasted on an expression of mock humility. "I'm very sorry, sir. It won't happen again. Please don't let me spoil your meal with your lovely wife there." He gave me a smoldering stare that went right to my groin, and then marched away. He was giving me shit, but it had a mean spirited edge to it. I wasn't completely out of the doghouse yet.

Gigi looked confused. "What was that all about?"

I rolled my eyes. "He's just giving me a hard time. He does stuff like that a lot. His sense of humor didn't mature much past eighth grade."

"He is a nice guy, though," she said, taking a sip of her drink. She wrinkled up her nose and sighed. "Oh damn, the prep cook is at it again. He's not very good, and this is the third time this week he's burned something. I may have to let him go soon. We don't need this right now."

I sniffed the air. I barely detected some hint of an off odor, but never would have noticed if she hadn't pointed it out. "Good catch," I said, "I guess you get tuned to that kind of thing when you work in a restaurant all your life."

"So, what do we do now?"

"That's kind of up to you," I said. "We can take this to the police, but we don't have much to go on. I can try to get you something more solid, and then you can go to the police. Or, I can go lean on Wallace and give him several good reasons to find something else to do with his time."

"Do people really do that kind of thing?"

"Come on, you know they do."

She looked mildly uncomfortable. "I think I'd rather have you put together some more information and we'll take it to the police. I want to be sure this is finished."

"Oh, it would be finished." I drank the last of my beer.

"All the same…" She gave me a stern look.

I grinned at her. "You're the boss."

I expected a sharp comeback, but her attention was focused across the room where there was some commotion. I turned to look and saw that several people were upset and getting to their feet, and in the corner, where a large potted palm stood, smoke was beginning to drift along the floor and billow up into the air.

A woman screamed and someone yelled, "Fire!"

Chapter 26

People crowded away from the corner as the smoke grew thick, and panic swept through the restaurant. At first it didn't seem so bad. It was a small area and if someone grabbed the fire extinguisher, we could get it contained. But then in the blink of an eye, the curtains on either side of the palm erupted in flames that shot all the way to the ceiling.

Patrons shrieked and rushed away in a chaotic scramble. An old woman was knocked down and Gigi leapt up to help her. All the while she was calling out assurances. "Please, everyone, just file straight out the front door. Try to stay calm."

The bartender got on the phone, and it was pretty clear by his gestures and the tone of his voice, he was calling 911. Some of the younger staff huddled at the back of the restaurant, as scared as everyone else, while the rest helped Gigi get people moving out the door.

My eyes stung as I looked around for the nearest fire extinguisher. The smoke was incredible and filled the room with white and gray clouds so dense it became hard to see what was going on at all. And the whole time, the flames spread with alarming speed, licking up the walls and flaring at the edges of the room when the tablecloths caught fire.

People around me had gotten confused and didn't know which way to go, so I turned them in the right direction. Gigi passed by me to help someone else, and I said, "You need to get the hell out of here."

"Don't be ridiculous," she shot back. She coughed hard, and followed a mother with two children to the door.

Everywhere I looked, people screamed and cried, and the air was so thick we could hardly breathe. I pulled my handkerchief from my pocket and held it over my mouth as I moved through the dining room, trying to make sure everyone got out.

Marco came in with the fire extinguisher and attempted to hose down the walls where the worst of it charred the woodwork. Wallpaper peeled off and caught fire as it fell. In the distance, I heard sirens and would have breathed a sigh of relief if I could have.

Gigi appeared again through the haze and grabbed Marco's arm. "Forget it," she hollered over the roar of the flames. "It's not doing any good. We need to get out while we still can. The fire trucks are almost here."

She glanced over at me and I nodded. I took one last look for anyone we might have missed, and then followed them out into the clear sunshine.

The three of us slumped against the hood of my car and gasped for air, coughing smoke out of our lungs. People huddled in groups on the sidewalk and around the parking lot, many of them still crying. Onlookers had gathered across the street.

I straightened up and looked for Seth. Across the lot, by the side of the building, the kitchen staff gathered in a group where they had gone after escaping out the side door. I searched the faces and got sick to my stomach when I realized Seth wasn't there. He wasn't with any of the groups along the sidewalk either, and a horrible chill ran down my spine.

I took off toward the front door of the restaurant and Gigi shrieked and grabbed my arm. "What the hell do you think you're doing?" she yelled.

"Seth is still in there."

I shook her off and ran back inside, holding my hand over my mouth. Half the restaurant was now in flames, and it was nearly impossible to see through the smoke. It didn't seem likely Seth would be in the dining room, since we'd just cleared it and the last I knew he'd been in the back.

Fighting my way through the heat and smoke, I went straight through to the kitchen. The lights flickered and went out as I ran down the hallway past the office. The lights in the kitchen were still on, though, and the door stood ajar, spilling sunlight into the horrific scene.

In the kitchen, I found Seth on the floor in a corner, dazed and coughing. He had a hand clamped to the side of his head and looked completely disoriented. I raced over and grabbed him, trying to haul him to his feet.

"Come on, buddy," I said. "We need to get out of here right now. Can you stand up?"

"Oh, fuck, Dino," he groaned. "What the hell is going on?"

"The restaurant is on fire, let's go."

I dragged him through the kitchen and out the side door without waiting for him to get his footing. He stumbled alongside me as we crossed the parking lot to the far side, and then fell to his knees, coughing and wincing with pain.

I got down on the ground and wrapped my arms around him, holding him tight until my heart stopped pounding and I could take a deep breath. My glorious day had turned into a nightmare. Fire trucks had pulled up while I was inside, and they had hoses out. One pair of firefighters aimed their water at the corner of the building where the blaze had burned out through the roof, while two more teams doused the walls that were still intact to keep them from going up too.

I kissed Seth on the forehead and shifted so I could sit. He leaned heavily against me, breathing hard, but coming around.

"What happened to you?" I asked. "How'd you end up on the floor?"

"It was that sleazy little fucker, Dino. Lester came tearing through the kitchen in a panic when all hell broke loose, and shoved me backward out of his way. I cracked my head on the edge of the stove when I went down. Everyone else was already out, so no one saw it happen."

I intended to have a little talk with Angelo about making sure his staff was taken care of, but that could wait. For the moment, I just needed to sit and get over the terror I felt when I realized Seth was still in there. "Jesus, Seth," I said, "I really don't need you scaring me like that. I think you just took another six years off my life."

"You know me, always good for a little drama." He looked up at me and smirked. Then he kissed me full on the lips, snaking an arm around my neck. "Thanks for coming back for me."

"Always," I said.

The noise of the crowd filtered back in, and I looked up to see Gigi coming over to us, with Marco close behind. "Dino, thank God," she said. "You didn't come back out, and I was afraid you'd gotten hurt. Seth, are you all right?"

I gently untangled myself and stood up, then helped Seth to his feet. He stayed close by my side, and I put a hand on his shoulder. Gigi seemed to notice, but she didn't say anything. I didn't either because it wasn't the time or place for explanations.

"I don't think you need to worry about firing Lester," I told her.

She looked stricken. "You really think they would go this far?"

Seth said, "Lester flew out of there like a bat out of hell, and damn near killed me in the process. He's long gone now."

"I…" Gigi was completely disconcerted, searching for the right words, and I felt responsible. "Where would he go?"

"I have a pretty good idea," I said, watching black smoke billow up into the sky. "And I think it's time we did something we should have done a long time ago."

Chapter 27

"Dino, what are you talking about?" Gigi eyed me with concern, and I know I made her nervous.

"If I was better at my job, I could have prevented this." Anger welled up so fierce in me, I practically choked on it. "I really thought we had more time."

"So did I. That's why I didn't mind putting you off until today. You couldn't have known they were going to do something this drastic."

"I knew it was a possibility."

The fire was mostly under control, and the building hissed and crackled as it cooled. An ambulance had shown up, and a few people stood around the back of it while EMTs treated minor cuts and bruises. One elderly woman was seated inside, breathing through an oxygen mask.

"You've got a lot to deal with here," I said. "I'll give you a call when I have something."

"What? Where are you going?" Gigi asked as I pushed past her. She followed me all the way to my car. "I think we have enough to go to the police with now, don't you?"

"Not enough to pin it on Wallace. Besides, I want a little personal payback." I turned to Seth. "Are you with me or do you wanna go over there and get checked out?"

"What do you think?" Seth's voice was low and about as dangerous as I've ever heard it. "I want to have a chat with Lester. And I'm responsible too, I was supposed to be keeping an eye on him. I should have known what he was up to."

Gigi grumbled with annoyance. "Oh, for Pete's sake. Neither one of you is responsible for this, and you don't have to rush off busting heads to make it better."

"Oh, yes. We really do," Seth said as he jumped into the passenger seat.

I went around and got in, starting the engine with more force than necessary, and backing out. It took a little jockeying to get around the fire engine and the crowds of people. Gigi followed behind and hollered rudely, "Now, that's the Dino I remember! Why be rational when you can use your fists?"

When we were clear of the throng surrounding the restaurant, I hit the gas and headed north. It was a good bet Wallace would be at Mickey's, and Lester would have gone running to report to him after starting the fire. If we didn't find him there, I knew where he lived.

Seth stared straight ahead, a grim expression on his face. I said, "You sure you're all right? You were pretty out of it when I found you."

"I'm fine. I have a splitting headache, but I'm gonna give it to Lester when we get there."

"Good." I rounded the turn toward Mickey's a little too fast and squealed the tires, which gave me a perverse kind of satisfaction.

"What about you?"

"I'm good. I wasn't in there long enough to really do any damage to my lungs."

"That's not what I mean."

I glanced at him. "What are you talkin' about?"

"You are in one hell of a rage right now, and I want to make sure you can do this without getting stupid."

"Ah, have you looked in a mirror lately? You're not exactly a model of self-control."

"Yeah, but I'm not defending the honor of an old flame."

"Maybe I'm defending the honor of a current one."

"It's cool, Dino. I'm not jealous. I'm with you on wanting to get even for Gigi, but I think you have a lot riding on this, and I don't want you going overboard."

"I know where the line is," I told him. "I might dangle Wallace over it by the balls, but I won't cross it."

"Okay." He nodded and turned his focus forward again.

I managed to get a lid on my driving by the time I pulled into the parking lot. I didn't want to go blasting in there and give Wallace enough warning to bail out the back door. Seth leapt from the car before it stopped rolling, and met me around back where we fell into step together.

Mickey's was mostly empty when we stormed inside. Just a couple of tables with people at them and some guys on stools. The TV behind the bar was running news coverage of the fire at Salvatore's, which pissed me off even more. The thought of that asshole sitting in there with a drink, gleefully watching his handiwork like it was entertainment made my blood boil. When I saw him, I grabbed him by the front of his shirt and slammed my fist into his face as hard as I could. It felt better than I'd expected it to, so I did it again. Then I gave him a shove and let go. He staggered backward and crashed into the bar. Two women gathered up their purses and darted out the door with startled gasps. The guys at the bar jumped and stood ready to join if the boss needed help.

Wallace looked up at me with wide eyes. He wiped the blood from his nose and comprehension dawned. "You're that asshole from yesterday," he spat.

"Oh, I'm so much more than that, Tommy." I towered over him and crowded him so he couldn't get up. "I'm your worst nightmare, and I'm the guy that's gonna put you in jail."

Back in the kitchen, someone shrieked and a moment later, Lester stumbled out in a panic with Seth right behind him. He waffled and tried to run, but Seth cut him off, then chased him around the dining room like a cat plays with a mouse.

"I don't have a fuckin' clue what you're talking about, pal, and I have no idea who you guys are." Wallace sounded bored, like we weren't worth his time and trouble.

I hauled him to his feet, then grabbed a handful of his hair and directed his attention toward the television. "You fucked up big when you started messin' with Gigi Sapora. What happened? You get tired of playing petty ante pranks and decided to up the stakes? You figure if she's burned out she'll be too scared to rebuild and she'll sell to you instead? Or were you maybe hoping she wouldn't make it out and then you'd have a really easy shot?"

Running through it all got me so mad, I bashed his head into the bar post without even thinking about it. That was all it took to get the rest of his gang involved. A couple guys jumped me and pulled me off Wallace, while a third one took up a stance in the front doorway. This was going to be an all-out bar fight, and nobody got to leave until it was finished.

I broke free from one of the guys and swung around to nail the other with a solid left cross. He bellowed like a moose and broke his fall by clutching a video poker machine. The other guy grabbed me by the elbow and yanked me back, where his fist met my face and he kneed me in the gut for good measure. I coughed, hard, but managed to gather up the strength to shove him backward over a table.

Lester streaked past me and then Seth, who tackled him. They crashed into a bunch of chairs, knocking furniture everywhere. "Pale, fucking big-headed weasel!" Seth snarled.

When I straightened up, Wallace had just gotten his head clear and was looking to take a shot at me. I ducked it and elbowed him in the chest. "You miserable son of a bitch!" I yelled.

He leaned on the bar, wheezing, but pulled a sardonic smile and said, "I don't have any idea what you're talking about."

Across the room, Seth had Lester pinned to the floor and sat on his stomach, pounding him high school style. Lester wailed incoherently and tried fruitlessly to fend off Seth's blows.

I turned back to Wallace and said, "I'll bet your pathetic lackey does, and it won't take much more of that before he's spillin' his guts."

Both thugs had recovered by that time and they tackled me so hard we all went down in a pile of flailing fists, taking Wallace with us. I cut loose with all the rage I had, and kicked or punched anything that felt human and wasn't attached to me. It had turned into a complete brawl, and even the guy at the door abandoned his post to join in the fight.

Every hit I took focused my anger more, and I locked onto Wallace as my target, punching him anywhere I could reach. Someone caught me across the jaw, and I tasted blood. My knuckles were bruised and raw, and my hands started to ache. Somewhere in the background, I became dimly aware of the sound of sirens.

Lester crawled over to the pile, whining. "Somebody called the cops, Tommy, what are we gonna do?"

Seth jumped on his back and leaned forward to get right in his face. "You're gonna go to jail where they'll teach you that it's *wrong* to leave people to die in a *fire*. Cocksucker."

"Shut your hole, Lester," Wallace snapped.

I punched him for it. Then one of the thugs punched me, and the whole thing started all over again. The sirens hit top volume and within minutes, cops flooded through the front doors. They started grabbing guys and sorting them out, including me, who got dragged out of the mess and pulled to my feet. Wallace and his thugs were lined up against the bar, while Seth hung from two cops, trying desperately to kick Lester, who was being held by a third one.

It took a few minutes to get everyone settled down so the guy in charge could gain control. "All right, gentlemen," he said, pacing between us. "Anyone care to explain what this is all about?"

Wallace piped up immediately. "These two barged in here and attacked us without any provocation."

"Bullshit," I barked. "These assholes are responsible for the fire that destroyed Salvatore's this afternoon."

"I've been here all day, and I have several people who will verify that." Wallace rubbed his jaw and I was pleased to note his shirt was streaked with blood. He also had a gash above his left eye from when I slammed his face into the post, which I admired. "Now, I will admit I was at Salvatore's on Monday night and had a lousy meal which I complained about. For all I know, that whore can't stand the heat and got her guard dogs to come up and get even."

"You son of a bitch." Anger shot through me, and I slipped the cop's grasp and smashed Wallace's face in one more time.

That was a mistake, of course, and I knew it would be. The cops had me pinned face down on the floor in a split second and snapped on the cuffs before my hand even stopped stinging.

One of the guys holding me down looked about twelve and had to be a rookie. "So who do we believe, Captain?"

The cop in charge scoffed and said, "Arrest everyone and we'll figure it out at the station. We got 'em all on disorderly conduct anyway."

They pulled me to my feet again, and I watched as Wallace and his thugs were cuffed and lead out of the building. Wallace bitched the whole way, threatening to call a slew of lawyers and politicians. Seth was smart enough to settle down and let them handcuff him quietly, while Lester sniffled uncontrollably and looked like he would burst into tears at any moment.

The rookie read us our rights. He looked so excited, it probably gave him a hard-on doing it. He also got to pat us all down, and I was glad my gun was still out in the car. I'm especially fond of that one and wouldn't like to have it confiscated.

When he was done, the cops led us outside and put me in the same car with Seth, which I was grateful for. It was getting close to dark, and the air felt humid and stifling. My jaw hurt, my cheek hurt, my ribs hurt, and I had a nasty headache. Squashing my hands between my back and the car seat didn't do anything for their circulation. They closed the doors and soon we were pulling out in the direction of the police station.

I slumped in the seat and took a deep breath. Seth sagged against my shoulder and sighed. In a quiet voice, he said, "Is it wrong that I got kinda' turned on watching you get manhandled and cuffed?"

"Do you ever stop?" I asked. "How can you make jokes at a time like this?"

"It's how I deal with stress, roll with it."

We sat quietly for a while, then he said, "Besides…I wasn't joking."

I cast a glance at him in the fading light, and he was grinning just slightly. It felt good to be back on speaking terms and have him close to me, even if it was in the back of a squad car. "I wouldn't know if it's wrong," I said. "You're the expert, you tell me."

Chapter 28

When we reached the station, they drove around back where the secure entrance was. The one you didn't really want to be taken through. It was dark, but they had the parking lot lit up like a runway. Wallace and his gang arrived just ahead of us and were already going in as we were helped from the squad car.

Inside, the cool air-conditioning was a welcome relief, but lasted only as long as it took to reach the end of the hallway and go downstairs where the holding cells were.

This was not the first time either Seth or I had been down there, and we'd both been on the wrong side of the bars a time or two. Mostly, though, I ended up there while dealing with clients. Once, it was Seth I had to go for.

At the far end of the booking desk, Wallace was giving the guy a hard time and screaming for his lawyer. Lester had tears running down his face, and kept looking to Wallace to tell him what to do, only Wallace was ignoring him. At our end, a large middle-aged woman with unnaturally blond hair and an abbreviated version of her police uniform slapped clipboards on the counter and started to give us instructions. She had her sleeves rolled up and her tie off, collar open to catch whatever breeze the weak fan behind her threw off. She came around and removed our handcuffs, then went back to her post.

"I need your driver's licenses, and anything in your pockets. All jewelry and loose items, except eyeglasses." She set two trays out for us to put our belongings in.

While we filled out the paperwork, she wrote up swift inventories of everything we had and gave us those to sign. Two big cops with all the hardware strolled slowly around the room, ready for action if anyone should take it into their heads to resist arrest.

"This really sucks," Seth muttered as we were led down to where they fingerprinted and photographed us. Although, he didn't seem to think so when I was put against the wall and handed the sign to hold while they took my mug shot. When it was his turn, he smiled broadly and flirted with the woman manning the camera.

Eventually, we worked our way through the gauntlet of formalities and were taken back to the actual holding cells. The guard locked us in with a couple hookers and a guy who reeked of booze snoring on a bench. Across the aisle, Wallace sat stiffly, gaze fixed on me with a stare that just about made up for the lack of air-conditioning.

I smirked and said, "I told you I'd get you thrown in jail."

"Yeah, well, we'll see who's still here in the morning."

One of his thugs grabbed the bars like an enraged ape and sneered. "You're gonna regret the day you ever walked into that place. I'll see to that."

Wallace got up and smacked him on the back of the head. "Shut up, you moron. You're going to get us in worse trouble than we already are." He pointed to the whole group of them. "Nobody says one more word until my lawyer gets here, and not even then, got it?"

I turned my back on him and went to sit down next to Seth. The fight was all drained out of me finally, and I just wanted to be still long enough for my head to quit pounding. Across the cell, the two hookers sat at the far end of their bench and chatted calmly as if they were waiting for a bus.

Seth groaned and leaned back against the wall. "What now, Dino?"

"Wait 'til we get to make a phone call," I said. "You need to call Molly to come bail us out. I'll pay her the money tomorrow. I'm going to see if I can't get in touch with someone who can help us nail Wallace."

"You gonna tell Gigi we took off and got ourselves tossed in the slammer for a bar fight?"

"Yeah. We probably owe her the chance to say 'I told you so' after we failed to prevent her restaurant from going up in flames. Besides, this is good for us."

"This is good for us." He twisted sideways and braced a foot up on the bench. "How, exactly, is this good for us?"

"First off, Wallace isn't going anywhere, so we don't have to worry about that. Second, now we have the police lookin' at him, and if we push hard enough, maybe we'll get them to find the proof I couldn't."

Seth nodded and rested his chin on his knee. "And if they can't?"

"Then I'll keep picking until I do. It's out there, I know it is. There's no way in hell he's not the guy."

We sat silent for a while, waiting and listening for any sign that someone was coming to get us. Seth stood up and paced around a little, said hi to the hookers who both offered him a jailhouse discount the next time they were all free. There was a lot more I wanted to say to him, but it wasn't the time or the place, and to be honest, I didn't want to wreck our apparent truce by bringing up a touchy subject. For the moment, I was content to pretend everything was fine between us. He came back across the front of the cell, dragging his fingers along the bars.

"What are you thinkin' about?" I asked.

He flashed me a sly grin. "Prison sex."

"Oh, why am I not surprised?"

"Boy would I love to get you alone in here..."

The door at the end of the hall slammed with an echo and everyone straightened up to see who was coming. I hoped it was our turn to make a phone call, but with the way my luck had been running, it was probably Wallace's lawyer coming to spring him so he could go get rid of any evidence before I had a chance to do a thing about it. What I wasn't expecting was to see Teresa Clyne stroll into view and rest her elbows on the crossbar.

"Well, well, well," she said. "Here's a sight I don't get to enjoy very often. Dino Martini, behind bars." Apparently, that sight was deeply amusing, because she smirked without shame and was enjoying every minute. "When I heard who they brought in, I had to come down and see for myself."

That was fine with me, because if she was there, and she was in a good mood, I stood an excellent chance of getting help from her. In the fifteen years we'd been friends, we'd had dozens of opportunities to help each other out, and proved that the cop-detective relationship doesn't always need to be an adversarial one.

"I really hope you're not just down here to sightsee." I stood up. "I was actually about to give you a call. Or that was the plan if they ever let us *make* a call."

"Oh, you were, huh? And what is it you think I can do for you?" She gave me an obvious onceover and said, "There's no way you can convince me you were falsely arrested."

"No, we were most definitely fighting, but it was for a very good cause."

"Now this I would like to hear." She put her fingers to her mouth and whistled, waving the guard over. He came shuffling down with his keys and she said, "You want to let his one out, please? I need to take him up for questioning."

The guard unlocked the door and slid it open far enough for me to slip through. Seth was right behind me, but Teresa put a hand on his chest and nudged him back in the cell. "Sorry, shortcake. You're going to have to hang tight for a little longer. I've got to do this through official channels."

"Aw, come on," he whined. "I don't wanna be stuck down here with nothing to do but watch the monkey house over there. That's not fair."

"I'll be back for you as soon as I can," she said. "But you've got to behave or there's not a lot I can do."

He cocked his head and looked annoyed. "Why does everyone always think they've gotta' tell me that?"

Teresa laughed out loud. "Oh, you're cute."

"Yeah, well, you're not." Seth pushed his face through the bars and pouted at us.

"Sorry, Seth." I gave him an apologetic shrug. It wasn't like I'd arranged this. "Let me get things straightened out, all right?"

"You owe me so big you can't even comprehend the sheer magnitude of it."

"I know." I gave him a pat on the cheek, then followed Teresa down the hall.

Instead of going to Teresa's desk like I'd assumed, she led me to a tiny room with a table, two chairs, and a big bright mirror that is never good for anyone.

I stopped in the doorway. "You're interrogating me?"

"We're having a conversation."

"This is an interrogation room. If this were a conversation room, there'd be sofas and a coffee maker."

She put her hands on her hips. "You want a cup of coffee?"

"Yes. I also want not to be interrogated."

"I'm not interrogating you, we're just going to have a talk."

"You, me and who else?" I asked, nodding toward the glass.

She flagged down a passing aide and asked for two cups of coffee. Then she took me by the elbow and steered me into the room. "There's a fire investigator in there and the cop who arrested you, and I told them you'd be happy to cooperate."

"I am, but cooperation is face-to-face."

She sighed and pushed me down in the chair, leaning close. "Why are you always so damn difficult?"

"I just wanna make sure that son of a bitch pays for what he did, and I don't want a bunch of cops gettin' sidetracked because I can't control my temper. No offense."

"None taken." There was a knock at the door. "Here's your coffee. I'll be right back."

Teresa left and the aide came in and set the cups on the table at arm's length like she thought I might be a serial killer.

A few minutes later, Teresa came back with the whole posse. "This is Inspector Holt, with the fire department. And this is Captain Miller, who you've already met. Gentlemen, this is Dino Martini, private detective."

Miller chortled and gave me a nod. Holt was a wiry guy with dark hair, graying at the temples, and gold rimmed glasses. He reached out to shake my hand. "Detective Clyne invited us to come and speak with you directly."

"I appreciate that."

Teresa carried in a third chair, and she Holt sat down across from me. Miller apparently preferred to stand.

He said, "You were talking up some theory about Wallace and the fire down in Pass-a-Grille, and I figured I better follow up on it. Clyne says you're a stand-up guy."

"Thanks. I like to think so." I took a sip of coffee and sat back. "It's not a theory. I'm dead certain Wallace is behind it, even if he didn't set it himself." I looked at Miller. "The sniffling weasel is the one who did the dirty work. He's been at it for a while, but it's only recently they did anything illegal."

Teresa rested her arms on the table. "Salvatore's is Gigi Sapora's restaurant, isn't it?"

"Yes. That's why I'm involved." She'd been around for the Gigi era, and was one of the people who thought we made such a great looking couple and couldn't understand why we ever broke up. Holt looked confused, however, so I said, "I will tell you right now that I'm an ex-boyfriend of the woman who owns the place. But that was ten years ago."

"And you're involved now because of your role as a detective?" he asked.

"Yeah. She didn't really know who else to ask for help, so she came and found me."

Teresa said, "Why don't you start at the beginning? What's been going on?"

"Gigi came to me a couple weeks ago because she thought someone was sabotaging her restaurant, but she wasn't sure. She wanted me to check it out. I did some digging, and we got Seth a job as a busboy, and sure enough, someone was hassling her pretty good."

"So why didn't she report it to the police?" Teresa asked.

"Nothing was big enough to warrant a complaint. Even all put together, it just comes off like someone pulling pranks. I finally tracked it all back to Wallace though Lester, who was working at Salvatore's. That was yesterday. I was talking to Gigi today about what our next move was, when the fire broke out."

Miller was pressed against the wall with his arms folded. "Why do you think he was doing those things?"

"To devalue the restaurant, so he could try to buy it cheap. Some big corporation is planning a luxury resort right behind it, and when it's done, that's going to be a prime spot to own a business."

"Can you share your case file with us?" Teresa asked.

"If Gigi okays it, which I think she will."

Teresa stood up and looked at Miller. "I think we might have enough for a warrant. You want to go with me?"

"Yep."

She turned to me and said, "We'll check out his restaurant first, and then his house. Do you have anything else that might help?"

I shook my head. "Not really. He's a slimy guy. So, what happens to me now?"

The look she gave me was apologetic, and she pointed straight down. I groaned and snagged a couple gulps of coffee before they took it away from me. She said, "Unfortunately, fist fights are not a recognized investigative technique, and we still have that matter to deal with."

"Which you seemed to imply you were planning to do."

"First things first. Let's go."

In the hall, the three of them made arrangements to go out to Wallace's, then Teresa led me back to the holding cell. On the way down, she stopped on the landing and said, "Okay, I can understand why you didn't come to the police with a bunch of pranks and nuisance charges, but this afternoon, when you were sure Wallace had started the fire, why didn't you come to us then?"

I raised an eyebrow. "Come on, haven't you ever engaged in a little police brutality for personal reasons?"

"No. Of course not."

"Kneed a wife beater in the nuts just before you stuffed him in the squad car?"

"Oh, forget I asked." She turned and continued down the stairs.

"Yeah, see? I knew it."

"Nobody likes a maverick, Dino."

"Yes, they do. Bookstores are crammed with stories about guys like me."

Chapter 29

Seth and I waited in the holding cell long enough that we were allowed a bathroom break, our phone calls, and still had time for a crappy dinner consisting of a dry bologna sandwich, potato chips, and water. We reeked like smoke, were stained with blood and grime, and to top it all off my shirt was ripped.

"Quit bitching about it, Dino. It's a shirt, not a work of art."

Since I already had our help taken care of, I used my phone call to try to check in with Gigi. Unfortunately, she wasn't picking up, and I figured she was either still busy dealing with the fire, or somewhere getting drunk. I left a message on her voicemail, letting her know I had the police looking into Wallace, and that I would keep trying to get a hold of her.

Seth called Molly and warned her that we may need bailing out, and she promised to be on standby. I was hoping we wouldn't get that far, but I didn't know how many strings Teresa might be able to pull.

Wallace and his gang had pretty well maintained their cone of silence, much to Seth's annoyance. I had to remind him Wallace actually had the right idea and we'd be smart to do the same. He didn't like that much, but mostly it had to do with him being bored more than anything else.

Finally, Teresa came back down the hall with the guard and they unlocked our cell. Seth jumped in front of me and stood right in the door. "Either you let me go with you this time, or no one's going anywhere."

Teresa hung her head to hide a smile. "All right, you got me, come on."

We stepped out and the door clanged shut. The guard waited while we all filed past, and then brought up the rear.

From behind us, Wallace finally cracked and shouted, "When in the hell am I going to get to see my lawyer? What kind of two-bit operation are you running here?"

Teresa turned around and walked backward, shouting, "We're not in the business of fetching lawyers, Mr. Wallace. I imagine you'll see him whenever he decides to show up."

* * * *

Upstairs, Teresa brought us to her desk to pick up some paperwork, and then split us up between two other desks staffed by the kind of fresh-faced young cops who still got a kick out of that kind of thing.

"These nice officers are going to take your statements. Then we'll see if we can't get you out of here one way or another."

"Wait a minute," I said. "You still haven't told me if you found anything."

"First give your statement, then I can fill you in."

"See, I know you found something, because otherwise you wouldn't need my statement."

"Well then, sit down and give it." She ended the conversation by turning around and walking away.

Lorring was the guy assigned to take my statement, and I rattled off the story all over again to him. I was exhausted and getting sick and tired of the whole process. I wanted to see Wallace locked up, then I wanted to go home, get a shower, and get things squared away with Seth once and for all. Across the room, he was gesturing wildly, and I wondered just how far from reality his version of the fight was.

When Teresa came back, she didn't look too happy. She collected our statements and looked at them quickly. Finally, she beckoned us over to her desk.

"All right," she said, standing close and keeping her voice down. "I tried to do what I could to get the charges against you dropped, but Wallace isn't having any of it. He's pissed, and he's insisting we throw everything at you we can. That's the bad news."

"So what happens?" Seth asked.

"Honestly, the worst-case scenario in this one is you get a fine and some community service. Wallace is calling it assault, we're calling it a brawl. It'll even out, trust me. It's possible the D.A. will waive all that if you can help out at the trial."

I smirked. "So there's gonna be a trial."

"That's the good news." She rocked back on her heels and looked rather proud of herself. "We found enough paper in his office to back up your sabotage story. There were property reports on Salvatore's and a bunch of schedules and invoices that belonged to the restaurant. He also had a whole file on the development project, so it looks pretty damning."

"Yeah, but what about the fire? All that other stuff isn't gonna amount to crap in the long run."

"We had to go out to his house with a warrant too, but that's where we hit pay dirt. He had all the right things in his garage to tie him to the fire, and Holt thinks they'll be able to prove the stuff is a match to the materials that started the fire. Wallace is in questioning right now, still denying everything, but it's not looking good for him."

"Yes!" Seth pumped his fist in the air. "At least I didn't singe the boys for nothing."

I rolled my eyes. "You were not singed anywhere. I'm pretty sure you didn't even see flame until we got outside."

"I burned my thumb on the stove during lunch rush." He held it up for me to see.

"Very courageous."

Teresa said, "They were about to question the kid when I left. You want to go see how that's going?"

"We can do that?" Seth asked, lighting up.

"If you keep your mouth shut and act like you belong there. It's not exactly protocol, but I doubt anyone will say anything."

Seth pressed his lips together in a tight line and raised his eyebrows.

"Very good," she said. "I'm impressed. Come on."

We followed her out to the hall I'd been down earlier, only this time, I got to be the one on the happy side of the glass. The only other person in there was a technician, who thought we hardly rated a glance.

Lester sat in the interrogation room, hunched over the table and sniveling. He was a mess. He looked completely strung out, and there were streaks on his face. He shook even though the officer in with him was doing the good cop routine.

"Look," the officer said, "we understand that you were working for Tommy Wallace and this was his idea. We just need to get the details from you."

Lester twitched and looked around wildly as if the walls were closing in on him.

"It's going to be much better for you if you cooperate with us. Otherwise, you'll just go down with him."

"It was just supposed to be smoke!" he shrieked suddenly. His eyes were red, and he sniffed loudly. "It wasn't supposed to do that. It was just to scare people. It was just a smoke bomb."

Teresa folded her arms over her chest. "That's it. We got him now."

In the interrogation room, the officer prodded for more details. "You set off a smoke bomb in the restaurant?"

"I just put it where he said. I thought I did right, but it wasn't supposed to start a fire."

"Where did you get the smoke bomb? Did you make it?"

Lester shook his head. "Tommy gave it to me. He said it was harmless. He told me it wouldn't hurt anybody. I never wanted to hurt anybody."

"Bullshit," Seth muttered, on my other side. "He sure as fuck didn't have any trouble shoving me into a stove and leaving me to die. Hey, Teresa, isn't that assault? Can I press charges?"

"Only if you want him to press them back. He's got witnesses, you don't."

"Geez, you're a hard ass."

"That's what my kids tell me."

Once Lester got going, he spilled it all. He sniffled his way through an explanation of how Wallace had paid him to get a job at Salvatore's and start doing whatever he could to cause trouble. He would report back to Wallace, and steal whatever looked useful, and Wallace would give him new assignments to carry out. Everything was exactly as we'd guessed, except according to Lester there was never supposed to be a fire. They just wanted to scare people and make them feel unsafe there.

Seth shook his head. "Hard to believe someone would do all that just to basically end up working in the same business."

"People do horrible stuff to each other all the time," I said. "Jesus, I have a headache. What time is it anyway?"

"It's a quarter to eleven," Teresa said, looking at her watch.

"When can we get out of here?"

"Pretty much any time. We're waiving bail under the circumstances. Besides, I know where you live." She gave me a faint smile. We were all getting tired, and I was glad it was over. "Come on, let's go downstairs and I'll get you signed out."

On the way down, Seth edged up to Teresa and said, "So…what kind of bribe would it take for you to get me a copy of Dino's mug shot?"

"You know, I just might be able to arrange that."

Chapter 30

Teresa was nice enough to give us a ride back to Mickey's so we didn't have to walk. It was a gorgeous night, but after the day we'd had, I just wanted to get home as quickly as possible.

"Dude, Matilda looks as bad as we do," Seth pointed out. Which was saying something because it was only in the glow of the streetlight that we saw anything. Soot had rained down on her during the fire and dotted her body and interior. It showed stark against the white upholstery.

I swiped my thumb along the edge of the backseat, smearing the soot into a pale gray streak. "No shit. This is gonna be hell to clean. I'm really glad I hit Wallace twice."

"We'll take it over to Uncle Suds. They do a great job, even if you do pay through the nose for it."

I shrugged. "Yeah, well. It's hard to feel really bad about it when I think what Gigi's facing right now."

"I know. But that can be fixed too, eventually."

I dug into my very own police-issued plastic bag and found my watch. "It's too late to call her tonight," I said, strapping it on. "We can see how she's doing tomorrow."

We slid into the front seats. I didn't worry about the soot, because it was already as ground in as it was going to be. Instead, I put my head back and closed my eyes, taking a moment to appreciate the quiet and the salt breeze. The air had cooled off to a more tolerable level.

When I sat up straight, Seth was watching me. I pushed the key into the ignition and took a deep breath. "You want me to take you home now, or…what? I mean, obviously you're speaking to me again, but how far does that go?"

He tilted his head and raised an eyebrow. "I thought you said I was getting you tonight whether I liked it or not." His tone was warm, but he wasn't flirting.

"I talk big sometimes."

"Shit, don't I know it."

"It's late, Seth. I really want to take you back to my place. What do you want?"

"It's not your fault, Dino."

"I coulda stopped it."

"Really? How?"

"I knew what was going on. I should've told Gigi to go to the police sooner."

"And what would they have done?"

I sighed. I knew what he was getting at, but I wanted someone to blame. Even if it was me. "They would have taken a statement, and maybe kept an eye on things if she was lucky. But, damn it, someone should have been able to stop him."

"I keep tellin' ya, you're not Superman…"

"Yeah, yeah, yeah. Your place or mine?"

Seth scoffed. "Yours, asshole, you know that."

It felt good to hear him say it. As I started up the car and headed north, he took out his cellphone and dialed. "Who are you calling?" I asked.

"Original Pizza," he told me. "You don't think a bologna sandwich constitutes dinner for me, do you?"

"I should have known."

"I'll order it now, and we can pick up as we drive by."

* * * *

When we got to my building, everything was quiet and mostly dark. A faint glow spilled from under Adele's door, but there were no other signs of life. Upstairs, Seth put the pizza on the counter and grabbed a couple of beers for us.

"I don't know about you," I said, "but I need a shower before I do anything else, including eat."

"Hey, that's cool. Pizza is good at any temperature." He grabbed a slice and followed me into the bathroom.

I felt odd with our fight still hanging between us, but I figured it had waited that long, it could wait another half hour while we got cleaned up. I downed a couple large swallows of beer while I turned on the water.

Seth balanced the pizza on top of his beer bottle while he stripped off his shirt and jeans. He had a dark bruise on his forehead where he'd hit the stove, but other than that, he didn't look any worse for wear. I was thankful for that. I wanted to reach out and touch him, but I wasn't sure I had the right. At least not until we squared things away.

Instead, he came to me and started to unbutton my shirt. "You really do look like shit, you know. You oughtta take something before you really start to ache."

"I already do."

He pushed my shirt off my shoulders and smoothed a hand over the dark shadow on my belly where Wallace's thug had kneed me. "You're not hurt, though?"

"No," I said, taking another sip of beer. "I'm fine."

Seth stepped up close and leaned into me, chest to chest, all warm bare skin. Best pain killer I ever had. I wrapped my arms around him and held him tight for a minute. I could have stood there all night.

"Come on," he said, "you can wash me down in the shower. It'll be step one on the road to forgiveness."

"I thought pulling your ass out of a fire was step one."

"Nah, that was just a show of good faith. You still have a lot of sexual favors in your future."

"You really know how to punish a guy."

He climbed under the water, and I finished getting undressed. I kicked all our stinking, soot-stained clothes into a pile to deal with later. Then I took another swallow of beer and got in after him. The warm water was marvelous, and I felt better the instant all that grime started swirling down the drain. Seth was already scrubbing shampoo through his hair and I did the same. I rinsed and we switched places. It was all very comfortable and friendly.

Then he gave me a lazy smile and handed me the soap. I lathered my hands and reached for his neck and shoulders. His eyes drifted shut and his head tilted back, while his body swayed slightly under my touch. At first, all I could think about was how much I'd missed him, and how scared I'd been, how incredibly relieved I was that he was speaking to me again. I kissed the bruise on his forehead, which showed even darker with all the soot washed off.

As I moved lower, however, my thoughts turned toward the physical and almost certainly more along the lines of what Seth had in mind. I knelt on the floor of the tub and ran slippery hands up his legs and over his hips. He put a hand on the tile to steady himself and looked down at me, eyes dark, with just a faint curve to his mouth. His expression made my pulse race and my skin go warm.

I washed his stomach and let the shower rinse the soap away, then leaned forward to suck water off his skin. He moaned and put a hand on my neck. It's not all that often I get him in a mood where he doesn't want to rush things, so I took my time. He was hard long before I got around to lathering him up and stroking his cock with soap-slicked hands. So was I, to be honest, and his panting and moaning went straight to my groin.

I took about fifteen seconds to soap my own body, then stood up and pushed him under the spray, kissing him deep and hot. We clung to each other, wet and slippery, necking like teenagers.

When I moved to lick his throat, he took a deep breath and said, "Look, I know we need to have a talk, and I'm sure as hell not letting you off the hook, but—"

"Sex first, talk later," I panted by his ear.

"That's supposed to my line."

"You're a bad influence on me."

We toweled off and took our beers to the bedroom, finishing them on the way. I didn't bother with the lamp. The light filtering in from the kitchen was more than enough, and I liked the mood it set. Seth climbed on the bed, and I was a step behind him, covering his body with my own as he lay down. I moaned and slipped an arm under his neck. I wanted him so bad I could taste it, and the more I touched him, the more I needed.

We knew how to fit our bodies together easily, and exactly how to move. The slide of soap was replaced with a delicious friction, and it felt so good it made me dizzy. Seth arched his back and ground into me with a low moan. "Oh God, Dino, I missed you."

"Yeah, really?"

"Of course, moron."

To prove his point, he pulled me down for a kiss that was as much eager enthusiasm as it was wanton sex. Then he hooked his leg over mine and ground against me in a way that was entirely about the sex. We were all warm skin and hot breath and thrusting bodies.

Seth tightened his arms and brushed his lips along my jaw line. That was all it took to have me coming hard, burying my moans against his shoulder. My body shook, and it wasn't only a physical release. All the tension of our fight, and the fire, and the long horrible day faded along with the last tremor. Those things still had to be dealt with, but I finally felt like it would be okay.

Seth rolled us over so he could take control, and I watched him, mesmerized. His face was set in blissful concentration and his neck and shoulders were flushed. He braced himself on his forearms, hands tucked under my back, and rocked his hips, picking up speed as he got closer. Then his mouth fell open and he ducked his head, swearing in a strained voice as he came. "Son of a *bitch*…"

After a minute, he dropped onto my chest, panting and happy.

It was well past midnight, and exhaustion was setting in. I wanted nothing else but to close my eyes and fall asleep, preferably like that, with Seth warm and wilted on top of me. I was obscenely relieved when he mumbled, "I'm beat. Let's talk about the rest in the morning, 'k?"

"Yeah, sure." I stroked my hand along his back lazily. "One of us has to put away the pizza, though."

"That's step two."

I smiled. "Just out of curiosity, how many steps are there?"

"You don't even want to know."

"I was afraid of that."

I rolled him off me and leaned in for a kiss. "It's a damn good thing I love you, you know?"

It only took a few minutes to clean up and put the pizza away. I spent a little extra time setting up the coffee maker, so there'd be some waiting for me in the morning. I knew I was going to need it.

When I came back, Seth sat in the middle of the bed with his arms wrapped around his knees. He watched me so intently as I came in that I froze in my tracks. "What?" I asked.

"Do you realize that's the first time you've actually said it?"

I had to think for a second. "That I love you?"

"Yeah."

"Well…out loud anyway."

He shook his head and gave me a wry grin, then moved over to make room for me. "It astounds me that you ever managed to get laid in the first place."

"Must be my brooding good looks. Some people like that kind of thing I hear."

"Yeah, yeah, yeah. You're just lucky I happen to be one of them," he said, settling in against me.

I draped my arm over him, and within minutes, we were both sound asleep.

Chapter 31

The next morning, we woke up and did it all over again, only in reverse order. Sex, then shower. Seth was significantly more awake, which meant he was also a lot noisier.

"Fuck, Dino," he panted, "I'm not gonna be able to stay quiet if you keep doing that. I mean, remember it for sure, just save it for my place."

"You know what? Go ahead and make all the noise you want." And I did it again, better.

Seth moaned indecently, and managed to focus his eyes on me. "Seriously?"

"Seriously. If Della squawks, I'll point out that I know all about her and the two pool boys from across the street."

"No shit, really?"

"You have no idea."

He shook his head. "She is like…my role model, I swear."

"Yeah? You want to still be goin' at it when you're her age?"

"I want to be doing two pool boys when I'm her age."

"Nice."

"Well, you'll be too old to fuck by then," he said with a smirk. "You can watch from your rocker and have fond memories."

I narrowed my eyes at him, then proceeded to put Della to shame and give Seth a few fond memories of his own. I'm reasonably sure the whole block heard him.

I took my shower while he recovered, and was sitting at the kitchen counter with the newspaper and a cup of coffee when he finally showed his face. He got two slices of cold pizza and a can of coke out of the fridge and came to join me. "That was completely off the hook, man."

"There are some parts of this I'm getting the hang of," I said with a shrug. All I could think about, though, were the ones I wasn't.

He cracked open the soda and took a slurp of it. "You sound awfully serious for a guy who just had mind-blowing sex."

I watched him for a minute, hoping I wasn't about to destroy the affectionate truce we had going, but we needed to get to it sooner or later. "I owe you a huge apology, Seth. I was a complete ass, and I wish I could do it over."

He chewed thoughtfully. "Yeah, you were, kinda'. But I'm not sure doing it over would really fix the problem. I mean, dumping me on the floor was just an accident. You were startled, I get that. That's not really the issue, though."

"I know it's not." I took a deep breath. "I know what you want from me, I'm just not sure I can be that guy. But I'm not ashamed of you, I hope you know that."

"I do. More or less. It would be nice if you could show it somewhere outside of this apartment."

"I can try," I told him. "That's fair. I want you to know I'm not ashamed of myself, either."

Seth raised an eyebrow. "I'm not entirely convinced of that. You spend a hell of a lot of time worrying about what other people are gonna think."

"Too much time, I understand that. I don't switch gears as fast as you do, but I'm not ashamed. And I'm not all wrong. There is a lot of hate out there, and people do get hurt."

"You can't let it control your life, though."

"You can't ignore it either," I told him.

He nodded and tossed his pizza crust at the garbage can. "So maybe we can meet each other halfway. I could stand to be a whole lot less pushy about it, I'm sure."

"That I think I could do." I reached out and caught his wrist to pull him close to me. "I'm sorry I ever made you feel like I was ashamed of us. A lot of that didn't have anything to do with who you are, or what I think about us being together, it's just the way I am. You know I tend to stay low profile."

Seth hung his head and looked a little sheepish. "Yeah, I thought about that over the past couple days. I know better, but I managed to convince myself it was all about being gay."

"If I meet you halfway, is that gonna be enough for you? I'll never be quite the 'fuck the world' kind of guy you are."

"I know. I can live with that, and it wouldn't kill me to be more patient, either." He hooked an arm around the back of my neck and butted his forehead against mine.

"Well, aren't we civilized," I said.

"That's what the two-day cool off period was for."

"Oh." I nodded. "You were just sparing us from ourselves."

"Something like that."

"You are so full of shit."

"Hey, it worked, who cares why, right?" He looked at my watch. "What's the game plan for today?"

"First thing is check in with Gigi. See how she's doin'. You want to come with, or do you need to be at the garage today?"

"I'm good. I don't have anything lined up until this afternoon."

"I'll call and find out where she is, then."

On our way down, we ran into Adele, who was coming in with her shopping bag. She eyed me critically, then Seth. There was a long, awkward silence and I had no idea what to say. More than likely, it was my own hang-up that made her seem critical. It's not like she was ever overly friendly.

She pointed at me and narrowed her eyes. "I meant it when I said no floozies."

"Ah. I see you've been talking to Della." My face got warm, and I was pretty sure I turned pink.

Adele let out a bark that could either have been a cough or a laugh. "You don't think she sat on that for more than twenty minutes, do you?"

"And... is this a problem for you?"

"Nah," she said with a shrug. "Fern is pretty scandalized, but as long as you don't start prancing around here in gold lamé shorts and singing show tunes at top volume, I think we'll be fine."

Seth burst out laughing and was so overcome with glee, he had to sit down on the stair.

I looked at him and sighed. To Adele, I said, "As far as floozies go, you're gonna have to make up your own mind. I may be pushing the limit here."

I kicked him in the shin and walked out the front door.

Not ten steps down the sidewalk, I ran into Della, tending the flower bed around our yard light. Seth came up behind me at the same time she stood up and said, "My, my, don't you two look relaxed this morning. I take it you're getting along?"

Seth smirked. "As a matter of fact we are."

"Yes, I heard that you made up." She gave us a very knowing smile, and that time I'm positive I blushed.

"Well, I heard you nailed two pool boys."

My mouth dropped open, but Della just laughed. "I'm not quite as spry as I used to be."

I jabbed Seth and muttered, "I can't believe you just said that."

"It's all right, sugar. I wouldn't dish it out if I couldn't take it."

"That's great. Look, we're running late, so we better be going now." I steered Seth the rest of the way down the walk, and tossed my briefcase in the backseat of my car.

Seth climbed in and said, "That was just one big gauntlet of embarrassment for you, wasn't it?"

"Yes, it was, and you could try not to enjoy it so much."

"Dude, I would have popped an eyeball if I had to hold that in."

Chapter 32

Gigi and I had agreed to meet at the restaurant because she would have to be there to meet with investigators and insurance agents. I wanted to see it anyway. I'd been too focused on other things to get a real sense of how much damage there was.

On the way down, our mood turned more serious, and Seth broached another subject we'd had trouble over before. "So…with everything that's happened, did you get much time to work on Molly's problem? I would understand if you didn't. I'm not giving you shit, but other than knowing you didn't get killed, I haven't even heard how the thing with Tony G went."

"Yeah, there's a story for you. Which we don't have enough time or beer for right now, but I can give you the condensed version. He had no trouble backing off Molly when I explained who she really was, and how things stood. I had to do a little work for him as a trade-off, but that worked out in our favor too."

"Oh, really?"

I pulled up to a stoplight and used the opportunity to grab my briefcase from the back and fish Tony G's photos out of it.

"He gave me these," I said, handing them over. The light changed and I drove on.

"Holy shit," Seth muttered as he studied them. "I knew Frank was a sleazebag, all right. I'm not even that lewd in public."

"Actually, you are. That's not the half of it, though. That woman isn't just any stripper. That's Frank's girlfriend, Roxanne."

"You know, for a while I felt a little guilty messing around in Molly's life. Now, not so much. I thought the fucker was just a money-sucking loser. I didn't really think he was sneakin' around on her."

"I met Roxanne the other night. They make a charming couple, and she'd like to keep it that way. I told her we'd be happy to help if she took care of Frank and his issues."

"Wow." Seth tapped the photos on his knee. "If this doesn't make Molly see reason, I don't know what will. Thanks, Dino."

"No sweat. I thought maybe we could go over there tonight and break the news to her. She doesn't really need to know you put me up to it if you don't want her to. This all came out of the meeting with Tony G, anyway, and she's the one who called me in on that."

"Let's see how she takes it first. If she's gonna be all grateful and stuff, I want some credit."

"And if she wants to kill me?"

He shook his head. "She won't want to kill you, you're just doing your job. Me, on the other hand…she'd kill me for a slice of chocolate cake."

We came up to Salvatore's and found the parking lot roped off, so I had to park on the street. The stench of burned wood and wet cinders filled the air. I could hardly stand to look. The entire front corner of the restaurant was gone, framed by the charred edges of the remaining walls. Debris lay everywhere. A crew was inside, pulling down loose timber and nailing in braces to stabilize what was left of the building. Beyond them, chairs and tables still stood at the back of the dining room. It was jarring and made the place look naked.

Seth and I stayed by the car for a minute, taking it all in. "Jesus," he breathed. "What a mess."

People milled around in the parking lot, conferring with each other, taking measurements and snapping photographs. I spotted Gigi talking to some guy with a clipboard.

"Come on," I said. "Let's go see how she's doing."

We walked over and ducked under the yellow tape. Gigi saw me and gave me a wan smile, but seemed genuinely happy to see me. She was dressed in jeans, but looked professional, and when I got close, I saw her eyes were red. She'd been crying, and I didn't blame her.

I gave her a tight hug and said, "I'm so sorry, Gigi."

"It's going to be all right," she said. "It's not really as bad as I thought."

"Looks pretty bad from where I'm standing."

She led us closer, so we could get a good look inside. "Actually, the bar wasn't damaged much. Only smoke and water. It will have to be refinished, but it should look as good as new."

Seth shaded his eyes against the bright sun. "You think you're going to be able to rebuild?"

"Definitely. The structure of the back corner is sound, which means we can rebuild it and not have to worry about zoning laws that were passed since it's been here. If we had to put up a completely new building, I don't think we'd be able to keep the docks, or stay as tucked in here as we are."

"What about the kitchen?" I asked. "That looks like it's mostly still there."

"I have someone coming out this afternoon to take a look at the appliances. Angelo thinks they might be all right with some new filters and fittings. There's a lot of electrical damage though, and I don't know if that harmed them or not."

"Are you covered if they're wrecked?"

She nodded. "Oh yes, we're going to be just fine. The worst part is that we'll have to be closed for a couple of months and people forget easily. I'm hoping we'll get our regulars back when we re-open. I'm thinking about expanding the dining room. If we return to our usual level of business, I think we can support it."

"You know, it would be poetic justice if Wallace ended up making your restaurant more successful in the long run," Seth said with a smirk.

Gigi smiled. "Yes, it would."

She turned to face us and her look changed to one of concern. "You both look terrible. Are you all right?"

"This is nothing," Seth told her. "We're fine."

"Nothing a night in jail couldn't cure," I added.

She winced. "I'm sorry about that. I appreciate everything you've done for me, both of you. It didn't end nearly as well as I'd hoped, but at least now it's over."

"Until we all have to appear in court."

"Don't remind me."

The guy with the clipboard came around the corner and called to Gigi. She gave him a wave, and turned to us. "I'm sorry, I better get back to work here. There's a lot we need to go over."

"I'll talk to you later," I said. "If you need anything, let me know."

"Thanks. Dinner for both of you is on me when we're open again. Any time."

"If you let Seth take you up on that, you'll be out of business."

That brought a smile to her face. I gave her a quick kiss and turned to follow Seth back to the car.

"Oh, Dino?"

"Yeah?" I stopped and went back to her.

"When you said you were seeing someone, but you didn't want to talk about it…" She glanced over my shoulder. "Did you mean…"

"Seth. Yeah." I figured I was blushing again, but I was starting to get used to it, so I couldn't really tell. I sincerely hoped I wasn't going to have to explain my new dating habits all day. "Kinda' caught me by surprise."

"It's not really any of my business, of course." She chewed her lip. "So, when you and I were together, what was it?"

"It was real, if that's what you're worried about. I still like women too."

"I was a little worried, I'll admit. I'd prefer to keep my memories of that part of my life just the way I have them." She looked relieved, and I was flattered. I mean, everyone likes to be worth remembering. "And you're happy?"

"I am," I told her. "It's been kind of a wild ride, but I am."

Marco arrived then, to help with the assessment, so I said goodbye and headed out to join Seth. When I got there, he was on the phone with the car wash, making an appointment for Matilda, and explaining to the guy exactly why they should bump the schedule and get her in first.

* * * *

That evening, with a clean car, an easy workload, and the promise of better days to come, I set out to break a girl's heart. Seth worked at the garage while I took Matilda to the car wash, and we hooked back up after five, so we could give the news to Molly in person. I wasn't looking forward to it, but I knew in the long run, it was better for her and I kept reminding myself of that.

The first thing we saw when we turned down her street was Frank's truck. Seth rubbed his hands together and said, "Oh, now we're gonna have some fun."

"I would like to remind you that you are currently facing charges of disorderly conduct and if you manage to get yourself arrested in less than twenty-four hours, they're not going to look too kindly on that."

Seth snorted. "Frank's too big a weasel to turn me in or call the cops. He knows I'd beat the crap out of him for that."

"He might not, but these people on the sidewalk probably would." I parked across the street from Molly's house and looked around. There were about four or five people standing on either side of the block, all talking in little clusters, and all focused on Molly's. "What the hell is going on here?"

"I don't know," Seth said, scowling. "If that fucker's done something to hurt her I'll kill him."

I grabbed my gun and followed Seth across the street while I clipped it to my belt. We heard shouting from inside the house, and I was starting to get a very disturbing picture of what everyone was talking about.

We got as far as the curb when the front door flew open and Frank ran out of it, tripped on his own feet, and landed in a heap on the walk. Molly was right behind him and lobbed a duffel bag at his head.

"You miserable son of a bitch!" she screamed. "If you ever set one fucking foot in this house again, I'll tear your fucking nuts off."

Seth stopped dead and clutched his heart. While we stood there like deer in the headlights, Molly disappeared into the house and within a few seconds, piles of clothing came sailing out and floated down over the lawn. She fired a series of shoes and boots from the doorway, every single one pegging Frank somewhere on his body. He tried to duck as he scrambled around collecting his belongings, but couldn't avoid her in such a tiny yard. She vanished again, and we heard her ranting her way through the house, using enough obscenities to put Seth to shame.

He grabbed my arm and said, "Who in the hell is that, and where's my sister?"

"Hey, I'm impressed. She really is a Donnelly. I used to think she was adopted."

"I guess I got my wish."

Molly came back and heaved a bowling ball into the yard, narrowly missing Frank, who finally had enough incentive to really move. She flung the bag out after it and went back for more.

Seth and I picked our way along the edge of the yard and approached the front door from the side, out of the line of fire.

He leaned toward the opening and called, "Molly? What's goin' on?"

The only answer was a stack of nudie magazines she hurled out the door, fluttering to the ground like pornographic birds.

"Oh my God, this is priceless," Seth said, watching with awe. He stuck his head in the door and yelled louder. "Molly, what the hell happened?"

She came out and dumped another laundry basket of clothes on the ground. "That two-faced motherfucker's been cheating on me. One of my friends was at a bachelorette party and saw him getting a bonus level lap dance from some circus freak." Seth was fighting hard not to laugh, and she punched him in the arm. "You think this is funny?"

"No," he said, losing the battle. He fended off another blow. "I've just never heard you swear like this before. I'm sorry."

She let it go and turned her ire back on Frank. "He's denying everything, the fucking coward."

Frank tried to protest, but Seth took a couple menacing steps toward him. "Save it, asshole, we know about your other girlfriend and how you've been shacking up with her on the side."

"*Girlfriend?*" Molly shrieked. Her face went pale, and her eyes were wild for a moment, then narrowed to slits.

"I met her, Molly," I said. "She's for real. You're doin' the right thing here."

More people had gathered to watch the show, and I thought she could maybe do it more quietly. But then, I'd seen their parents fight and they learned from the best.

"He's got a fucking *girlfriend?*"

She turned to stare at him and in that second, I realized things were about to get ugly. She tensed, and just as she leapt forward to attack Frank, I grabbed her around the waist. The last thing she needed at the moment was to get herself in trouble, or give Frank a reason to want to do anything but get the hell out of there. She swore at me and thrashed in my arms, but I ignored it and held her off the ground, hoping she'd calm down. Instead, she got angrier, and in her fury she threw back her head and bashed me right in the eye. We connected with a sickening crack and both went down in a tangle.

"Damn it," I groaned, rolling onto my back. "Why do all the Donnellys gotta' give me black eyes?"

On the plus side, getting her bell rung took the fight out of her, and Molly sat up rubbing her head. "Oh God, I'm sorry, Dino, I didn't mean to hurt you. I just wanted you to let go."

"Yeah, I know. Don't worry about it. That was not really the smartest move I've ever made, either."

I pushed to sitting as Seth came over, and he bent down to touch my face. "Geez, are you all right?"

I winced. "I'm fine. I've just got one hell of a headache now."

"Hold tight." He patted me on the shoulder and went past me into the house.

While he was gone, Molly got up and started to lay into Frank again, who was frantically trying to gather all his stuff. There was no way I was getting in the middle of that again, and I sat on the top step to watch. Seth appeared and dropped onto the stair next to me. He had three cans of beer in his hands.

"Here," he said, handing me two. "One's to put on your eye, the other is to drink." He leaned over and planted a light kiss on the hurt side of my face and opened his own beer. "I ordered a pizza. It should be here in about half an hour. I have no intention of leaving until Frank does, and this looks like it'll go into extra innings."

"Good plan," I said. We toasted beers and settled in to watch the mayhem.

Meet the Author

Elle Parker likes her heroes snarky and human, and she writes with a realism that incorporates humor and everyday detail into steamy and exciting stories. Although she writes a few forms of erotica, her first love and primary focus is M/M Erotic Romance. She works hard to create characters you can't help but fall in love with.

Most of the time, Elle can be found in her home in the north woods of Wisconsin, working on her latest novel, or spending time with her husband and teenaged kids. When not writing, she likes reading, brewing beer and swimming with the loons. Unless it's winter. In that case she grabs a book and drinks the beer.

Elle's Website:
http://www.elleparker.com/
Reader eMail:
elle.parker@ymail.com

Don't miss the book that started it all.

Like Coffee and Doughnuts

Dino Martini might accept his friend Seth as a lover—if they can stay alive.

Dino Martini is an old-school P.I. in a modern age. Sure, he may do most of his work on a computer, but he carries a gun, drives a convertible, and lives on the beach. Best friend and mechanic Seth Donnelly will back him in a fight, and there's not a lot more Dino could ask from life. Until his world is turned upside down.

A dangerous case and a new apartment are just the start. His friendship with Seth has turned into a romance, only Dino has never had a boyfriend before. Can he handle this sudden twist? Just as he begins to believe it's possible, he loses Seth in more ways than one...
Read on for a special excerpt!

A Lyrical e-book on sale now.
http://www.kensingtonbooks.com/book.aspx/30205

Chapter 1

When I went into Ed's Garage looking to get backup from my friend Seth, I knew immediately my job was going to be harder than I'd thought. Seth and his latest "date," a blonde with short spiky hair and pretty legs, were tangled up on top of a red Ford Torino necking like the world was coming to an end. Neither one of them had a shirt on, but she wore a black and pink polka dot bra. She also wore a pale green skirt under which Seth's hand had disappeared. My timing wasn't good, but I was glad I hadn't come any later.

She saw me first and gave me a pretty smile, apparently not too disturbed by a stranger walking in on her fun. Seth was doing something to her neck that might have been kissing, but reminded me of the way he ate.

She prodded him and said, "Hey, we've got company."

When Seth raised his head, he looked surprised, but that quickly changed to irritation when he saw who it was. He didn't need to say a word for me to know exactly what he was thinking.

I smiled. "I thought you had to have the hood *up* to do a tune up."

"Not when we start with me first," he said. "Don't you have someplace better to be?"

"I'm sorry, I had no choice. Believe me, I did not want to do this, but duty calls."

"Tell duty to call back in about an hour, Dino." He went back to what he'd been doing.

"You're Dino?" the girl asked, lighting up. "I've heard about you."

"Dino Martini, at your service," I said. "Nice...bra."

"Thanks." She grabbed a fistful of Seth's hair and pulled him up to look at her. "Don't be rude to your friend. He's obviously here for something important."

"He's here because whatever job he's got going this evening involves a high likelihood of him getting his ass kicked." He turned to look at me. "Am I wrong?"

I shrugged. "Hard to say with a case like this, but I don't like to take chances."

"What now?" Seth looked defeated already, which was good, because it meant this wouldn't be nearly as difficult as I'd thought.

"Cheating wife," I said. "You know how those can be."

"Yeah, yeah, all right."

Seth Donnelly is about five foot seven, has an unruly mop of carrot colored hair, and although he's thirty-three, he often acts like he's twelve. He's my mechanic, but he's also been a good friend for a lot of years, and there's no one I'd rather have next to me in a fight.

He slid off the hood of the car and told the girl, "I guess I'm gonna have to catch you some other time."

"That's okay," she said, climbing down and pulling her shirt on. "I have to get to work anyway. Can you look at my car tomorrow?"

"Sure, bring it by after three."

She gave him a quick kiss, got in the Ford and drove out, turning left, toward the beach. I was willing to bet she worked in one of the tourist bars down in John's Pass.

"Sorry about that," I said, turning to Seth.

"No sweat. Buy me dinner and we're square. She's cute enough, but her brother's the one I'd really like to nail."

I shook my head. "You bring a whole new meaning to the word 'sleaze', you know that?"

"Oh, come on, it's not like that. She knows. She's just in it for the fun and the free service on that wreck she drives. Did she look especially brokenhearted to you?"

"No," I admitted. "I can't say that she did."

"So tell me about the case," he said, grabbing his shirt off the workbench.

"Not that much to tell. This guy's had me following his wife for a while, and I finally caught her cheating on him with a long haul trucker. Turns out she's been meeting up with all kinds of them off a website called The Hot Trucker's Hookup."

"No shit, are you serious?"

"Yep."

"Sweet deal for the truckers, man. They can line up something everywhere they stop."

"That's pretty much the idea," I said. "They've got quite the little community on there."

I had followed Amy Ware all the way out to Florida's Interstate 75 and wound up spending an afternoon playing "Peeping Tom" through the ground floor window of a cheap hotel. On my fifth pass, I nearly swallowed my cigarette. She had her guy trussed up in a horse's harness and reins with the thing in the mouth and the whole nine yards, and she was ridin' him for all he was worth. I took easily fifty shots of that.

I'm kind of a mix between the old school P.I. and the modern "private investigator," which means I do my fair share of computer searches and background checks on top of the more traditional tailing of cheaters and mystery solving. But I drive a Mustang convertible, I carry a gun, and I live on the beach.

Well, close to the beach.

You are what you drive, they say, and I am a 1966 model of stylish sophistication with a sporty rakishness and a lot of muscle. Instead of Vintage Burgundy, though, I'm your average Italian color, and I have maybe a moderate amount of muscle. When I was a little younger, I had the classic Italian greaser look going on. Now I don't have quite enough hair on top to pull it off, but I'm told I still look pretty damn good.

I named the car Matilda because of her white ragtop, which makes her look like an old lady. She is, without a doubt, my most prized possession. I bought her eight years ago, after an especially lucrative case, and while she was in pretty good condition to begin with, Seth and I restored her to the level of perfection she exists in most of the time these days.

Outside, Seth dropped into the front seat next to me. He looked in the side view mirror and scrubbed his fingers through his hair. That's what passes for styling for him. He plucked his sunglasses out of the collar of his shirt and slid them on. It never fails to impress me how he can make slovenly look good.

"You goin' in carrying on this one?" he asked.

"I don't think so," I told him. "This guy is money. If he gives me trouble, it's going to be of the fist swinging variety, which is why I wanted you along."

"Are we gonna run it the usual way, then?"

"If you expect to be fed."

Certain people do not take bad news well, and if they can't lash out at the object of their anger, they'll often take it out on the closest thing available. I generally happen to be sitting across from them at that point, and I've learned to take precautions.

If the guy is big enough, or bad enough, I won't hesitate to slip my gun into a holster. Most of the time, I just bring Seth for backup. He may be small, but he's wiry and he likes to fight. Best of all, he'll do it for the price of a steak.

For situations like this, I prefer to arrange the meet in a nice dark bar. They're noisy, so you're not likely to get overheard, and you don't look out of place. Plus, it feeds the average Joe's romantic vision of a private eye. People seem to like it better if it goes down the way they see it on TV. And who am I to argue? I like bars.

The "usual way" is I go in first to find the client and get settled, and about five minutes later, Seth comes in and takes a seat at the bar where he can keep an eye on things. Nine times out of ten, nothing happens and he gets to enjoy a beer and flirt with the bartender, but on the rare occasion some idiot decides to take a pop at me, it's nice to know he's got my back.

I'd chosen a dive called Henry's, well outside of Ware's territory so there'd be little chance of him running into someone he knew. Not like it would be tough to explain, but I hate to put a guy in that position right after he's found out his wife is the Calamity Jane of the eighteen wheeler set.

I parked around back as usual. No sense in advertising what I drive if there's a chance there might be trouble. I grabbed my briefcase, which held the folder of photos, and climbed out of the car.

"See you in a few minutes," I said.

Seth saluted me and slouched in the seat.

Inside, Henry's was busy, but not packed. Mostly old guys with nothing better to do, or blue-collar types shaking off the workday. I spotted Ware in a back booth, clutching a glass of scotch or bourbon. He looked pretty grim. Of course, he had to know it was bad news. It doesn't take a face-to-face meeting for me to say, "Hey, your wife is pure as the driven snow and only has eyes for you, and by the way, I have some lovely shots of her shopping for Bibles."

I sat down across from him and set my briefcase on the seat. "Good evening, Mr. Ware."

A cute waitress with a ponytail and a low-cut shirt came over, and I ordered an amaretto on the rocks.

"Cut to the chase, Martini." He took a sip of his drink. "Amy's cheating on me, isn't she?"

"Yes, sir, I'm afraid so."

Seth strolled past me and plugged the jukebox, messing around with the touch screen for a minute before he took a seat at the bar. His way of letting me know he was in the room, since Ware had left me with my back to the door.

"Who is it?" Ware asked.

"Unfortunately, I wasn't able to determine that in such a short time frame," I lied. Since the guy was just one of many, I didn't see the need to share that information with Ware. "It's highly unlikely he's anyone local."

The waitress brought my drink, and I spent about half an hour explaining the deal with the truckers and the website to Ware. I also gave him instructions on how he could do a little sleuthing of his own on his wife's computer. He asked me if that was something I could be hired to do, and I told him it was, but I'd need access to her computer for a while. He said he'd hang onto my card and think about it.

When there wasn't much left to say, I brought out the folder and passed it across the table. He stuck it into his own case without looking at it. That's pretty common. Most people don't want an audience when looking at candid porn starring their beloved for the first time.

At this point, I usually like to say something sympathetic and heartening, maybe give them a bit of advice. I was just opening my mouth when a beer bottle whizzed past my face and bounced off the wall, nearly hitting Ware.

People were shouting and a couple of bar stools crashed to the floor. When I turned to look, a guy the size of a tank had Seth pinned like a bug on the bar, one meaty hand clamped around his throat. Seth gripped the guy's forearm and kicked his legs in the air, trying to score a hit or get away, I wasn't sure which. The ponytailed waitress bounced around, swatting at the tank with a bar rag and begging him to stop.

Ware looked horrified and shot up. "I think I should go. Listen, thanks for your time and trouble," he said, stuffing a check into my hand. "If I decide to have you do that computer thing, I'll get in touch."

I gave him a nod and a pat on the back and sent him on his way. Then I turned back to the scene on the bar.

"Rick, honey, come on," the waitress was saying. "He didn't mean anything. He's just a customer, babe, they say stuff like that all the time, you know that."

"I know his type," the tank roared. "All these guys think they can hit on you just because you bring 'em drinks. It's time someone taught 'em a lesson."

Seth squealed something in protest, but his throat was too constricted for anyone to make it out. He flopped like a fish out of water.

I drained the last of my drink and took a deep breath, then stepped up to the moose and tapped him on the shoulder. "Hey jack, why don't you let the little guy go, he wasn't hitting on your girl."

"Why don't you mind your own business?"

"This *is* my business," I snapped, getting up in the guy's face. I may be skinny, but I can intimidate the hell out of people when I want to. "I can personally guarantee he wasn't hitting on her, so why don't you get your fucking hands off him before I really get mad."

There was a crowd of people standing around us staring. I could see them all mentally calculating the odds of me against Rick the Caveman. The bartender hovered near the phone just in case. But see, I fight smart, and I know how to knock guys like this off their game.

"You can guarantee that?" he sneered, pausing in his attempt to strangle Seth. "And just how are you gonna do that when you weren't even here?"

"Because he's my *boyfriend*, jackass, and if you don't get your filthy paws off him, I'm gonna kick your ass."

A hush fell over the room, and Rick looked down at Seth like he was suddenly holding a rattlesnake. He yanked his hand away, and Seth immediately started wheezing air.

"You mean...you and him..." Rick tried to puzzle it out.

"That's right." I pulled Seth down off the bar and held him tight against me while he got his breath back. "And if I ever catch you trying to feel up my guy again, I'm gonna have to teach *you* a lesson. You got that, asshole?"

Rick's face turned pink and then red. He looked like I'd sucker punched him. "I was *not* feeling him up!"

"Yeah, that's what they all say." I went over to grab my briefcase, and came back pointing at him. "And yet time and time again, I got some big ox like you putting his hands all over my friend and I gotta' step in and break it up." I wrapped an arm around Seth and squeezed him. "Are you okay, baby?"

Seth sniffed. He was struggling not to laugh. "He hurt me, Dino. I was just having a nice beer and talking fashion with that girl and suddenly he was all over me."

I gave Rick a withering stare. "For shame," I said, steering Seth toward the door. "I really can't get over some people's manners. Think they can do whatever they like."

I glanced over my shoulder on the way out to see Rick dumbfounded, the bartender looking relieved, and the waitress trying not to crack up. Everyone else was already back to business as usual.

Seth fell into the car laughing his ass off. He rubbed his neck where Rick had grabbed him. "You realize half the bruisers in this town think we're dating?"

"Well, I am about to take you out and buy you dinner," I said, starting up the car and backing into the alley.

"Sure, but that's for services rendered."

I gave him a sideways glance. "Yeah, that makes it sound much better."

Seth smirked and hung his arm over the side of the car. Clearly, he wasn't traumatized by the incident.

"What did you do to set him off, anyway?" I asked.

"Oh shit, I was just flirting with the waitress a little. It was harmless. I told her those jeans must be from outer space because her ass is out of this world."

"Oh my God, did you really bring a lame line like that?"

"Sure," he said. "Us goofy little guys can get away with shit like that. People think it's cute."

"Cute and goofy are not what I'm generally going for when I approach women."

Seth rolled his eyes. "Because you're such a ladies man."

"I can be. I just have standards, is all. I'm very selective about who I choose to spend time with, whereas you'll fuck anything that moves. And several things that don't."

"Touchy, touchy," Seth said, reaching over to pet my hair. "It's all right, honey, you have a nice ass too."

I shoved his hand away. "Shut up and figure out where you want to eat."

"Aw...come on, Dino," he purred, crawling across the seat to breathe on my ear. "You chased off my sure thing for the night. The least you could do is take her place..."

A shiver ran down my spine in spite of myself, and I turned to give him the stony look I usually do when he gets this way. When I said he'd fuck anything that moved, I wasn't kidding. He's game for anything and anybody, and it doesn't matter what goodies they have on their plate.

"Dinner?" I reminded him. "Ideas?"

He sighed. "How about...the Oar House? I could eat a burger."

* * * *

After dinner, we went back to Ed's. My car was piled with the last load of boxes and suitcases from my apartment. The building was being torn down to make way for more condos, and Seth offered me his couch until I could find a new place to live.

The garage is a small red, white and blue auto shop located right next to the marina on the Intracoastal Waterway, between Madeira Beach and St. Petersburg. Seth more or less runs the place, since Ed has taken to spending all his time buying stuff at junk auctions and selling it on eBay.

When I pulled in, Ed's dogs were yapping and running around the parking lot. One is a pug with the coloring of a Siamese cat, and the other is an old mutt whose forehead is so flat she couldn't possibly have a brain inside.

I shut the engine off, and Seth got out of the car. He cast a glance over the mound of stuff in the backseat and shook his head. "Matilda looks like a pack mule, man. That is no way to treat a venerable old lady."

"Although you are absolutely correct, I would like to point out that this car is the exact same age as me, so watch it with the 'venerable old' talk. Where in the hell did you learn to use the word venerable, anyway?"

"I use words like venerable," Seth said, mildly disgruntled. "And Matilda is forty-one, that's like...ninety in car years."

"She may look like an old lady, but inside she still purrs like a kitten."

"Same as you," Seth said with a wink.

"I have never looked like an old lady." I grabbed the nearest box, shoved it into Seth's arms, and took another for myself, following him through the shop to the back room where the rest of my stuff was stashed. It took us three trips to get everything inside. The only things left in the car were my suitcase and garment bag, a box of stuff off my desk, and my laptop computer.

Seth took the box and I grabbed the bags, and we climbed the wooden stairway that ran up the outside of the garage to an apartment built over it. This was Seth's place. And mine, for the foreseeable future.

The steps creaked alarmingly and bounced more than I generally liked in my climbing apparatus. "Don't you worry about these falling off?"

"Naw," he said, pausing to lean on the railing and look back at me. "I used to, but that bugged me, so a couple of years ago, I spent about half an hour out here jumping up and down for all I was worth to see what would happen. Turns out they're more solid than they seem. Here I'll show you—"

"Do not jump on these steps right now, or I will smack the shit out of you."

Seth grinned and ran the rest of the way up.

Seth's monkey-like qualities extended to his living habits, and I never failed to be a little dismayed when I went into his apartment. Junk was littered everywhere. Magazines, pizza boxes, beer cans, laundry. Dirty dishes and open cereal boxes covered the counter in the kitchenette. The coffee table was spread with newspaper and sported a vast array of engine parts and beer cans. Behind that, against the wall, was a massive brown sofa with fat, low slung cushions. It was...pristine.

"You cleaned it?" I asked, disbelieving.

"Yup." Seth beamed. "I even pulled out the cushions and vacuumed all down in there. I knew you'd freak out about sleeping on it if I didn't."

"Since when do you own a vacuum?"

"I brought the Shop-Vac up here. Does the same job, right?"

"It would appear so," I said, putting my bags down on the one clean surface in the entire apartment. "Now all I have to worry about is what might crawl out of the darkness to get me in the night."

"Yeah, well, I think there's a box of doughnuts under the chair. You can toss those to distract it."

"You are disgusting, you know that?" I unzipped my garment bag and laid it out on the sofa. "Where can I hang my clothes up?"

Seth stared at me blankly.

"Got some space in a closet? I need to hang these up or they wrinkle."

"Um, right." Seth pivoted on his heel and kicked a path to the tiny coat closet by the door. He pulled a few computer boxes out of it and bounced them into a corner. "You need me to make some space in the bathroom for your curlers and make-up?"

"Fuck you. Normal people hang their clothes up. This is the usual way in which grown-ups do things." I bent down to look under the chair. "Are there really doughnuts under there? This is not a healthy way to live. Seriously."